To Sarah

C000015572

NOT SO INNOCENT

Lynette Heywood

Enjoy babe!

Fisher King Publishing

NOT SO INNOCENT

Copyright © 2017 Lynette Heywood

Fisher King Publishing Ltd,
The Studio,
Arthington Lane,
Pool in Wharfedale,
LS21 1JZ,
England.
www.fisherkingpublishing.co.uk

A CIP catalogue record of this book is available
from the British Library
ISBN 978-1-910406-59-5

For my beautiful mum and dad.
For the unconditional love given to us.
For putting food on our table.
For going without to make sure we were warm.
For fighting for what is right.
For creating a family so strong it's unbreakable.

Acknowledgements

This book is about three friends, friends who are loyal to the core. A lot of the book is based on my childhood, growing up in a Manchester community where everybody has your back.

For me the learning of loyalty comes from my beautiful friends and family. While I cannot name you all here, you know who you are and the importance you hold in my life.

To Gary and Joanne - my first love and my first best friend. For Billy, Niall, Billie, Sian and Jacob for bringing such happiness to our lair.

From very early on it was apparent that we were all we needed. That is us, our family.

None of this would be possible without mum and dad. My rocks; all our rocks.

For those who have parted from my life, those who have been cruel, and those who thought I was never good enough, I thank you too for helping me to survive, contributing to my strength and helping to keep my fire going.

But for those few who have felt the penetrations of my solitude, who have lifted me when I've needed to be lifted and brought me back down to earth when also required, those who made every step lighter to take and held my hand whilst doing so, you're still there and always will be.

For Heaven-Leigh, Joel and Marlow, the words have not yet been invented for whatever it is I feel for you. I just know that you three touched my very core in a way that no other could.

To my wider family I love you all.

*All I want is to watch you rise and rock and flex
your strong arms whilst I arch hard against you,
and submit and permit and insist and understand
that this is absolute nirvana...*

Prologue

The trial was imminent. My life felt like hell. After everything that had gone on, we'd managed to survive all these years; now it all seemed pointless. There had been no mention of the past, no mention of what had happened to us, to me, to my family.

As far as I was concerned he got exactly what he deserved.

The three of us were on trial. On trial for something that happened over twenty years ago. On trial for something that had to be done, something that had ruined our lives and left us tarnished forever. We were on trial for murder.

The jury, seated, unyielding as they sat with rigid stares. Their human shapes appeared like unfeeling androids; emotionless. What did they think now they had heard our story? Did they understand? Probably not. No matter the circumstances, murder is murder. It's against the law, it's not allowed. We had tried to justify our actions. We thought it would be ok as long as we didn't get caught.

The victim had a lot to answer for and deserved to die. He was evil, foul, predatory animal with no redeeming features. The world was a better place without him. That didn't change the fact that we were on trial for his murder and our chances of getting off were slim. Our lawyer had a good reputation but the prosecutors had the evidence.

Our families were there to support us but I could see the questions in their eyes. From the dock I looked up at my children. Each of them had tears in their eyes, pleading silently. I felt the bile rise to my throat as the judge addressed the jury.

'Have you reached a verdict on which you are all agreed?'

I held my breath as the foreman gave the jury's verdict; 'Guilty.'

Everything became a blur. It was surreal. I felt like I was floating high above myself, above the court room. My vision became fuzzy and I could only just hear the judge utter my name. Then my sentence, life imprisonment.

I woke with a start. I was sweating and my hair was drenched like I'd just been caught in heavy rain.

It was the same dream I'd been having for over two decades. I felt sick as I looked over at my true love. I couldn't live with this secret anymore. I wanted everybody to know the truth. I wanted this out in the open once and for all. It was the same every time I had one of these nightmares, a nightmare so close to reality. It was getting harder to hide the truth.

I got out of bed, went to the kitchen and turned to my saviour, the kettle. As I watched the steam rise into the air I recalled the events of over twenty years ago. That night my life changed forever; it filled me with the stench of guilt and repentance. I transgressed, or did I? Either way it's too late now, too late to go back. Never live with regrets; always try to make the right choices.

That's easier said than done when you're not so innocent.

Chapter 1

Ella Parker - in the 1970s

My name is Ella Parker. Actually, Pamela is my given name, but I prefer Ella. Pamela? My parents must have been having a laugh.

I grew up in the southern most districts of Manchester on one of the UK's biggest council estates. On paper, it wasn't the best start you could wish for in life. In reality, there was beauty in the way that we were brought up; a sense of security, the community behind you. The deprived came together, fighting and struggling most of their lives to get by as best they could. They all experienced bad times and learned how to deal with disappointment. When you needed help they understood and empathised. Commonality between people could be a remarkable bond; you had to have been born there to fully understand it.

When times were tough they were really tough. The lack of money meant a lack of food, warmth and clothing. Then there was the lack of education. Our schooling was sparse and knowledge of how to do better was never really shared. Some people managed to escape but most never left their roots.

My family were firmly in the latter category. The one thing they did impart to me was how to love and be loved. I think that's the most important thing in life; to love and be loyal to those who shared your blood.

My parents were hard-working and honest as the day is long, but we had nothing. The things we had to overcome just to get by were tiring. There must have been an easier way to survive.

I was the eldest of four children. Next came my brothers Henry, then George and finally my beautiful sister, baby Josephine; Josie for short. It was chaos getting ready in the mornings. Dad would light the oven on the gas cooker and leave its door open for us. It would be our only warmth after getting out of bed and we'd all gather in the kitchen.

We'd be shivering and moaning all the way down the stairs. The fire in the living room must have used too much gas or I'm sure that would have been lit too, but the oven was enough.

Often the clothes horse would be on the rug drying our clothes. The washing would be dry and warm, having had its turn in front of the oven. We'd try to get in between the wooden rails and let the bed sheets or towels wrap around us to keep us warm. Mum would go ballistic but I don't think she minded really.

Dad would have already left. He used to get up in the dark to go to work and it would be hours later before he would return, also in the dark. He worked hard at an abattoir somewhere near Gorton. I remember it had a sculpture of a bull's head outside.

My mum must have toasted two loaves of bread a day. It would be stacked high on the table, with the thinnest scrape of butter on each slice. Sometimes, not often, we had cereal but we never went without breakfast. Mum's life objective was to keep us full so we'd never feel the pang of hunger like she had as she grew up. There were so many folks around that, due to lack of money, didn't eat as well as us but our mum always made sure we were properly fed. She'd go without so that we could eat. Even at an early age I knew that she was special. I promised myself that when I was older I would get rich and buy her nice shoes and warm boots with fur inside.

One particular winter, mum walked me to school. Henry had only just been born. I was raging with jealousy at the thought I had to go to school while he could have mum all to himself.

My school uniform consisted of a vest top and a pair of purple cotton bell-bottoms. Despite inches of snow, I didn't wear a jumper. At least my black wellingtons kept my feet dry. Those and the six pairs of odd socks.

I had a big thick coat, a scarf and a pair of socks on my hands to keep me warm. Well it wasn't really a pair; just two socks that may once have been white. At least it all kept the cold at bay.

I remember my mum wearing a thin raincoat but no scarf. I looked down at her feet and saw her American Tan tights peeping out of her sandals. I shuddered and looked up adoringly at her. She just got on with it. She was never forthcoming with cuddles but she made up for the lack of them with her actions like always making sure her kids were warm.

The snow was thick that particular year, it was hard to tell where the pavement ended and the road began. The trees glistened in the light, the sky was pale blue and the sun shone brightly but no heat could be felt from it.

Every morning, near our house, there was a little girl playing on the green. She looked over and I looked back. I was intrigued by her; she was so pretty. I guessed she must have been a bit younger than me or else she would have been going to school.

There was always an older boy in the background. I knew who he was but I didn't know what he was doing with her.

He was Peter Lawrence the local freak, I had no interest in him at all; neither did she by the look of things. She always looked immaculate. She had a fur muff, which was pretty unusual around our way, and a matching fur hat. She wore a red coat with black buttons down the front and fur around the collar. She was little and round with hair of white curls that could be seen sticking out of the front of her hat.

One day, she smiled at me. I was immediately aware of my own outfit and unconsciously tugged at my worn blue quilted anorak and half-smiled back between my curious stares.

'Mum, why doesn't that girl go to school like me?' I asked.

'Oh I don't know, I think she's too young yet,' my mum replied taking a guess at the reason.

I thought about it all day long and was jealous that I couldn't play out instead of having to go to school. I never saw her mum or dad or anyone else with her, just Peter Lawrence lurking in the background. I didn't like him; he gave me the creeps.

Day after day I used to see the little girl just happily playing on the green, balancing on the concrete 'No Ball Games Allowed' post and skipping happily along. I used to feel more and more curious wondering why she didn't go to school when most children our age did.

Anyway I had bigger things to worry about. Even at six years old I felt the pressure my parents were under. I often listened to their chats and, as ludicrous as it might sound, I'd offer my advice. They never criticised, just engaged me in their conversations. From being very young I understood their pain and where it was hurting.

One night I tiptoed downstairs. Dad must have heard me and he met me halfway down.

'Get back into bed,' I heard mum shout.

'Aw leave her Chris, let her come down if she wants,' said my dad.

He reluctantly let me go into the living room and there they were playing with our new Christmas present which was plugged into our large TV.

'Wow,' I said taken aback.

They were playing a game. It was called 'Pong' according to dad.

Mum explained that they'd been to bingo and she had won £200, so they had gone to a warehouse to buy all our Christmas presents. I felt very superior when dad explained that no-one else on the estate had one of these. We would be the first.

The next day I was brought back down to earth as normal life continued.

'Ella love,' Mum was shouting for me. 'Go and ask one of the neighbours if they've got a shilling for the electric.'

I stood and waited for a pound note or something for the neighbours to exchange for coins.

'What are you waiting for? I've got no money. Just say I'll pay them back tomorrow when I get my family allowance.'

I had to make a decision on which neighbour would have a spare shilling. I would choose a different neighbour to last time.

I'd spend many evenings knocking on neighbour's doors trying to borrow a shilling. I didn't mind it once I was inside and they'd agree to a loan. I preferred the older neighbours, their homes were warm and cosy and smelled of cooking. Sometimes they'd offer me warm cakes or hot scones fresh from the oven. I enjoyed the comfort and the chats. They'd ask me about which pop stars I liked and if I had a boyfriend.

When I went home mum would be pleased that I'd not only managed to get a shilling but also something to eat as that meant there was one less mouth to feed.

Then there were times when we had to sit in the dark. I remember the electricity going off and yet again mum hadn't accounted for it. It felt like we sat in darkness for hours but it couldn't have been that late as we were waiting for dad to come home with his wages.

It wasn't just the gas and electric issues we had to deal with; there was also the loan man. I hated him. He scared me and was always mean when he came to the door. My mum was tough though and told him to 'bugger off' on more than one occasion.

If she couldn't be bothered telling him herself, she would use me to do it for her. 'Ella, tell Norman I'm not paying him this week,' she would say.

Norman would send me back to ask why she wasn't paying him that week.

'Go and tell him because I'm bleeding not that's why.'

'Because she's bleeding not Norman, that's why,' I'd repeat, then shut the door in his face.

He once almost frightened me to death by peering through our letter box. He had big wrinkly eyes and they looked right at me.

'You're a cheeky little bugger, Ella Parker, just like your mother. A cheeky little bugger,' he shouted. My mum raced up the hall, opened the door and went off her head.

'How dare you, you cheeky bastard? Don't you dare talk to my kids like that! She's a good girl. She was just doing what she was told. Now get lost.'

Off he went with his orange book, but he was back the following night. Mum was still fuming, 'I can't be bothered with this, get behind the couch,' she instructed. So baby Josie, mum, the boys and me all sat huddled behind the sofa.

Norman shouted through the letter box, 'I know you're in Mrs Parker.'

'He knows you're in, mum,' I whispered.

'Ssshhh,' she hissed.

He shouted again and made baby Josie jump; she started screaming the house down.

'For god's sake,' said mum in despair, 'Ella, empty the back of the telly and pay Norman. Tell the bastard not to come back until next Friday, when your dad's been paid.'

I emptied the coins from the back of the telly and gave them all to Norman. Just as I was shutting the door mum yelled for me to get a receipt. Norman scribbled on a piece of paper and ran off down the path.

One Sunday mum was cooking dinner and our aunty turned up out of the blue with her latest fella. Mum was fuming and took me to one side.

'Ella there's not enough food, but I don't want her to know that. Nosey cow she is. Just make sure you say you don't want any and tell Henry to do the same.'

So we sat there while everyone ate a big yummy Sunday dinner. Henry and me pulled mock faces and feigned dislike at the look of the hot steaming roast beef that dad had brought home from the abattoir. When the huge apple pie was brought out our mouths were watering; we jumped up and down with excitement.

'What?' Mum stared at me and Henry. It was a look that told us not to even think about answering back. 'You pair can bugger off. You didn't want your dinner, so you're not having any pudding.'

That's how it was for me and my family. We struggled to

get by but we had each other.

Poor but happy we were; just poor but happy.

Chapter 2

Bess Holland - in the 1970s

My name is Elizabeth Holland, or Bess as my dad likes to call me. My life was very normal; or as normal as can be growing up on one of the biggest council estates in England.

Normal until my mum deserted us leaving me and my alcoholic father to pan it out.

I never knew they were so unhappy. Things never seemed so bad to me; but then I wasn't the one married to a drunk. Although I eventually grew to adore my dad, I didn't blame mum for being fed up with him. How on earth she managed to have a child I don't know, he was rarely sober.

I always felt safe with my mum. She was beautiful and had a warmth about her, a glow that seemed only meant for me. Her beautiful face, her elegance; she was almost ethereal, a soul who was put on this earth to adore me and I adored her.

We never wanted for much. Dad was a grafter. He supervised builders and held all his meetings in the local pub, 'The Lion' which was just around the corner. That's part of the reason he was more often drunk.

Mum wasn't from the estate, she was different to all the other mums. Every morning she would be up bright and early, she always looked immaculate. She'd have breakfast ready and we'd sit down and eat together. All the cups and plates matched and they were always laid on a freshly pressed table cloth. The kitchen smelled of baking or cooking. My mum's upbringing had been strict and her father had instilled in her good manners which had never left her.

After breakfast I played on the green for an hour or so.

'The fresh air is good for you,' mum used to say. 'It'll put some colour in your cheeks and give me a chance to tidy the house.'

Peter from next door would always come out and join me. He was a big daft oaf of a lad who used to annoy me, always around when I just wanted to be on my own.

Every morning I'd watch the children go to school, although I didn't really understand what school was. I just knew that at a particular time each day, a posse of mums and their children would cross the main road to the big building with the high wire fence.

There was one girl I'd see who intrigued me. She was always happy, skipping along next to her mother, holding onto a large red leather pram, chattering away. She had straight, jet black hair cut sharp into a little bob with the the most crooked fringe.

I thought I heard her shout something to me one day but I couldn't be sure so I just smiled. She was very pretty, very natural and her face sparkled. She seemed to speak with her eyes. I was mesmerized by her, an instant love for someone I didn't even know.

Most days that was my routine. Breakfast, then playing on the green whilst the other children went to school then I'd spend the afternoons with my mum doing jigsaws or colouring books. I was a happy child.

Then everything changed.

I'll never forget the day my mum left. She had yet another massive row with dad. He'd just returned from the pub, it was late and mum said that she'd had enough. Dad may have been a grafter, but after his meetings he always came in staggering, stinking of booze, falling about and urinating in places he shouldn't.

She screamed that she'd had enough, she was leaving him. I was in the living room in my night clothes. She came over to me, kissed me, then told me to go to bed and she'd pick me up in the morning. So I did. I went to bed. My heart was aching as I knew she meant it this time; we were leaving dad. I felt sad about leaving our house and I felt sick that mum didn't love my dad anymore.

I had a restless night but in the morning I got up, got dressed and waited for mum to come and get me. She'd already packed a suitcase with all my clothes in it.

All day I waited, looking out of the window, jumping up every time I saw movement from the corner of my eye. To make it easier to see out of the window I even sat on my case for a few hours. At one point I ran upstairs and looked out of mum and dad's bedroom window because I could see right down the road from there and would be able to see her when she came.

I waited all day until my dad finally told me to go up to bed; she wasn't coming.

I was devastated. The wave of sadness hit me from within. I got onto my bed and hugged my pillow, rocking while I cried myself to sleep. All the time I was trying to explain to myself why she hadn't come back for me. Perhaps she had made a mistake, got the day wrong or something.

I repeated the process the next day, and the day after, until eventually weeks had passed until it finally dawned on me that she wasn't coming back. I didn't get it. I never understood it because she'd even packed my case.

I never got over it. The solidity of my life was over for good.

Dad loved me and brought me up as best he could. He cared for me in his drunken way but, from the moment mum left, I felt alone in the world. Dad was difficult to communicate with. He was always drunk or tipsy and never looked me in the eye. I missed my mum incredibly and my heart ached for her. The emotions I faced were certainly too much for a child. I knew I'd have to face the big bad world alone because my mother was gone and I was left with my careless, miserable, drunken dad.

From that day forward, I looked after myself. I made my own breakfast, lunches and dinner. At first I didn't know where to start but it wasn't long until I could fix a meal. There was never much food but thankfully I didn't need much. I used to keep the house in order. I had a routine and made sure that I cleaned up after myself; after all there was no-one else to do it.

We had a great big double top load washer. I had watched my mum many times so I knew the drill. You had to lift up the lids and fill one of the compartments with water using a hose. I had to stand on a chair to connect it to the tap. Every Sunday I used to wash seven pairs of knickers, seven vests and whatever else I'd worn that week. I'd dry them on the back of the kitchen chairs, on the side of the bath or anywhere else I could hang them. At the time it was just my life, it was all I knew so I just got on with it because I had no choice.

Social Services weren't interested in my situation and I had my Nana who used to pop by when she could. When she did, I was so pleased to see her. She'd help out but she'd always complain about my mum. It hurt that she felt that way but I was grateful she was there.

One day she sat me down and explained that the law said I had to go to school as I was five years old. I remember asking who 'the law' was and she simply said the police.

As I walked up the big stony path to my new school, my stomach hurt, and my legs trembled in fear. It was a lovely crisp day, cold but the sun shone brightly. I shivered as I looked toward the huge building. There was a large field on my right hand side with perfect cut grass and white painted markings for a football pitch. It had goalposts without nets; nets would get stolen.

I remember how lightly the other children were dressed given the weather, but not me. I had a fur muff to keep my little hands warm. It was daunting going to school but I was looking forward to it. I didn't know what it was all about; I was so naive. I just knew there would be hundreds of other children there. I already knew that because I used to see them going to school every day and coming back; all with their mums and brothers and sisters.

I saw a familiar face; the girl that used to pass by the green with her mum and the red pram. I felt strangely drawn towards her, she was so smiley and beautiful. I headed over to her and I felt a spark. Straight away the connection between us was deep. As our eyes met it was intense; we were both speechless almost as if were searching each other's soul. An immediate bond formed which would glue us together for the rest of our lives. She was friendly and approachable with the biggest grin I had ever seen and it warmed me to the core of my body.

She made that day at school complete. She took me under her wing and introduced me to her friends. I soon became part of it all, and popular too. Thanks to Ella Parker.

I loved school. I loved the noise, the smell, the wooden desks and wooden chairs, the blue shiny floor and the parquet block flooring in the great hall where we all met for assembly and to sing hymns. I sang at the top of my little voice; it was amazing.

I loved how the teachers treated me. The female teachers reminded me of my mum and I grew to love them all. I loved interacting with the other children. I loved learning, and reading out loud.

I got lots of attention because I was different from the other children. I hadn't realised how poor the neighbourhood was. I didn't look like the others. I was always dressed perfectly and even had matching outfits so I stood out from everyone else. Compared to the others I had lots of shoes and clothes, which I soon began to understand was completely out of the ordinary. The other girls became very interested in me but there was also a lot of jealousy.

The settling in period was lengthy and I still had knots in my stomach for weeks after that first day. I was in awe of the number of children in one place and sometimes I just wanted to go home. I'm not sure why, maybe the comfort and familiarity of that place. Fortunately, with my new best friend always by my side, life wasn't so bad. I never thought I'd laugh or smile again but I did. Things that happened in school were funny and made me giggle, especially where Ella was concerned. She was cheeky but loveable and not many could be cross with her for long.

My life in school and living on my own with my dad was such a contrast to when mum was living with us. I loved school but it was difficult not to think of the times when the house had felt full of people and I wondered if the pain would ever subside.

As night fell and darkness spread, my thoughts would wander and I would lay awake thinking of my mum. No matter how hard I fought, I couldn't get her out of my head. Sometimes I'd picture her dead and buried and other times

I'd imagine her coming for me. I'd wonder where she was, and who she was with; it was constant. Night after night my head hurt from it. My dad never spoke to me about it but I could see the sadness in his eyes which made me feel sad too. Sometimes I hated my mum for not loving me enough to come back; sometimes I hated my dad for letting her leave without me, and sometimes I hated myself.

Returning home one evening there was a man at the door. He said he'd come to empty the meters. He did so but left a load of money piled up on the side. I didn't pay much attention to it at first but later when it was still there, I picked it up and put it in a little plastic bag under my bed.

That night Dad came home, pissed as usual, and asked if the meter man had been. 'No', I lied.

I looked at his face, his red skin, his red eyes, and the saliva in the corner of his mouth, it sickened me. It was then that I decided that as soon as I could I was leaving. I'd save up and move away from him. I wondered if I would be able to. He had no one, even his own mum wasn't bothered; she only came round because of me.

He threw an envelope full of notes onto the table. I stared at it wondering what he planned to do with it. Soon I could hear him snoring and thought about the money. I took some notes from the envelope and put them under my bed in the little plastic bag with the money from the meter man.

Early the next day I was woken by dad's shouting.

'Elizabeth? Bess, Bess!'

I jumped up in panic. I'd never heard him in such a state. I ran downstairs, 'What's up dad?'

'Bess I put my wages down on the table last night and now some of its missing, have you seen the rest of the money?'

'No dad,' I replied. I tried my hardest not to let my

expression change.

He looked at me but didn't question me further. He rubbed his chin as he often did when he was thinking. 'Shit,' he said, 'I must've spent more than I thought last night.'

He gave me a shopping list and half the money and told me to go to the post office with Nana when she arrived to pay some bills and get the food.

So it continued. Every week my dad brought his wages home and I took one of the notes and stashed it. He was none the wiser. Did I feel guilty? No, he should have been more careful and he did nothing for me, I had to do it all myself. This was my escape money, my future and I needed it.

I'd lay on the sofa with a blanket over me and as soon as dad stumbled in, I'd feel secure enough to go to my bedroom. I often wondered whether he'd know about it if someone got into the house. Still, he was there and that was enough.

One night I was already asleep and dad woke me coming into my room. I wasn't sure what he wanted, so I pretended to still be asleep. He tripped over the rug and almost knocked himself out. He just sat at the end of my bed and sobbed his heart out. I heard him speaking, slurring his words, 'Oh Elizabeth, Bess my Bess, please don't ever leave me. You're all I've got, please Bess, please Bess, please.'

He leant over and stroked my head and kissed my cheek. One of his tears fell onto my face. I felt warm and safe for a moment and then so sad that our worlds had been rocked so much. If dad wasn't always drunk I probably wouldn't be so alone. He stumbled out of the room, and I too sobbed, I sobbed for him, I sobbed for my mum, but most of all I sobbed for me.

Chapter 3

Vanessa Brown - in the 1970s

I'm Nessa Brown. Our house was the biggest type of house on the estate. Having said that, there wasn't much variety as nearly every house looked the same, differentiated only by the colour of the doors. Ours had four bedrooms; it had to. There was my mum, my dad and six kids, three boys and three girls. I was the youngest and probably the most protected, although I didn't know it at the time.

Although it was a big house compared to others, it was one of the scruffiest. The brown dusty curtains remained closed most of the time. Inside the walls were covered in smoke-stained yellow anaglypta wallpaper and the floor had brown and orange carpets that were never hoovered. Clothes were strewn all over, dirty clothes at that.

I was a cute child, with auburn hair as straight as a die and a fringe that my mum cut most Sundays. I had big brown eyes with lashes that got caught on my fringe if it ever got too long.

Each morning it was a case of first up, best dressed. It was total utter chaos. Usually Jane, my eldest sister, woke first and made sure we all followed suit. Our feet would freeze on the terracotta stone kitchen tiles. We'd take it in turns to get our clothes from the heap piled on the kitchen table. We'd rummage through the pile to find something to wear. If our clothes weren't there or someone else had put them on, then we'd have to make do with what we wore the day before. If that went on for a week, then so be it.

Every morning I'd get myself dressed and if the bathroom

was free, I'd wash and if it wasn't, I couldn't. You'd think that because I was the youngest that the older kids would look after me but they didn't. It was dog-eat-dog in our house.

I rarely had breakfast. Being the youngest meant there was never anything left by the time I'd found something to wear and nobody would ever save me any.

Mum rarely did any shopping and none of us had any money so we'd steal stuff where we could. Often I'd wait for the bread to be delivered to the local shop then sneak a loaf off one of the trays in the back of the van. Then on the way home, I'd take a bottle of sterilised milk from a neighbour's doorstep.

One particular morning it was snowing. Outside looked beautiful. It was as though someone had come in the middle of the night and covered everything in cotton wool. The trees were white, the ground was white and the sky was white. I couldn't help staring until the brightness was hurting my eyes, but I liked it.

I knew I couldn't go in my usual attire or I'd freeze to death. I had no chance of finding a wollen jumper, let alone a clean one and my coat was paper thin.

I couldn't risk waking my mum. Dad worked at the hospital so he'd already left. I put on a jumper that belonged to my brother, Andrew. The jumper was longer than my skirt and the sleeves almost touched the floor but at least it would keep me warm. As I was going out of the front door, Andrew shouted at me to stop. He ran towards me and pulled me back by my hair.

I remember kicking him and screaming, 'Mum, Mum, Mum.'

'What's all bleeding the fuss? You've gone and woke me

up,' she yelled.

I looked at my brother hoping he would relent on hearing mum's voice but he was fuming and wanted his jumper.

'Get that fucking jumper off now,' he shouted loud enough to wake the dead. I screamed back at the top of my voice.

'If you make me come downstairs I'll beat the bloody pair of you,' mum shouted. She meant it too.

She didn't have to tell us twice. We ran as fast as we could out of the front door. Andrew was not happy about me wearing his jumper but luckily he was more interested in getting out of the way of a good hiding.

That was a typical morning at the Browns; chaos and then school for more chaos. My older siblings went to senior school, Tom and Faya were in the juniors and I was in the infants.

They all had red cheeks and big smiles as they threw snowballs at each other. As usual I walked behind them in a world of my own. I was doing little skips, dreaming and looking up at the white sky as if I was talking to God to make my dreams come true. I was a dawdler; everyone said so.

I was thinking about the new family that had just moved into the area. They spoke funny and the children had just started at our school. The three brothers all had the devil in their eyes especially the middle one, Si. He had the cheekiest face I'd ever seen. He seemed untouchable, unapproachable, wild, feisty and naughty; a whirlwind, his own tornado, a self-made dust devil, tumultuous, a confused gale of whatever he was rushing towards. He was all of that but also the cutest person I'd ever clapped eyes on. If I looked hard enough I could see myself in his eyes. That wasn't easy as he hardly ever looked at me and when I looked in his direction he'd quickly look away.

Before I knew it I was in the school playground. I looked around for Ella Parker, my friend. I knew she would be with the new kid, Bess Holland. They'd very quickly become inseparable. Lovely as Bess was it stung slightly. Ella had always been my best friend so I felt a bit disgruntled. It was as though I was the odd one out, the loner who never seemed to be able to have anyone to myself. I didn't dwell on it though.

I spotted Ella and Bess in the smaller playground, Ella's mum was with them. She took Ella to school every day. I thought Ella was so lucky. Chris Parker was such a lovely mum who obviously cared about her children. I longed for my mum to be like Chris and daydreamed that Ella was my sister and Chris was my mum. Perhaps my own mum was bored to death with kids; after all I was her sixth. I saw Ella kiss her mum goodbye and skip away with Bess.

I started to walk faster, as fast as I could in four inches of snow, so I could catch up and enjoy the fifteen minutes playtime with them both. I passed Ella's mum and said good morning. She looked cold; she didn't even have proper shoes.

I jumped down the two steps that led into the playground and passed the nursery to my left, with its two huge big red doors. I was aware of all the mums, children and prams passing by as I hurried along. I asked myself why dads didn't take their kids to school. It was a rare sight to see a dad at school in the seventies.

I was deep in my little world when I suddenly heard the sound of chanting. 'Nessa Brown is a clown. She's a tramp, tramp, tramp.'

The emphasis on the word made me shudder, maybe because that's what I thought I was too. It went on; 'Scruffy, scabby tramp'. They continued to chant until they were right in front of me.

I was intimidated. I wanted the ground to swallow me alive and the dull ache in my stomach was getting stronger. I recognised the small crowd that gathered in front of me. Where was my sister Faya? She'd floor the lot of them when she found out what they'd said about me.

I saw Si but he wasn't joining in. In fact he looked mortified whilst the rest were enjoying the scene, fascinated at what my response would be. I looked the bullies in the eye, took a deep breath and attempted to walk past them but it didn't work. One of the girls grabbed my hair, pushed me to the freezing floor and sat on top of me. She scratched my face and stared at me whilst she let saliva fall from her mouth towards my face. The hairs on the back of my neck stood up as it landed near my eye.

I felt ridiculous, embarrassed and humiliated but didn't know what to do. I was in shock. I looked around me and could see the children in the nursery playground only meters away. I looked back at the older girl on top of me, making sure I would remember her horrible wicked face as she went to raise her arm. Then I heard it, a gruff little voice, 'leave her alone. Yeah? Get off her, you bully.' She fell back and a feeling of relief rushed over my body.

It was him, Si Bailey. As I looked at him, he looked toward the floor, his face red. I wanted to look at him forever, absorb his face but I also wanted to die there and then.

Then I heard a more familiar voice shouting, 'Get off my sister right now.'

It was Faya. She dragged the girl away from me and slapped her hard across the face. I was crying because of the commotion and because I had snow up my back.

I saw Ella and Bess with a teacher, who was screaming for the girls to stop fighting. It was Bess who ran over to me first. She gently wiped my face and hugged me tightly. The bully girl tried to run away from the scene but as quick as a flash Ella stuck her leg out and sent her reeling across the playground. She went flying on to her back with her legs in the air, giving the whole playground a good view of her dirty underwear. Even I started laughing as Ella shouted, 'Skidder, Skidder Barker, not Linda Barker, Skidder Barker'. The name Skidder Barker stuck from that day forward; she deserved it.

Bess Holland was carefully brushing me down. The tears in her eyes told me that she would be my friend forever; Ella too. I could feel the loyalty oozing from their pores.

They were my heroes. As I looked across the playground I saw my other little hero, Si, swaggering away with a walk that was far too confident for his age. I felt warm as I watched him and knew there and then that I would love him for the rest of my life.

I dreamily imagined that when I married Si I would love him and kiss him and hold his hand. We'd be perfect together; not like my mum and dad. They made a strange couple. It was obvious they didn't have much time for each other. They were more like enemies than husband and wife, always whispering about one thing or another and we were never welcome in the same room as them. So of course it made me curious as to what the big secrets might be.

One night I heard mum hissing at dad. She was furious, fuming. 'If you go into the bedroom again, it'll be the last fucking thing you do,' came my mum's sharp tongue.

They were sitting in the kitchen. Something was definitely going on. Mum wasn't happy. They were both holding cigarettes. Dad's hands were a deep golden colour and his nails were black. His grey hair was stuck to his head with grease. Mum had flat, brown, mousey hair, with three rollers in the front. She was frail and always looked tired with big black bags under her eyes.

'Make us a brew woman, and stop nagging,' said dad. Mum threw a pan at him which bounced off the wall and just missed his head. There was a kerfuffle; it didn't sound nice.

I slid along the hall wall away from the debacle that was my parents. I sat with my knees hunched up and wondered what they had been talking about. Mum was hopping mad; she was always hopping mad but this time she was worse.

My ears pricked up as mum's voice became raised again. 'You're a dirty bastard Derek Brown, a dirty fucking bastard.'

I heard our Tom come in. 'Ssshhh,' I whispered and put my fingers over my lips nodding towards the kitchen. He knew what I meant, that I was listening to something. He tiptoed across the hall which made me giggle out loud.

Suddenly I felt a blow to my head. It was my dad.

'How fucking long have you been there, you nosey little bastard?'

Tom was mortified as my nose started to bleed and ran over to protect me but Dad lashed out at him too.

'Get up them fucking stairs the pair of you, now. Go on get out of my sight,' he yelled.

The incident stayed with me all night and was still in the back of my mind the following morning. I had no marks on my face but my nose was sore and I was hurt that my mum had let it happen. I still believed that underneath all the ranting and raving she must love us really. Dad lashed out at us all except Faya but that might have been because she always kept out of his way.

Not long after the bullying incident my life changed completely. It was freezing so we were wrapped up in our blankets on the sofa trying to keep warm. Tom's blanket stank of piss so we were hitting each other and arguing. I wanted him to move. 'You stink of wee,' I said with a sense of disgust.

Mum's hand came out of nowhere and slapped me across my face. I jumped in shock and felt the tears welling up in my eyes. I hated her sometimes and I'd had enough of being attacked recently.

I huddled further into my blanket. We'd all been entertaining ourselves playing hide and seek before mum and dad had asked us to go into the living room. I'd been crouched in the airing cupboard next to the hot water tank for what felt like hours waiting for our Tom to find me. Unfortunately Faya had locked the door to frighten me and snapped the key in the lock. Initially we were too scared to tell anyone but I became more and more aware of the heat from the hot water tank and I was starting to feel sick and short of breath.

I shouted to Faya for help, but she was panicking. In the end my older brother, Paul had to take the door off. Mum and dad were fuming. 'Come on for Christ's sake,' my mum cursed, 'your dad and me want to tell you something.'

So now we were all sitting on the sofa with our blankets around us. I rubbed my cheek which still stung from the slap I'd received. I looked at mum and dad to let them know I was ready to listen to what they had to tell us.

Nothing could prepare me for what came next.

It was mum who spoke as dad looked on. She calmly announced that they were finding it difficult to clothe and feed us all. As a result the welfare officer had agreed that we needed to go into a foster home. Not all of us; just me, Tom and Faya.

'Where are we going?' asked Tom.

'It's on the other side of the estate,' said mum.

The estate was ten square miles so it could be anywhere.

That night I crawled into bed. It felt as though my life had come to an end. I was scared about what was going to happen to us.

It couldn't get any worse, I thought. My head felt like it was in a vice and was about to explode. I couldn't believe what was happening. What about my best friends, Ella and Bess? What about Si?

It made me feel ill. I threw up and covered the mess with a towel. Then I fell asleep, hoping that when I woke in the morning it had all been an awful dream.

The next day it became a reality. Mum made sure that we dressed in our party clothes which, if truth be known, were ready for the bin. There was a beep from outside and dad nodded. As I watched everyone hugging and saying goodbye to one another I noticed that my parents looked sad. They just stared straight at us. Surely they had a choice. I hated them but at the same time wanted to run to them and hold them tight and beg them to let us stay.

I was the first to go out of the front door and walk towards the big red car. The door was opened by my new foster parents, Pat and Kenny Davidson.

I was immediately greeted by the smell of rich leather. The car was beautiful, the dash board was made of walnut and the steering wheel was white. I could imagine driving it with leather gloves on my hands.

I was pulled gently onto my new foster mother's knee. It was uncomfortable and I grimaced through my tears all the way to our new home. Through the sparkling clean windows of the beautiful red car I watched our old world pass by.

The next few days were strange for everyone. My heart ached for home but I did feel better that my brother and sister were with me. I still couldn't believe my parents could do this. I couldn't forgive them. Our Faya took the longest to settle. She has always been moody I thought as I watched her whimpering on her bed one evening. Tom was feeling it too; at least we had each other.

We should have been going to a new school but it didn't work out. They'd been waiting a week and half to get everything sorted. During this time I'd been fretting about my friends. I was worried about what they'd be thinking and wondering if they knew what had happened to me.

On the Friday of the second week, the Davidson's had some news for us. They told us that we were going back to our old school on Monday. I couldn't believe it. The new school had lost all the transfer forms and it would take weeks to find them. I couldn't wait to see my best friends again and this time I'd never leave them.

Chapter 4

Ella

It was 1977 and the Queen's Silver Jubilee. Everyone was getting ready for a huge party that was happening on our street. The kids were running excitedly in and out of each other's houses, helping with bowls of food, plates of sandwiches and crisps. The atmosphere was amazing. The sun streamed across the union jack bunting that draped from bedroom windows and between lamp posts. The men were charged with carrying out kitchen tables and there were makeshift chairs in the form of beer crates donated by the local pubs. White sheets were placed neatly over the tables while record players on window sills blasted out the hits of the day. There was dancing, laughter and loads of fun to be had.

The whole estate seemed to have dressed up for the occasion including of course Bess, Nessa and me. Mum had splashed out on new jumpsuits for me and Josie. My brothers were wearing flared trousers, pumps and white vests with 1977 embroidered underneath a silver crown. Ness was wearing blue bell bottom jeans and a red vest top with a white belt made from one of her foster mother's old blouses. Bess, immaculate as always, wore a white cotton jumpsuit with red wedges and a blue belt.

The love and camaraderie of the community was something that would stay with us forever. Nothing this exciting had happened to us before and we all sat in a great big line facing our friends and families enjoying the celebrations.

Halfway through the afternoon the heavens opened and

we laughed as the rain soaked everything and everyone. Luckily it was just a shower and the sun came out and shone through the rain making a spectacular rainbow. I imagined a pot of gold and I hoped that one day I would find it.

Eventually the party moved to the local church hall and everyone mucked in to carry food and drinks; pop for the kids, beer for the dads. The boys carried the record players and the whole neighbourhood walked together to continue the celebrations.

The girls were secretly thrilled that the Bailey brothers had also made their way there. So too had Peter Lawrence, although he was on his own. Mind you, he was always on his own. He never looked like he wanted it any other way; he just didn't seem interested.

We approached the Bailey brothers with Peter looking on. Nessa still had a soft spot for Si Bailey ever since he saved her from the bullies when she was six years old. She had strong feelings for him and knew that for all his swagger and cockiness, deep down he was a beautiful person. Although he was usually as rough as his brothers he always went really shy in her presence and she took this as a sign that he really did like her.

The Baileys had moved here from somewhere down south and were pretty wayward, especially Si, always fighting. Nessa saw a vulnerable side to him and that made her love him dearly. Sadly he never looked at her or spoke to her. Not at the party, not in class at school, not even when he walked past her in the street. Occasionally he would inadvertently catch her eye and it would melt her senses, but before she could respond he'd put his head down and walk on. She described how he made her feel warm inside and she always wanted to be friends with him. She would brush past him in school just to feel the electricity between them but she would never try to speak to him and always loved him from a distance. I knew this because she was my dearest friend and we shared everything with each other.

I danced with the oldest Bailey brother, Matt. Si and the middle brother, Anthony, sat with the girls but as always Si didn't say much. That was until Peter Lawrence came over and started to tease Nessa. He was hounding her, getting personal about her circumstances and was clearly embarrassing her and making her feel uncomfortable.

Si suddenly grabbed hold of the table where they were seated and launched it at Peter. Peter flew back in shock and landed flat on his backside, got to his feet and ran off. Nessa was thrilled that Si had done that for her.

Gradually the party died down. Everyone had had enough of the fantastic day and piled out of the church hall and into the quiet evening air, drifting off to their homes among the streets of the estate. The rain had stopped so it was a pleasant walk.

I was in a world of my own having danced with Matthew Bailey. He was older and cooler and I'd had a really good time. He made me feel special and no matter how hard I tried to stop them, I could feel the little butterflies fluttering in my tummy.

Nessa didn't sleep. She thought about Si Bailey all night desperately trying to recall every moment, every word that was said. Not that Si had said much, he'd just lost it, but secretly she was glad and hugged herself tightly.

Bess, meanwhile, had helped her father up the stairs and into bed. She remembered to lay him on his side so he didn't choke. She had such big responsibilities at such a young age. When she was sure her dad was asleep, she got her stash of money from under her bed and counted it.

My brothers were shattered and Josie was hyper. Dad was making a fuss of them. I thought about the attention they always seemed to get from him but I wasn't really jealous. I loved my dad very much. He worked hard for us and was a bit different to the other dads. He had no shame in taking us out to the park and he'd love to pick us up from school given half a chance.

It was nearing midnight and my dad, who was also called Chris, had let me stay up to watch the big white dot on the telly screen fade into nothingness.

Mum was looking out of her bedroom window, her head full of rollers with a scarf over them to keep them in place. This was a regular ritual of hers but tonight she couldn't believe what was happening; it was pandemonium. There were police cars everywhere and I heard her call down to my dad. 'Chris, there's something going on out there and it doesn't look good,' she said.

Dad went to the front door and was greeted by a commotion which appeared to be happening over the road.

'Bloody hell, Christine, you'd better come down and see this,' he said.

Well she didn't need to be told twice and nearly broke her neck running down the stairs.

'Jesus, woman,' said my dad, 'you're like a rat up a drainpipe.'

She went out the front door, passing dad and headed to the scene. Flashing blue lights and black police vans were parked along the street. A police officer approached her as she got nearer.

'You can't come in here love,' said the officer

Mum told him she was concerned that a close friend of

the family might be involved but he wasn't convinced and sent her away. She spotted one of the neighbours heading towards our house. It was Jean Wright from up the road. She would know what was going on. She joined mum outside the house. The two women were delighted to have such drama so close to home. Mum got two stools from the kitchen and put them in the garden next to the front door so they had front row seats.

The women were horror struck however, when word had finally got out what had gone on. Jean Wright couldn't hang around. She dashed back to her house as she needed to wake her husband up to tell him the gossip.

Mum came inside and spoke to dad, 'Chris, put the kettle on while I get Ella to bed.'

I wasn't happy; I'd been waiting for ages to find out what had gone on over the road and now I was missing out on the action. I stormed upstairs in a huff.

I pressed my ear to the floor as hard as I could. It was muffled but I could make out what they were saying. Mum spoke in a voice clearly full of revulsion. Allen Owen was the neighbour over the road and the centre of tonight's activity. He was a porter at the local hospital and it transpired that he had been caught with his pants down. I could hear my dad chuckling and asking if it was with one of the nurses.

'No, Chris, not with the nurses,' mum explained, 'with the stiffs, in the morgue.' My stomach wobbled inside. I'd heard enough and imagined the scene in my head. I felt a bit sick and got into bed and thought of the shame and shock for the families of the dead. I never knew that a person could do that. I couldn't wait to tell the girls.

The mood had changed downstairs. I could feel it even from my pillow. I was never going to sleep now anyway and was trying to take comfort from the mumbled conversation downstairs. I could hear mum putting on the kettle and lighting the oven for warmth.

I had an unsettled feeling in my stomach. I got out of bed and tiptoed onto the landing. If you looked straight down the stairs there was a tiny window at the bottom. There were never any curtains and it always frightened the living daylights out of me as I imagined a pair of eyes staring in from outside. The voices downstairs were raised now. Dad was not happy.

I was careful and dared to take three steps down then bent my head over the banister. I could see into the kitchen. I heard dad say, 'You've gone too fucking far this time Chris.' I listened intently as he continued, 'How could you tell Jean Wright about Ella not being mine?'

A wave of dizziness swept over me and I lost my footing. I fell to the bottom of the stairs and immediately my parents ran into the hall to pick me up. They were panicking big time and checking me over.

Dad looked at my mum and picked me up.

'I don't care what you say; Ella's mine,' he said vehemently.

I held my dad tight as he carried me upstairs and put me to bed. As I drifted off to sleep my head was in turmoil trying to make sense of what I'd heard. I couldn't help wondering, if my father wasn't Chris Parker then who was?

Chapter 5

Peter Lawrence

The curtains on the windows were grubby. They were never opened and instead of white they were dark grey with a thick layer of dust. If you touched them the dust would jump out, shoot to the back of your throat and choke you.

The house looked unused, like it had been left to rot. It was stale and damp with water dripping from the gutters onto the outside wall which created a green thick slime that coated the bricks.

The street light flickered giving the effect of a film noir set. The orange glow lit up my walls which were covered in old posters of bare chested women waiting to be fucked.

I lived on my own. I probably wasn't supposed to but dad had fucked off. My mum had fucked off too, years before. Johnny, my brother, was doing time in prison. He'd wiped a family clean out. Too handy he was with a knife, that boy, and I should know I had the scars to prove it; fucking lunatic. Then there was my sister. Well fuck knows where she was, probably in care. Dad still paid the rent on the house so no one bothered me.

I tried to fit in but nobody wanted to know. Those three girls stuck together like glue but it was Bess that really did it for me. She was sweet, pretty and I always wanted her in a way I wanted those girls in the pictures on my wall.

I could see her house from where I sat. We lived next door to each other, but my house was on a slant on a corner, so I could see right into hers. My balls ached for Bess. I wanted her.

That Nessa Brown made me look a right fucking idiot at the party, playing the fucking victim to get attention from Si Bailey. She was obsessed with him but he was a fucking nobody; probably a queer. He was a dead-leg, a nothing, walking around like he owned the place. He probably didn't even like the Brown slag and she was hanging round him like a fucking leech, fuck knows why. He needed sorting out that was for sure.

I sat in my room, my stinky sweaty room. I had an ache in my groin, a feeling like my whole body was going to explode and I wanted it to explode all over one of those slag's faces. I laughed out loud at the thought of Si Bailey's reaction if I did.

I needed to sort out that Nessa Brown and find a way of getting to them. They fucking hated me and never want anything to do with me. Bess used to play with me when she was little, before she got involved with those two. They warped her mind about me.

As I peeped through the window staring at Bess I vowed to get back at Nessa Brown for showing me up, the fucking bitch. Yeah I'd get her back, fucking tramp. Only problem was that if you hurt one, you hurt them all and I never want to hurt Bess. I'd find a way to sort it though, somehow.

Chapter 6

Nessa - in the 1980s

We entered the age where it was important to look good but it was also embarrassing. Ella's poor breasts were out of control and she tried to hold them in as best she could. Our skirts and dresses had gotten shorter and shorter.

We'd do anything to follow fashion and try and look good but it was hard when there was no money around. Someone at school had an older brother who stole two left moccasins from the shopping centre. Ella was given them and she tried convincing herself that no-one would notice the difference. They were modern and that's all that mattered. Brand new shoes, just a pity they weren't a pair. She wore two left foot moccasins just to look cool.

Our parents didn't care about fashion. There was too much going on, too many mouths to feed.

We decided we needed jobs. We'd hung around the shops for years so we knew all the shopkeepers. Mike Bishop was a community policeman but also ran NSS, the local newsagents. When the three of us walked in together and asked for a job he handed us three paper bags full of ink and filth.

'Come on girls, if you really want to earn some bread, you're going to have to get your hands dirty.' He told us.

Bess was mortified. 'Sorry girls,' she said, 'I'm not delivering papers for nobody.' She stormed out of the shop. Me and Ella looked at each other and laughed. 'Well I'm up for it,' we said together.

And so it was. We had sixty papers to deliver each morning

before school. Ella's brothers had old, run down, Raleigh Boxer bikes that we used. By the time we had finished the round we'd be absolutely black.

Ella was given the high rise flats that looked out onto the large shopping centre. The buzzers on the security doors never worked so she'd have to wait until someone was going in or coming out which sometimes took a while. When she did get in the lifts were full of shit and piss and stank to the high heavens. So for £3.50 a week Ella Parker would run up fifteen flights of stairs all the way to the top, six blocks in all, to deliver her papers. And all before 9am just in time for school. Well not always in time for school.

I thought I'd got the better deal but soon changed my mind when the old English sheep dog at number 8 Brinkash Avenue started terrorising me. I walked slowly, very slowly, each morning up the tarmac drive which led to the house. It had a nice stone edge to it. The colourful flowers in the garden amazed me, all orange and in straight rows; it really did look beautiful. But I soon forgot my surroundings as I spotted the horrible creature salivating and trying it's hardest to squeeze out of the small window to get at me.

I was convinced that one day it would escape. As I got the morning newspaper out of the bag, the dog would disappear but I'd hear it breathing heavily on the other side of the door. I'd stand shaking my head. My breathing was heavier than the dog's. My skin prickled hot with fear at what was to come. Every day, as soon as I put the paper through the letter box, the big bastard pounced and snatched the paper before I had chance to finish pushing it through. I was terrified of that animal. Having delivered the newspaper, I would run as fast as possible up the garden path to get as far away from it as I could. I wish I'd got the tower blocks instead. I hated that dog with a passion but I did it every day before I started school for £3.50 a week.

I'd meet Ella back at the shop, both our faces black from the print. We'd each get a drink on credit until we got paid. Then we'd go and get Bess who would listen and laugh at our stories.

It was worth it though. After two months Ella bought a pair of Adidas Kick trainers from her wages; a left one and a right one. I spent as I went. I used to buy drinks, sweets and records so I never had anything left. I did manage to buy some brown cord material and I asked Pauline to run some elastic through the top and make it into skirts for me and the girls. Things were looking up.

I left school in the eighties and was ecstatic. Ella and Bess had gone through more or less the same subjects as me. We'd done nothing but laugh, wind up the teachers and smoke behind the prefab. This was a prefabricated structure which divided the school into who was cool and who was a knob; ironically you were considered a knob if you didn't smoke.

If I had put my mind to it, I could have achieved anything, but I didn't. I was too busy having a good time and my heart was never in it. I spent my days trying to persuade the girls to play truant. We'd get the number 102 bus to Altrincham and go stealing from Boots the Chemists. We'd use what we took as birthday gifts for our family or share them between us. I'd forge my foster parent's signature on notes to say why I'd been off school and that was it, no further questions asked.

I was still at the foster home. I'd live there longer than I had with my mum and dad. Kenny and Pat had become parents to Tom, Faya and me and it hadn't been too bad. We were always well fed and even if our clothing left a little to be desired we were ok, certainly compared to some. There was always a stigma about foster homes in the eighties. They had an aura about them and a misunderstanding about the children who were in them. There was this belief that they were ill disciplined and therefore violent and untrustworthy which was true in some cases. I was sure there were other reasons we had been put into care but they had never been explained to me. There were times when I would call to see my birth parents after school and it was like we'd never been there. I always felt like I was intruding. Mum and dad didn't speak to one another and the atmosphere was dire so I never stayed long.

In the evenings Pat allowed me to hang out with the girls. We'd sit in shop doorways, smoking and giving cheek to anyone who could take it. We'd meet up with the Bailey brothers and other friends and just have a laugh about this and that. Si was never able to have a conversation with me and looked intense if I ever caught his eye. He made me shudder. He had a profound effect on me and I could never understand why, nor could I talk to him, it was strange. I came to the conclusion that he must have hated me or he'd surely speak to me, wouldn't he?

One evening the boys told us a tale about smoking a joint. Ella, Bess and me looked at each other intrigued and then asked them what it was like, where had they got it from and did they have any?

Matthew Bailey said he knew where to get it from if we were up for it. I felt nervous and excited, I was sure it'd be ok. Bess shook her head and said no way but Ella was torn.

'Come on Ell,' I pleaded, 'it can't be that bad.'

'It'll be dead funny, come on let's have some,' said

Matthew.

He didn't have any on him but he said that if we all clubbed together we could buy some.

We turned out our pockets and managed to find just over two quid. Then of course we had to decide who was going for it.

'Can't we all go?' I said.

'Don't be fucking daft, they'll get nicked and we'll get leathered for encouraging them,' said Matthew all experienced in these matters.

'No, you go Nessa, you're the bravest,' he said all fired up.

I remember in my subconscious feeling Si's concern at the suggestion of me going which egged me on even more.

'OK, what do I say?' I agreed.

Matthew showed me where the house was. God it was rough; all the houses were but this was dog-rough. There were bin bags everywhere and the grass had grown right up to the windows. There was a black lad on the doorstep smoking what looked like a spliff. I jumped out of my skin when an enormous Alsatian started barking its head off as I approached. I stayed calm. The black lad just stared at me. I was shitting myself but I wasn't going to let him see that.

'Alright,' I said.

'What do you want?' he replied and smiled a sly twisted smile that made me freeze on the spot.

'A two pound wrap,' I said still trying to be cool.

'Two pound eh? What of?' he replied.

I couldn't believe it, why didn't he know what I wanted and just have it there ready for me?

'Matthew Bailey sent me so whatever he normally has,' I said.

I was sweating and shaking. What was I doing? My heart was in my mouth and my tongue was dry.

'Don't know him,' he said and passed me the spliff.

I stared at it in my hand for a long time and then decided I'd better smoke it. So I took a drag of my first spliff and inhaled it deep, deep into my lungs and held it there for a few seconds. My head felt like it was going to explode. I felt dizzy and not quite together. I stared at the spliff and took another long, deep drag of it and felt my eyelids go heavy. I felt strange and everything seemed a bit slower and all of a sudden the world seemed to have a soft focus to it. Somehow it was easier to breathe and I felt in a total state of relaxation.

I took another drag and went cross-eyed. The lad looked at me in shock. He was clearly amused and I found the look on his face hilarious. Suddenly I found myself bursting in to laughter, uncontrollable laughter.

'Oh my god,' I said, 'I'm so sorry.' I couldn't stop laughing and then we were both rolling about on his doorstep laughing our heads off. He handed me my draw and when I went to give him the two pounds he waved it away, 'nah, you've made my day. I love a watching a virgin being broken in.' I could feel my face redden and I left.

When I got back the others were waiting with concerned faces.

'Fucking hell, Ness,' Matthew shouted, 'where have you been?'

I nearly laughed again but managed to control myself. I told them the story whilst we took turns with the spliff. By the end of it we were all stoned, sitting in a shop doorway in the summer haze laughing our heads off. Even Si, whose glances towards me made the hairs on the back of my neck stand on end. His eyes met mine once or twice, his deep dark brown eyes. His soul was beckoning me. If I caught him looking he'd look away sharpish. I was confused and tried my hardest to catch his stare but he never looked me directly in the eye. I never could catch him. He obviously didn't feel it like I did. My eyes welled up. It hurt, I didn't know why; I just knew I loved him.

I saw Ella and Bess most days; evenings too. We really were a threesome. There was none of that three's-a-crowd malarkey. I didn't feel closer to either one of them and vice versa. We'd been through a lot in our young lives and shared everything. We were typical of our age, talking about boys and not just the Bailey boys. We reminisced about being little, spoke about our problems. We would usually end up in Ella's as, unlike Bess and me, she had a normal family.

We'd sit listening to Ella's records while her brothers and sister tried to overhear our conversations; just a typical girl's night in. I'd often get the bus home and the girls would walk me to the bus stop.

One night the bus was taking ages to come. We shared a cigarette and had a joke with some of the locals as they passed. We all knew each other in the area despite the size of the estate.

It was still light, but the sun was setting and the world had an orange glow to it. As deprived as it was, the area where we lived was alive with trees and grass; it looked beautiful in the misty evening glow.

I noticed the local young lovers, Skidder Barker and Francis Peters arguing as usual.

'Jesus,' I said, 'they've been together for ages.'

Apparently they'd shagged, thought they were in love and got engaged, but they were always fighting. The three of us watched what could have been a comedy sketch and laughed loudly when Skidder launched Francis into the bushes and kicked him hard right between his legs.

'Ouch,' we said in unison.

'Go on Skidder,' Ella shouted.

Skidder threw her engagement ring into the bushes but was immediately full of remorse.

'Aw, no,' she shouted. 'Now look what you made me do, you bastard. I've lost my ring. Help me find it.'

Next minute she was on all fours searching for her cheap engagement ring. We roared with laughter as all we could see was her bony rear-end sticking out of the bushes. At least this time her knickers were clean, thank god.

'They're mad,' I said still recovering from my laughter.

Just then the bus appeared. The girls gave me a kiss as I jumped on still laughing at the image of Skidder's arse and Francis crawling alongside her as they searched for the engagement ring.

I went up to the top deck and was greeted by the smell of stale smoke. I liked to sit at the front so I could see the journey ahead. As a child I would stand at the front of the bus holding onto the silver bars.

I didn't see him as I sat down. I was still waving to the girls. I didn't see him as I looked over to the other side of the road where Skidder and Francis were still franticly looking for the ring. I laughed to myself and leaned back sighing.

Then I saw him. Peter Lawrence. He was staring right at me.

'Hi,' I said casually. I managed a smile, he just nodded.

It occurred to me that he lived near Bess so trying to be polite I asked him where he was going. He frowned clearly not wanting to answer any questions.

'Not sure', he mumbled and we sat the rest of the way in

silence. I could feel his eyes boring into the side of my face. As I neared my stop I seriously started to wonder where he was going. He made me feel quite sick with the tension he created.

I stood up for my stop, pressed the bell and went down the stairs. I could sense he was behind me, could feel his breath on my neck. When I jumped off the bus, I took a step to one side to let him pass me by but he stopped too. I started to walk and as I did so it was as if he was walking with me.

I turned to him. 'Where are you going, Peter?' I said abruptly.

'Just wanted to walk you back,' he replied.

I was taken aback and dreaded to think how he might react if I said no.

'Erm, ok then,' I said reluctantly.

We started to walk together but I picked up my pace and tried to leave him behind. Suddenly he grabbed my hair and pulled it hard. I yelped, his face was intense and for a moment I felt very afraid. To my relief he let go and demanded I walk with him and talk to him. I felt so uncomfortable. I just made general chit chat, more from nerves than any interest I had in him. Then he mentioned Bess.

'Do you think Bess Holland will go out with me?' he asked.

I nearly laughed in relief that it wasn't me he wanted but also at the thought of Bess's reactions.

'Erm, I'm not sure. Do you want me to have a word?' I said just to get him off my back.

'Yeah,' he replied, 'deffo.'

He asked me to walk through the park with him but I didn't want to. My gut instinct was on high alert at his request. I explained that I needed to get home as I was on a curfew and my foster parents would go mad, if I was any later.

He totally ignored what I'd said and went on to tell me about his home life. How his mum had gone missing when he was six years old and how he had a soft spot for Bess because her mum had left her too. I was careful not to imply anything about his mum but I remembered they had been looking for her body at one point; it had been on the local news. I also remembered stories about his dad going to identify a body, so god knows what happened.

He carried on talking, telling me how his older brother, Johnny, had killed a whole family and was in prison, and that he hadn't meant it. I suddenly felt very scared at the thought of being alone with a murderer's brother so I cut the conversation dead. I explained that I had to get home quickly as I was late. With that I ran off as fast as I could. I didn't stop until I got to our front door.

Later that evening I stood and stared out of my bedroom window and watched the world go by. The estate was huge. Orange street lights peeped through the trees. I could hear planes flying overhead, the whistling of the turbines and the reverse thrust of the engines as they came into land at the airport only a short distance away. The street lights at the airport were much taller and they were white. They gave me the sense of it being a foreign land.

I thought about everyone I knew and loved including Kenny and Pat who were fabulous with me, my brother and sister. I wanted things to be so much better for all of us. Even though we were loved and cared for, I knew there was a better life outside the walls of this estate.

There was a tap at my door. I opened it to be greeted by Faya.

'Come in,' I said.

She explained that she needed to talk to me about things that had been playing on her mind for a long time. I looked at her and noticed how tall she had become. She was wearing a striped cotton night-shirt which showed off her beautiful long legs. She was coming up to twenty now and I realised she was a young woman, no longer a kid. I felt very much in awe of her.

She sat on the bed and began a story that revolted me to the pit of my stomach and shocked me to the core. She told me how our dad used to force her to do things, horrible, terrible things. How could he? I listened to her closely, I never questioned her once and I believed every word she said.

She told me that dad had made her put his 'thing' in her mouth, how he'd watch her in the shower and call her in whilst he was bathing. I burst into tears but she didn't stop. She explained that she'd told mum and how difficult that had been but she'd become scared that it would happen to me. Dad completely denied the allegations so mum ignored the conversation and stood by him. Yet a few weeks later we had been carted off to live with Kenny and Pat.

We were both crying now and I thanked her for saving me from the monster that was our dad. We held onto each tightly and I felt my sister's love for me. I loved her more than anyone that ever lived and she loved me. From that day forward we shared a closeness that wasn't there before, a sisterly love that could never be broken.

Chapter 7

Bess - in the 1980s

For me leaving school wasn't that exciting. It had been my escape, the only interaction I had with kids my own age and I'd enjoyed every minute of it. It certainly took a lot of pressure off my home life. The situation at home had never resolved itself. Mum never came home nor did she ever get in touch and I couldn't remember the last time I'd seen my dad sober.

I was sixteen and I was not prepared to forgive the woman who had once been so central to my life. There were so many times growing up when I'd needed her.

The most confusing time for any female is when they are changing from a little girl to a young woman. It had been particularly traumatising for me. I had no idea what was happening and I couldn't approach my dad; there was no way he'd be able to cope with it.

I started my period at ten years old and was distraught. I was doing cross country at school and I remember feeling something running down my leg. I looked down to see red sticky blood. I gasped in shock and realised that all the other kids had spotted it too. Luckily Ella and Nessa came to my rescue and saved any dignity I had left.

Thank god my Nana had already bought me some sanitary towels. They were about two inches thick with great big loops on either end. I never knew what the loops were for but for the rest of the week I felt like I was walking with a pillow between my legs. I actually believed that all women were walking around after the age of ten with a big pillow stuck between their legs. I was mortified. I thought I would just bleed until I died.

Fortunately, Chris Parker took it upon herself to explain the reality of it. We were all upstairs in Chris's bedroom while she told us about periods, cycles and lots other words that I couldn't quite grasp.

'So you just pull this paper strip off the back and stick it in your knickers,' Christine explained as the girls stuffed their fists into their mouths, desperately trying not to laugh. I didn't think it was funny but their faces were, and that was enough to make me laugh. I went into the toilet, pulled down my knickers peeled the paper strip off the back of the sanitary towel and stuck it straight onto my privates. The itch it caused all day was unbearable and when I'd told Christine later she was in hysterics, so were Ella and Nessa. I didn't laugh as it wasn't easy or painless to pull it off my newly developed pubic hair.

There were other things that my dad couldn't handle and other times when I needed my mum. It had become more and more obvious that I needed to wear a bra. My nipples were sore through constantly bobbing up and down in my school shirt. Again it was Nana that saved me and got me a cheap bra from the market. It was the ugliest thing I'd ever seen. The straps were huge and there were two saggy bits where my boobs didn't quite reach

'It'll last you that will,' she said and was dead chuffed with herself. I wore it for weeks with an old vest over the top so no one could see it through my white school shirt.

After that games and PE were out of the question for me. I either had a sanitary towel stuck to the hairs on my fanny or blood running down my leg and a bra that my dad could have used to carry concrete around his building site.

I couldn't face it so I would sign a letter as if from my dad excusing me every week. I was sad as I enjoyed PE. I was a fast runner, strong swimmer, a brilliant goal attack in Netball and generally a good all-rounder but I'd have died before letting anyone see the bra.

Dad continued to prop up the bar in the Lion or have his head in the toilet on his return. He would sit in his armchair watching the telly with his slippers and papers next to him and for a minute I'd think he was sober. I used to pretend he was and imagine what it would be like to have a normal dad.

I'd rise early every morning and make sure the house was spotless. I'd put the pots away from the night before and wipe the bath and toilet; I hated anything being out of place.

One of the things dad had managed to do was open a savings account for me at the local post office. Every single spare penny I got I would put in there. That way I could always make sure I had some money for emergencies. My savings had grown over the years; my little blue book with GPO written on the front was getting quite full. I just wanted it to grow and grow and one day I'd be able to escape.

Would I really be able to leave my dad when that time came? It was an argument I'd have regularly in my mind. It was an odd set up, not me living on my own with my dad, but the fact he was always in a world of his own. My heart ached for him and I loved him, yearned for his attention, his affection, anything, but it was never to be. It was as if I reminded him of her which I probably did. It wasn't fair.

The summer I finished school was hot. I wasn't having a six week holiday as I was one of the lucky ones that already had work. I'd had a Saturday job with a local hairdresser for years and my boss had agreed to take me on full time doing a youth training scheme known as YTS. Although I was lucky,

I was also gutted to be missing out on the fun the rest of them would be having. On the other hand they wouldn't be getting paid and I would.

My boss was gay. His name was William and he was a nightmare. The other girls were older than me and I was intimidated by them. William loved me because I was hard working and always did as I was told. It was detrimental to my relationship with the others, they hated me, but I didn't care, I just got on with it.

My first full day at the hairdressers proved to be a trying one. William introduced me to Mrs Lee, a rich old Jewish lady who had owned the local book shop. He'd told me about her in the past and how they had to treat her like a queen as she was very affluent.

Whenever Mrs Lee came in, Will would get out his best China tea set which had belonged to his mother. Only Mrs Lee could use it as it was very precious to him. He always put it away straight afterward.

That day I was tasked with going up to his flat above the salon and preparing 'a proper cup of tea' for Mrs Lee.

'Remember, don't give her a cup if it has a chip in it,' he reminded me as I set off. 'Put it on a tray with some of those nice biscuits and whatever you do, don't drop my mother's china or your life won't be worth living.'

Jesus, by the time I reached the kitchen I was quivering with nerves. Mrs Lee was proper stuck up and I couldn't believe that I had to make her a cup of tea. Why me? Anyway I did as I was told. I made the tea and set it out on the tray with the biscuits. Unfortunately I started to shake as I got to the top of the stairs. I had visions of me dropping the tray and then that's exactly what happened. I lost my footing on the top step. I didn't fall but the tray slipped from my grasp and bounced gracefully down each step straight to the bottom of the stairs and into the salon where Mrs Lee was having her hair washed.

She immediately jumped up looking like a drowned rat and started to scream about hot tea and splinters everywhere. I just froze to the spot not quite believing what had happened. I stood there shaking, waiting for Will to start shouting and sure enough I didn't have long to wait. He rushed to the back of the shop and I could hear him screaming dreadful abuse. I couldn't bear it. I just ran down the stairs and out of the door. 'You dozy, dilatory, gormless bastard,' he was shouting, 'Don't you ever come back.'

My first full time job lasted less than a day.

I had an idea where the girls would be so I went to look for them. They had made their way to Chorlton, a place just outside Manchester where there was a Marina crowded with locals. They had huge cassette players blasting out loud music. Everyone was in denim shorts and had towels and bottles of pop. I found Ella and Nessa and joined them. They were next to a few of the old school crowd. Skidder and Francis were there, totally smashed, smoking weed till their faces were green.

The girls were ecstatic to see me.

'What's up?' Ella said. 'I thought you were in work.'

I explained what had happened and was doing an impression of Will mincing about the shop screaming 'you dozy, dilatory, bastard,' and Miss Lee screaming. I described the state she was in when she shot up as bits of china and hot tea hit her.

I don't know what I expected but they all roared with laughter which made me laugh and the more I thought about it the harder I laughed. On the bright side at least I got to spend the day in the sunshine with my two best friends.

We made our way back to the estate. It wasn't far but as we were in a big group it took longer than it should have. Every now and again, someone dropped off to go to their own neck of the woods. I didn't want the day to end so I asked Nessa and Ella if they would like to sleep at my house. They looked shocked.

'What about your dad, Bess?' Ella said; she was concerned.

'What about him?' I replied. 'He'll be pissed out of his brain. He won't even realise we're there.'

The girls were excited. We'd have the house to ourselves most of the night. Nessa told Pat she was sleeping at Ella's as she didn't think they would agree to her staying at mine.

It was on. The girls were sleeping at my house. I was so excited. I pinched a couple of bottles of dad's beer and put a record on the player. Not too loud but loud enough that we could have a dance to it; and dance we did. We had a right old boogie. Ella was soon drunk although she'd only had a few swigs of beer and Nessa wasn't far behind but I needed to stay in control just in case there was any hassle when dad got in.

'Hey Bess, guess what?' Nessa said. 'Peter Lawrence followed me home the other night and all because he fancies you. He asked me to ask you to go out with him.'

Nessa went into detail about Peter's strange admission of love for me and we all started laughing. I explained that I thought he felt sorry for me because we both had to grow up without our mums.

'So what do you reckon Elizabeth? You want to go out with him?' said Ella. She already knew the answer. I told her to shut it and to get another beer down her neck.

She laughed as she took a big swig and as she did there

was such a racket coming from the front of the house. I looked at the clock and realised that it would be dad. I grabbed the beers from the girls and put them under the sink so he wouldn't see them.

He was noisier than usual and I was sure I could hear groaning. My heart stopped

'Something's wrong,' I said to the girls. I just had a feeling. I ran down the hall and found my dad collapsed on the floor.

He was flat on his face and as I turned him over I could see he was cut and his eye was swollen.

'Dad,' I cried, 'Dad, who did this to you?'

I looked up at the girls, 'Help me get him up.'

'What happened, Mr Holland?' said Nessa trying to talk to my dad as she helped him up.

He shooed her away. Ella opened the front door.

'What are you doing El? Where're you going?' I shouted. I thought she was going home and leaving us to deal with the situation but she wasn't. She'd gone outside to see who was about.

We managed to get dad seated in his chair. I cleaned his face with tears in my eyes. Tomorrow I would tell him, tell him how much I loved him and tell him that he had to help us both and stop drinking. He muttered something about Peter Lawrence and was looking for his wallet. He'd obviously been mugged. My stomach sank at the thought that it could be Peter but we didn't know for sure. I couldn't quite believe it.

We made dad copious amounts of tea and tried to sober him up to see if he could remember anything about what had happened but he couldn't. I think the shock of it all was starting to sober him up. His face looked better and you could just about see his beautiful blue eyes.

'Do you think it was Peter?' Nessa asked me later.

Ella said she wouldn't put it past him but I didn't want to believe it. I mean, fucking hell, he practically confessed his love for me to Ella so why would he hurt my dad? Nessa wanted to phone the police but I decided against it. I was afraid they might realise I'd had to bring myself up and my dad would get in trouble.

Dad looked much better the following morning and was actually enjoying us girls fussing around him. It was nice to see him joking with Nessa and bossing Ella around. It was even nicer to see him smile.

I sat on the arm of the chair while he sipped his tea. I needed to say something.

'Dad, I love you so much. Please don't ever put yourself at risk like that again, you could have been killed,' I said. I was trembling as I spoke.

He stood up from the chair and took me in his arms and squeezed me so tight that I went a bit dizzy. The girls had tears in their eyes too, and I could see my dad starting to well up. It was a moment I would remember for my entire life and it made me forget about the mother who left me with the drunken father. Well for a minute anyway.

Later that day, the YTS people got in touch again. They had found me a new placement and by the end of the week I was back at work in a different salon.

Chapter 8

Ella - in the 1980s

'Ella, Ella,' my mother's voice was getting on my nerves. I knew she wanted to me to get up to sign on but I just couldn't be arsed. I'd just finished school for god's sake, what difference would £14 a week make that I never had before?

'Ella, Ella,' she called again.

'Fuck me,' I whispered under my breath. 'OK. I'm getting up,' I screamed back down the stairs.

'Come on,' she repeated. 'You won't get your stamp paid if you don't sign on.'

'You don't get a stamp, mum, you get a giro,' I retorted.

'Your national insurance stamp, you daft cow,' she replied.

I didn't care about any stamp or any giro to be honest; I was sure it would all fall into place. I hated the whole business of growing up; it was too much like hard work.

I stared out of the window. The hazy sunshine reminded me of school. I watched the younger kids playing outside. Some kicked a ball between them; others were riding up and down on their bikes. I felt sad that I couldn't do that anymore. Well I could, but not with as much freedom as they had.

I looked around the bedroom floor for clothes. We never had wardrobes in our house. Clothes weren't put on hangers, we didn't have any. I didn't have many clothes anyway. It occurred to me then that I couldn't get away with just wearing my school uniform every day anymore.

I went downstairs to look for something to wear. There

was usually stuff in what should have been our pantry. I opened the pantry door and screamed at the sight of my mother smoking a cigarette.

'Mum, what are you doing?' I said gobsmacked.

'What does it look like I'm doing?' she said, as the smoke bellowed out of her nose and mouth.

'Aw mum,' I said laughing. 'Dad will kill you if he finds out.'

'Well he better not bloody find out then,' she warned me.

I had never seen mum look so vulnerable, it made me laugh.

'Get your arse out of here and get signed on,' she said, looking at me sternly.

'Not before you give us a drag of that,' I said, nodding at the fag in her hand.

We both stood in the smoke-filled pantry laughing at our naughtiness; mother and daughter sharing a cigarette. Dad would have gone mad.

I grabbed some jeans and my green and blue Levi's jumper. It was my pride and joy even though it was from the market and probably not even genuine Levi's. I still felt cool when I wore it, which was a rarity.

I stepped out of the house and took in the beautiful blue sky. The birds were singing in the trees. I felt a pang of self-awareness, the little girl I used to be was disappearing fast and I didn't like it. I knew I was going through the next phase of my life and was finding it hard to grasp; it was frightening. I didn't want to grow up, get a job and move away from my family.

I could hear lawn mowers in the distance and the noise of the motorway behind our house. I started walking and eventually reached our high school. For a moment I stood still and looked through the railings. I was going to miss school, not that I enjoyed it much, but it was a massive part of my life. I reflected on some of those special times as I walked.

It was boiling in the sun so I pulled my jumper over my head and tied it around my waist. My lemon vest top was a bit mucky but at least I wasn't roasting. My visit to the dole office didn't take long. I signed 'P. Parker' on a dotted line and that was it.

Two days later my first giro came through the post.

'Hey mum, I got £28,' I was elated. I felt rich. 'What do I do with it?' I said.

'You'll have to get it changed at the post-office. You can get my family allowance while you're at it,' she said, and she got her long yellow book from under the cushion.

I walked up to the post-office in the gorgeous sunshine, not paying any attention to my surroundings, just feeling the warmth of the sun on my neck and arms. When I got there the queue was out of the door and almost up to the wall of the Lion where semi-clad men were sitting having a pie and a pint for lunch.

I saw Mr Holland and he waved at me. I smiled; he was a lovely man and I really liked him. After the night of his mugging, or whatever happened, he had really calmed down. He still drank most nights but not quite as much and it made a difference to Bess, who was much happier and that made me and Nessa happy too.

The cronies that were with Mr Holland started whistling at me and shouting things. I was mortified and felt my cheeks flush. I hated this attention from men lately. I was beginning to resent being anywhere near them. How dare they whistle at me? I was a young girl, the dirty old bastards. I stuck two fingers up to them and took my place in the giro queue.

Half an hour later with mine and my mum's money securely in my pocket, I went over to chat with Mr Holland. If those men said anything else to me I'd kick them in the bollocks.

While I was chatting to Mr Holland I heard a group of older lads behind him all talking about the shabeen that had been going on all week in the flats at the back of the local park. A shabeen was an illegal rave or party generally frequented by people of Caribbean origin. I heard them say there was plenty of booze, birds and weed and that it was at Dougie's flat.

'Is Bess on half day today?' I asked Mr Holland.

'Aye, she is Ella.'

I said goodbye and ran to her house to find her. I told her about the shabeen and was trying to persuade her to come.

'Bess come on. Oh my God, it'll be ace; we'll have such a laugh. Our folks won't know. We could stay here, your dad wouldn't even know.'

The minute I'd said it I knew it was the wrong thing to say, and she knew that I knew because she went very quiet. The next few minutes were going to be a bumpy ride.

Nessa's knock on the door interrupted the tense silence.

'Ella, I've just been to your house,' she said as she came into the room. 'Your mum's going mad for her money. She's sent Henry to try and find you and he's going mad as he was supposed to be going out with his mates. She thinks you've lost it and are too scared to go home without it.'

I laughed but double checked her money was still safe in my pocket.

I told Nessa about the shabeen and Bess's mood seemed to lighten.

'Why don't we all stay here?' she said. 'My dad won't know,' and I smiled, then she smiled back. I don't know why but that smile made the butterflies in my stomach flutter their little wings hard inside me. I was probably just excited.

The plans were in motion. All we needed to do now was convince our parents to let us stay at Bess's.

Kenny and Pat were a doddle compared to my mother and father. My God you'd think I was asking to stay at Peter Lawrence's house. Mum was really hard work. She didn't miss a trick and had an answer for everything. If it wasn't for my dad, I wouldn't have been able to go anywhere or do anything.

She had insisted on walking up to Bess's to get her family allowance from me. I raised the topic of the sleepover with her. 'God mum, we're staying here for the night, we're not leaving the country,' I said and managed to convince her. Josie was laughing behind mum's skirt.

Mum and Josie finally left and Bess immediately turned the stereo up to full blast. We all danced and sang along to 'Sunday Bloody Sunday', and started to raid Bess's wardrobe trying to find something suitable to wear that would make us look older.

We couldn't afford to dress up back then but we knew how to apply makeup and Bess would style our hair.

We left the house in the late evening sunshine and went to see if Mr Holland was still at the pub. He was.

Bess persuaded him to get a load of bottles of lager for us explaining we were off to a party and would all be staying at his later. He was completely fine with it all. I was jealous that she could do whatever she wanted whilst I had to practically beg every time I wanted to go anywhere. We stayed at the pub for a couple of hours. We could hear the music from the jukebox inside the pub. Fleetwood Mac's 'Albatross' in the background made the warm evening feel even warmer and the camaraderie from the punters was brilliant; you wanted for nothing. It was like being amongst family.

As the bell for last orders rang we were chatting to some of the lads who were going across to Dougie's party. They were only too happy for us to tag along so we headed off to our first shabeen with the lads from the pub including the landlady's son, Conny. My stomach was in knots and I felt so nervous.

Bob Marley songs filled the white musky stairways of the flats. You could smell the weed, mixed in with dry piss, a mile away. When we got to the top of the stairs, only the top half of the door was open and a big black man, who I recognised as Dougie was taking money off people for letting them in. I still had my dole money on me, so at least we could pay our way. Dougie stared as we approached the door. He sucked his teeth. 'Who said you could come here?' he said in his deep Jamaican accent. Before we could answer Conny jumped in.

'They're sound mate, she's Holly's daughter,' he said. For once Bess was proud of who her dad was.

The rooms were lit by orange bulbs that barely provided any real light. People were drinking and smoking. A couple of black girls were bumping and grinding in a corner, but the music was easy to get lost in.

In the kitchen they were selling bottles of beer for fifty pence and spliffs for two quid along with Bluebols, the liquor of choice at that time. I was feeling up for anything. I could tell by Bess and Nessa's faces that they were too. We filled up on Bluebols and bought a couple of spliffs. There were other drugs on sale but I thought of the consequences if my mum ever found out. I was in deep enough so I just watched as people heated stuff on a spoon or sucked powder off foil. I watched their faces as they went full pelt from earth to heaven as quick as a flash. Their change of demeanour even went as far as their voices and the whole night became a smoky haze of people moving in slow motion.

'Hey Ell,' a voice came from behind me. It was Conny. I stumbled into him, he felt warm and safe. It made me feel quite emotional. The music was hitting me hard now as it became louder and more and more poignant or so I thought in my stoned, drunken state.

Conny was getting the wrong end of the stick, but I liked it. I wanted him to get the wrong end of the stick. I wanted him to wrap his arms around me and make me feel safe. I breathed in his masculine smell. He bent down and kissed me. I was hungry for his mouth and kissed him back hard and with the sound of Barrington Levy banging out in the background we made our way to one of the bedrooms. I knew it was wrong but the feelings I was experiencing pushed away any doubts I had.

I was hot between my legs. I'd felt it before but not like this. It was almost a throbbing sensation. Conny pulled my jeans down to my ankles, pushed up my vest top and rubbed my tits. 'Oh my god,' I was panting. I wanted him now. He sucked hard on one of my nipples, I moaned loudly.

'Fuck me,' I demanded. He didn't have to be asked twice. He quickly undid his belt and ripped off his jeans as fast as he could. I couldn't believe the size of his dick and before I knew it, he was pushing it inside me.

'Ouch,' I yelped as it went in but the feeling soon became warm and his hardness was making me breathless as I started to enjoy the hot thrusts of his large cock. I succumbed by arching my back high and pushing myself with the flow. He pulled it out and started moaning loudly as he wanked off all over me. He kissed me on the head and pulled his jeans back up. He grabbed a nearby piece of clothing and wiped his spunk off me. 'Do you want a drink kid,' he said.

'I think she's had enough Conny, don't you?' It was Nessa at the door. The look she gave me was filthy. 'What the hell have you done, El?' she mumbled in shock.

I don't remember much more of the night. I had flashbacks of Nessa and Bess trying their hardest to hold me up. I remember that they were fuming and swearing and calling Conny a bastard.

I woke up on a cold, hard floor and couldn't move my head. At first I was convinced I'd been attacked and beaten up. I saw blood on my jeans and panicked. I stood up quickly but the room started to spin.

I realised I was in Bess's kitchen. I took deep breaths but my vision was blurry and I was clammy with cold sweat. I picked up a bottle of milk from the table and drank the lot. My God, I felt like I was dying.

Carefully I headed upstairs, afraid that if I blinked my head would cave in. I needed to see if the girls were there, and that they were ok. Then I remembered what had happened. I closed my eyes and it all flashed through my head. 'Fucking hell,' I whispered out loud, my stomach lurched and it gripped me hard. What had I done?

Why had I done that? That feeling gripped my stomach again. Oh my god, I had lost my virginity to fucking Conny who went drinking with my best friend's fucking dad.

What would my mum say if she found out? She'd go berserk.

Chapter 9

Peter Lawrence

I was there. I sat there grinning and holding my cock in a dark corner of a room that was filled with coats and empty cans of lager. I'd gone in to have a rummage through the pockets; see if any fucker had been daft enough to leave any money in them. I certainly got more than I bargained for.

Watching Ella Parker getting fucked and rubbing her tits up and down in that Conny's face had left me feeling dazed. I pulled hard at myself while they did it. They couldn't see me sitting at the back of the room, crouched next to a chair. I imagined it was me sticking it in her. I almost yelled as the spunk shot across the room. Just in time before her mates ran in to spoil the fun. Bunch of stupid slags they were.

Chapter 10

Ella

It kicked off big time; mum went ballistic. I was right, she went mad. She'd been nosing in my diary, which was bang out of order, and read all about my one night stand. She went mental and wasn't going to stop until she got her answer. She kept going on and on, constantly asking 'why.' All the time, why had I done it and why him?

I didn't really have the answer. It hadn't felt wrong at the time, something just took over my body and I wanted him. I didn't regret it, but how could I explain that to mum? I'd said the same to the girls too and they didn't get it although once they had calmed down they wanted all the details.

Mum was going on. 'Are you even listening to me, Ella?' she screamed. I didn't reply. I turned to walk out of the bedroom, fed up with the interrogation that was taking place, but she stopped me.

'I haven't finished yet,' she shouted.

'God mum, it happened, just leave it now,' I said.

That made it worse. She was furious and without thinking slapped me hard across the face sending me flying onto the bedroom floor.

I was shocked and sat touching the hot sting on my cheek. I felt tears of frustration welling up in my eyes. I'd expected all hell to break lose but not this. Mum was screaming now, salivating at the mouth. She was threatening to get Conny and break his balls.

'You're a slag, Ella. That's it now. No one will have any respect for you. They'll think you're a dirty cheap nasty little slag and they'll all want a go.'

Aghast, I felt anger like I'd never felt before. Fuck off, I didn't deserve this, not from her of all people, not from my mum who was had always been my rock. I couldn't help myself.

'You fucking hypocrite. You fucking hypocrite,' I screamed.

I was breathless in my anger. 'Is that what happened to you when you shagged my dad; my real dad?' There it was I'd said it and there was no going back.

The shock on my mum's face was enough to shut her up. It frightened me but at least it calmed things down for a bit.

Later me, my mum and dad, all had a good chat. The question was on the tip of my tongue but I didn't dare ask and nobody volunteered an answer. That question, the inevitable question. Who was my real father?

I found a job in the local factory making hosepipes of all things. I'd made it clear to all and sundry that it was only a stop gap until I could find something better but that stop gap was earning me a fortune. A hundred and ten pounds a week which in the eighties was mega bucks for someone my age.

I looked forward to 1pm on Fridays when the bell rang to indicate the end of my shift. We would down tools immediately and head along to the Supervisor's office. Friday was pay-day.

After collecting my money I would run up to the lockers, get changed then head home for the weekend.

I got friendly with a girl called Joanne who worked with me. Sometimes we'd sneak up to the toilets for an unauthorised cigarette break. We'd both climb up onto the back of the toilet and suck the life out of an Embassy Number One King Size. We'd blow the smoke out of the open toilet window.

One such time the door suddenly burst open and Sheila, the Supervisor, with her fat side-kick, Pauline, barged in, sniffing the air. Although smoking was banned on the premises, there was an unsaid rule about smoking in the toilets and most people tended to turn a blind eye. These two wouldn't bend for anyone. In fact it was like they had a lifetime ambition to catch someone and give them a good leathering.

The rest of the women in the changing rooms were going through the usual gossip, slagging anyone and everyone off. They stopped in horror as the gruesome twosome started banging on the toilet door that we'd locked ourselves in.

'Hope you're not fucking smoking in there?'

Me and Joanne stared at one another with a look of horror on our faces. Joanne's eyes nearly popped out of her skull and her mouth dropped to her chest. She had taken a great big drag of her ciggy just as Sheila banged on the door. In her panic she started to choke on the smoke. I wanted to laugh but I didn't dare. I couldn't be arsed facing these two bullies and certainly didn't want to be up in the office facing disciplinary.

The more I looked at Joanne's face the funnier it was becoming. In desperation Joanne stuck her head out of the window and tried to cough out the smoke as quietly as she could. I thought that her guts were coming next and rubbed her back while she too was trying to stifle a fit of the giggles.

The next bang on the door made us jump out of our skins and caused Joanne to cough even harder. That finished me off; I couldn't help myself and laughed so hard my snorting sounded like a pig on heat. The sound caused Joanne to laugh herself into a coughing fit.

I tried to stuff my fist into my mouth to stop myself laughing; tears were streaming down our cheeks. We both had our heads as far out of the toilet window as we could get them. Joanne sounded like a dying sea lion.

Supervisor Sheila was not amused.

'Fucking taking the piss whoever's in there,' she bellowed at the door. 'Fucking joke this place,' she added. They both stormed out still shouting and cursing. 'We'll find out who it is sooner or later and when we do, God help them.'

'What are you up to next weekend?' I asked Joanne once we'd finally stopped laughing, 'Do you fancy coming to Blackpool?'

Chapter 11

Nessa

We had made a plan to go to Blackpool one Friday when Ella got paid. She was the only one of us with a load of money. We were going to eat, drink and be merry, see the illuminations and stay in a bed and breakfast. We couldn't wait.

The only problem was Ella had invited a girl who she worked with to come too. Someone called Joanne. Bess pulled a face when she found out and took me to one side almost in a state of panic. I knew she felt uncomfortable when anyone else was in the mix and I was secretly pissed off at Ella. She knew what Bess was like and the night had been planned for ages.

We got a taxi to the local train station. Although we didn't have much money between us we were frivolous compared to our parents; they wouldn't dream of getting a taxi anywhere. They'd worked too hard to blow their money away but we were bit more free with ours.

As we approached the station I couldn't believe my eyes. Si Bailey and some of his mates were waiting for the Blackpool train. My heart skipped a beat, I started to shake and feel dizzy. Only he, only Si Bailey, ever made me feel that way. He put his head down when he saw me approach and again I felt the frustration. Why would he never look at me? I felt like asking him but I didn't.

Ella went bounding down the platform towards them. 'Got any weed?' she shouted.

I looked at Bess, rolled my eyes and smiled.

The night was a roaring success. We were bladdered and ended up in a pub called the Manchester. Well we had to, didn't we? The lads had joined us and were chatting up all the girls in the pub. Joanne had made it quite clear that she fancied Si and was all over him like a rash; he was enjoying it too. I felt sick to the pit of my stomach as I watched her with him.

'I can't relax while she's all over him,' I told Bess who was busy looking for Ella.

'Well go and speak to him babe,' Bess said impatiently.

Ella came bounding over to us. 'Hey there's a club upstairs and I've got a load of free tickets. It's called Sequins and you can skin up in there. They're not arsed.' She turned to Joanne and shouted over 'We're off to Sequins. Come on, and keep your hands off Jay.'

Ella looked at Si. 'Oi, Jay, you lot coming?'

Me and Ella got up on the stage next to the DJ and were dancing to Madonna like a couple of professionals, or so we thought. We were soaked in sweat from head to toe and laughing at our own antics. Ella was pretending she was part of the DJ set and I was dancing just as hard.

It was obvious you could get anything you wanted in this place. Our group found a corner and drank copious amounts of lager. It wasn't long before we went onto pints to save going to the bar as much while the boys did the skinning up.

The night was rocking. Joanne was still talking to Si who now didn't really seem interested. I hated the thought that he was there and I couldn't just go over and speak to him. What was up with me? What was up with him?

Bess went and sat between Si and Joanne and I felt relieved. I laughed as Ella carried on freaking out to the music. With a bottle in one hand and a cig in the other she was having a blast.

Later that night, we munched our way through dirty burgers whilst taking in the famous Blackpool Illuminations. The atmosphere was amazing, so many different colours. The trams all lit up and the scenery vast. Then there was the smell of fish and chips, candy floss and the noise of the busy slot machines in the arcades. Separate gangs of men and women with corny 'kiss me quick' hats and plastic boobs; it was alive. It told me immediately where I was; there was no place like it. The huge funfair was still in full swing and you could hear the music and the infamous laughing clown, the whole place made me smile.

We were walking along the prom, or more correctly, being blown down the prom. The lads were staying close by so it made sense for us all to walk together. They'd not even got started yet, even though none of them could stand up properly. Ella insisted on going to an all-nighter and was threatening to run in the sea.

'Oh, sort your head out, Ella,' said Bess who was getting irritated by her attention seeking.

''Ere look,' Ella squealed, 'A pool club. We could get a beer and have a laugh.'

Everyone agreed. As Ella walked through the door she tripped on the first step and fell all the way to the bottom of the stairs, missing all the steps in between.

We just stood gobsmacked. It was Bess who moved first, 'Ella, you ok?' she shouted running down the steep flight of stairs towards her, followed by Joanne and me.

By now a crowd had gathered around Ella, who was lying on the floor.

'My god, don't just stand there.' Bess panicked, unable to control her anger.

She rolled Ella on to her back. Her eyes were open but she was obviously having trouble with focusing through blurred vision.

'Come on babe, get up,' Bess said. Ella winced as Bess pulled her arm, but she managed to struggle to her feet, seemingly none-the-worse for her fall.

The crowd cheered as she stood and groggily asked if we could join in and play pool. And we did, right into the early hours. We drank and potted balls while in the background the jukebox played a collection of Bob Dylan songs. The atmosphere was rowdy and a fight broke out between one of Si's mates and an older bloke who was dressed like a biker. A bottle had come into contact with someone's flesh as there was broken glass and blood everywhere.

Si quickly pushed us to the back of the room and broke through a locked door at the back of the club. One by one he managed to get us all into this now unlocked room. Oh my god he was such an alpha male, so protective and authoritative. The feeling of love that rushed through my body was incredible. We followed him, panicking as the crowd began to throw bottles and punches. The guy who had started the fight caught up with us. 'For fuck sake, let's get out of here,' he shouted.

We found ourselves in the cellar. Luckily there were steps with a door at the top which we hoped would lead us out to the street. The walls were lined with crates and crates of beer so everyone grabbed as many as they could on the way out. I dropped a crate on my foot and yelped in pain.

'Y'alright?' Si asked as he ran over to me.

He looked really concerned. The pain in my foot quickly subsided. I felt hot and faint. He always had that effect on me.

'Ere, Vanessa,' he said. He always called me by my full name. 'Give us that,' and he took the crate from me.

I couldn't take it anymore; my face was bright red, enough to light up the dark passage we found ourselves in. I looked away. I put my head down and stared at my feet. I couldn't have looked at him even if I'd have wanted too. I held onto his waist as if guiding him through the passage towards the exit door. There was no way I was letting go of his strong muscular back. I smiled as he led me to safety.

Si banged the door hard with his shoulder. He fell headlong onto the street with two crates of beer in his hands.

The relief was immediate as we all piled out laughing and screaming and thinking about the trail of disaster we'd just left behind. At least we had loads of beer as a consolation prize.

I stared at Si. I wasn't going to take my eyes off him because, in this moment, he was mine. He looked at me very quickly before putting his head down. He had helped me and I didn't want to let him go. The fire in my tummy when he was near me was too much. He made me weak at the knees. I tried to catch his eyes again, but the moment had gone. Nevertheless I wasn't moving from the heat of his body, no matter what. He was standing with me, not moving and I could feel a force, a strong force like it was pulling me toward him. I knew that deep down there was something there, something I couldn't turn my back on.

Everyone grabbed their beer and crossed the main road to the beach which, in November, wasn't the best idea. The sea was black and angry and huge waves gave us a soaking from the spray. The wind was raging, and we were all freezing. The girls were dancing trying to keep warm, but the lads were having none of it so we decided to dump the crates of beer and leg it back.

As we got near our B and B without saying a word or looking at me, Si wrapped his big arms around me. I felt a surge like an electric shock going through my whole body. I felt like I was re-joining something. I was somewhere I belonged. He made me feel safe and whole. As the girls reached the boarding house his grip tightened and I didn't want to go in. I pulled him towards me. He didn't kiss me on the lips as I hoped and expected but hugged me tightly to his chest, holding the back of my head. It was as though he still couldn't look at me. He finally released me, kissed me on my forehead and went off into the night.

I was devastated. I felt lost and lonely as I watched him go. I didn't know why but I had a tear in my eye. I longed for him to turn around. Ached for him to look at me or change his mind and run back to me, but he didn't.

I joined the girls in their room. They were totally pissed, stoned and knackered and lay on the beds fully clothed and half dead. Ella said she felt the room spinning around her before rushing into the bathroom and clinging tightly to the toilet bowl as she gagged and retched. Bess ran over to rescue her, as she always did, and gently rubbed her back.

What Ella wasn't aware of when she woke up in the morning was that we'd shaved her eyebrows and blackened her teeth with a permanent marker that I had in my bag, she looked an absolute sight.

We were excited for our traditional full English breakfast and as we sat down people were staring at Ella, nudging each and other grinning.

'What's everyone staring at?' said Ella who had started to giggle. 'Do we look that bad?' We howled with laughter. Ella went to move her arm but winced in pain, and spotted herself in one of the tiled mirrors that were all around the dining room.

'Jesus, you bastards,' she roared.

No washing or combing of the hair could make her look anymore presentable later on that evening as she sat in the casualty department waiting to get her arm x-rayed with me, her mum and Bess.

'You're a fucking disgrace, Ella,' her mum said squeezing her tightly. A big smile broke out on her face. 'But you're my disgrace, and I fucking love you,' she added.

Chapter 12

Bess

It was bitterly cold and the windows were frosted up on the inside. The council kept promising us central heating but never committed to a date. They were also in the process of putting double glazing in properties across the estate to reduce the noise from aircraft from being so close to Manchester Airport but they hadn't gotten around to our house yet.

I was getting ready for work. Dad had left early that morning and put the fire on ready for me. My heart went out to him. As far as I knew, he'd never missed a day's work and I had to admire him for that. Mind you he'd never missed a day off the booze either but he wasn't half as bad as he was when mum left us. For a minute, as I often did, I wondered what she was doing and where she was living. What if she was dead? What if mum had died? Would I be upset if she had? I pushed the thought from my mind. I was confused as ever about why she had left.

I stared at my reflection in the mirror and knew that I looked like mum with my long blonde curls right down my back. My piercing blue eyes were my dad's, there was no doubt about that. I wasn't sure where I'd inherited my huge breasts from though. They were getting bigger by the minute and I was finding that men were no longer looking into my eyes when they spoke to me. Rather they'd speak directly to my nipples even though they were safely hidden underneath my clothes.

I'd continued with hairdressing, even after the unfortunate

incident at William's. I was working at a salon one day a week to keep the tax-man happy and the rest I did from home or at clients' houses. My phone never stopped ringing day or night. People weren't bothered what time it was, they wanted their hair doing and they wanted it doing now. I was proud of myself, proud of my situation and proud of what I'd achieved considering my background and circumstances.

I finished getting ready and drove to my appointment for that day. The Butchers were a large family so it was a lot of work but they paid well. They never tried to 'do me' as others would. There were several times when I'd done a whole household and then when it came to paying, the excuses would come. 'Shit Bess, I didn't realise but look there's no money in me purse love. I'll drop it round later,' or, 'can I pay you next week when I get the family allowance?'

Sometimes I'd get offered favours in place of money. 'You do my hair and I'll get my son to decorate your front room.' The cheek of some people and the favours I was owed. I'd heard all the excuses and would hear them time and time again, but gradually I was learning how to get people to pay without them kicking off.

The Butcher's house had a great big number 49 painted in white gloss paint on a brick on the front of the house. It was a tip. It wasn't dirty, just really untidy, but there was love and warmth in it. The kids were little sods who never went to school and drove the local shopkeepers mad nicking anything they could get their hands on.

Lynn, the matriarch, greeted me at the door with a cup of tea in her hand and a cigarette hanging from her mouth.

'Hiya love,' she said smiling. 'Come in. I've made you a brew. How's your dad?' Has he got himself a new woman yet?'

I rolled my eyes at the question; I'd heard it a thousand times before.

'No Lynn, I've told you, I'm his only woman,' I replied, winking.

As soon as they heard their mum talking to someone, all the kids flocked into the hall, straining their necks to see who it was. It was as if they never got visitors; as if they'd never seen a person at all.

Lynn chastised her eldest, 'Jesus Katie, wind your neck in love. You'll get frigging whiplash. It's only Bess come to do our hair.'

I smiled as I walked in, 'Come on then who's going first?' They were a beautiful looking bunch of kids I thought.

'Well one of you will have to go first,' Lynn shrilled as they all ran off. 'I've not washed mine yet. Katie, come and get the stool out and let Bess cut your hair. It's a fucking mess.'

Lynn turned to me, 'Sorry if it's full of nits, I've not had chance to do it, this week,'

'Hang on Lynn; I'm not cutting their hair if they've got nits, no way. Jesus, my other clients will catch them,'

'I haven't got nits mum, honest,' said Katie. She was stunning with gorgeous white hair and the biggest brightest blue eyes you'd ever seen. She looked like she was wearing jet black mascara on her lashes and black liner on her lids. She was certainly beautiful.

'Come on Katie, let's have a look,' I said, dreading what I was going to find.

I turned to her mother. 'It's not on Lynn, you should sort this before I come round,' I said.

Katie sat still while I trimmed her hair. 'How old are you now Katie?' I asked, genuinely interested. They would tell me every couple of months but I'd always forget by the time I came back.

'I'm twelve now,' she said biting down on her lip.

'Wow, nearly a teenager, where's the time gone? It flies, hey?' I said.

As we were making conversation, her younger brother David came in the room. 'Ah you look a right knob head,' he said

'Thanks David,' I replied.

'Not you Bess, I meant Katie,' David clarified.

'Yeah but I'm cutting her hair, so I must be making her look a knob head,' I said making Katie laugh.

'Do you want any swag, Bess?' said Lynn as she reappeared. She had her business head on now. The way she tilted her head and moved her mouth as she was promoting her 'swag' made me laugh. She looked like she was trying to be a gangster, like Ma Baker or someone.

'What've you got?' I asked.

'A load of meat from the Co-Op. Steak and all,' she replied.

'Yeah go for it. Give us what you can and I'll make sure Nessa and Faya Brown get some.'

I spied her youngest son, Tony, jabbering away in the corner. 'Who's he speaking to Lynn?'

'Tony, who are you speaking to now?' Lynn asked. There was no reply. 'Fucking mad that kid, he makes it up as he goes along,'

'My friend,' he said in a tiny little voice. His beautiful blue eyes were shining as he looked up at his mummy. He made my heart melt.

'What's your friend's name' I asked sincerely.

'Shitehawk,' he whispered gently.

'What?' we all cried at once.

'Shitehawk,' he said louder, and Katie started to laugh.

'He's got it off me mum. That's what she calls me dad all the time,' and we all started laughing.

I was in stitches. 'An imaginary friend called bloody Shitehawk, I've heard it all now.'

It was a full day's work at the Butcher's but I finally left with a big bag of various meats and the cash Lynn had given me for doing their hair. Lynn's love for her family had made me think about my mum and I decided to ask my dad if he'd heard off her lately. I wanted answers. I wanted to know where she was, and why she'd left me.

I still felt there was something odd about leaving your child. I could say with my hand on my heart that Lynn Butcher would kill for her kids. She wouldn't leave any of them, I knew that for sure, so why did my mum leave me?

I jumped in my car, a bright red Vauxhall Nova. I loved it. I'd bought it myself out of the stash of money I'd saved over the years. I felt guilty sometimes but then thought of everything I'd endured as a kid and justified it as wages off my dad.

I pulled up at our house and Peter Lawrence was standing as if he had been waiting for me. I tried to ignore him. I couldn't be bothered with Peter. I still wasn't sure whether it had been him that mugged my dad and I didn't trust him as far as I could throw him. Nessa told me years ago that he'd followed her home just to tell her he fancied me. We'd all laughed about it at the time but Peter's presence had always unnerved me.

I had my head down as I walked past him, but he called over to me, 'Oi Bess, how you doing? How's your dad?'

'Why do you want to know, Pete?'

'Just asking,' he said. 'Here let me help you with that,' and before I could stop him, he grabbed my hairdressing gear and the bag of meat. He walked gormlessly alongside me bobbing his head up and down. He had spit gathering at the corner of his mouth.

I wanted to avoid letting him in to the house but as I opened the front door he walked straight in and stood in the hallway. I could hear dad in the kitchen which was unusual but it made me feel less on edge. Peter's body language was really invasive and he kept 'accidentally' touching me as I was putting my stuff away.

Dad must have heard me come in and walked out to meet me, 'Alright Pete? What you up too lad?' he said.

'Er, nothing, Mr Holland. Just gave your Bess a hand with her bags,' he replied.

My dad went back to the kitchen and Peter turned his attention back to me. The hairs on the back of my neck stood on end. His eyes gave the impression that the light was on but there was nobody home. He gave me an anxious feeling in the pit of my stomach.

'Not heard from Ella Parker for a bit. Is she still shagging about?' he said.

I slapped him hard across the face. I had no idea where it came from on.

'Sod off out of my house, you tosser,' I shouted and he left rubbing his cheek and staring at me in shock.

I was still shaking when dad and I sat down for tea

'Are you alright Bess?' Dad asked with a look of concern on his face.

'Yeah, I'm fine. I just hate that Peter Lawrence. He gives me the creeps' I said.

Dad sighed. 'That's a bit harsh love. He just helped you

with all your bags.'

I ignored my dad's comments. I was right, Peter Lawrence was a first class weirdo and it wasn't just me who said it.

'Dad, I need to ask you something.' I said taking a deep breath. I didn't want to hurt him with my next question.

He smiled warmly. His smile was beautiful when he was sober and he was sober tonight for some reason. 'What is it, love?'

'Where's my mum? Do you know?'

Dad put down his knife and fork and looked stunned at the question. I had never raised the issue before; we just never spoke about it. He looked helpless as though he didn't know where to start. I was afraid that he might be thinking that I didn't love him anymore. I felt sad asking him the question but I just needed to know.

There was a pause, he cleared his throat and then he spoke. 'Bess, I really don't know what went on. Me and your mum had always got on, but then towards the end...' he paused again. 'Well we argued a lot, probably because I was always at the pub.'

I noticed he put his head down in shame and I hated putting my dad through any pain.

He continued. 'I just thought we'd had a row and she'd be back after a few days, I never thought she'd leave forever.' He looked at me with sad eyes. 'But your mum did love you. I've never understood why she never came back for you. It's a mystery to me. Maybe she couldn't face coming back straight away. Maybe she needed some time. But to not come back at all? Part of me never wanted her to come back. You were all I had left. I couldn't bear the thought of losing you as well. But as true as I'm sat here, Bess, I have never heard from your mum again. In answer to your question, I don't know where she went or where she is now. I just know she never came back.'

I was totally and utterly gobsmacked. I'd half expected him to say that he spoke to her once a week, reported back on my progress. I suppose I had just hoped that they were in touch and he'd be able to give me more of an explanation.

'So have you ever looked for her?' I asked.

He caressed his chin as though he was deep in thought. 'Yeah love, I did. I look in the phone book sometimes. I've even been to the library. There's no trace of her, love. God, I'm sorry, I don't know what to say.'

'Oh dad we have to find out, you know. I can't cope not knowing whether she is dead or alive. I don't care why she never came back for me. I just want to know that she's safe.'

In some ways I wished I'd never asked the question as it made everything worse. I thought she hadn't come back because she couldn't be bothered which gave me a reason to hate her, but dad had just confirmed that she did love me. Something must have happened it was strange and I was determined to get to the bottom of it.

Chapter 13

Nessa

Faya's time had come to leave the safe warm nest of Pat and Kenny's. She worked hard running a market stall and rented a flat from the council next to the local park. The neighbours were a mad bunch; drug dealers, single mums, single lads, all struggling in their own ways.

She asked me to move in with her. She didn't want any money off me until I was working full time so I jumped at the chance. I was sad to leave my foster parents as they'd been good to us all. Tom had already moved down south; he'd had enough.

Our little flat was cosy and I loved living with my big sister. When she got home from work I'd jump up and make her a cup of tea and then we'd chat about what we'd been up to.

'You alright,' I shouted happily as she walked in one night shivering from head to toe. She headed towards the fire.

'Yeah I am, babe, but I've got some news for you,' she said.

She told me that she'd just walked past the Bailey's house and it was empty. All the curtains had been taken down and there was rubbish left on the front; rubbish they'd left behind apparently. The front door was boarded up. She'd asked a neighbour who confirmed that they had gone back down south.

I didn't know what to say, I felt gutted, I was so in love with Si and he knew it. Even if he didn't feel the same, he'd known me all my life so how could he just disappear without even saying goodbye?

Faya saw the sadness in my eyes and hugged me. 'He'll have his reasons,' she said as if reading my mind

That was it. He was gone. The boy I had looked at every day in school in the hope of catching his eye. The boy who'd defended me from the bullies in the infants and rescued me from Peter Lawrence at the jubilee celebrations. The boy who held me tight in Blackpool and lit a fire in my belly like nobody else could. He had gone. He'd just disappeared from my life with no warning and no goodbye.

I stayed in that night and rented 'When Harry Met Sally' from the local video shop; I had no need for company. I was in no mood to talk to anyone but I was glad that Faya was in the other room. By the time the film had finished I was even more convinced that me and Si should have been something. It was not right. There was a surge of electricity so strong when we were near; surely he felt it too.

Before I went to bed I decided to call Ella. I explained that Si had left, just like that, and that I knew it sounded pathetic but I was gutted. True to form Ella sorted my head out and we talked, laughed and cried until the early hours of the morning.

The next day it took all my strength just to open my eyes, I felt that knackered. I lay there and remembered my dream with sadness. I'd dreamed that I was back in school and that Si Bailey was fighting as usual. He had blood on his face and I was crying. I ran over to him, but he'd put his head down and ran away from me. As I turned to walk away with tears streaming down my face, he screamed 'Vanessa' and ran back towards me, dishevelled with blood everywhere. I woke up before he got to me.

I stared at myself in the mirror. I had tears in my eyes; it was a bit dramatic but I knew what I felt. I grabbed the side of my face with both hands and pulled it so the big black bags under my eyes disappeared. I wasn't good looking but I wasn't ugly. My long, straight, auburn hair was shiny and everyone all my life had commented on the colour; I thought it was boring. My eyes looked like they were ready to pop out of my head. I thought I resembled Anne Boleyn. I was stocky with a bit of weight that hung on my hips. No wonder he never liked me; I was nothing special. I felt sad again. Why on earth had he left without even saying goodbye?

The knock on the door broke my thoughts. I told myself to get over it. Let's face it, he was bad news and he was going nowhere with his attitude. Then I remembered the tightness of his arms holding me in Blackpool and my tummy did a somersault. I loved him. Only I could love a man who'd never even spoken to me. I knew it was deeper than words could say and I was sure that he knew it too.

It was Bess at the door. She had bags full of goodies. In some ways I was envious of Bess, she always had stuff given to her, but Bess being Bess she always shared. She would bring half of whatever she got to me and Faya and I loved her for it. I looked at her beautiful face, her eyes were usually sparkling but today she looked troubled.

'Hey, come in, babe,' I said. 'What's up?'

She told me about the conversation she'd had with her dad and that she was worried sick about what could have happened to her mum. I was as taken aback as she was. It was something that we'd grown up with, but not something we'd talked about too often. It was far too sensitive to bring up. In many ways we were similar and our parents not wanting to know us as young children had left quite a damaging effect on us.

I thought briefly about my own parents. My father, the bloody nonce, and my mother, his wench or whatever she was. I wasn't interested in them anymore. I had Faya and my best friends. My life would have been complete if only I had Si too. The idea of him made my tummy lurch again.

'So what can we do Bess?' I asked, realising that all this time poor Bess thought that her mother hadn't loved her and now her dad was saying she did.

Bess looked thoughtful.

'Nessa I don't know where to start. I don't know what's gone on but I can't rest now. After dad saying that my mum loved me, and he was surprised that she'd left me, I just have to find out what happened. I'm going to have to get dad onside, maybe speak to Nana too. I was at the Butcher's house yesterday doing their hair and it made me realise something wasn't right. Lynn would never leave her kids and can you imagine Chris Parker leaving her rabble? Why would a mother leave her child if she loved them? So I don't know. I just know that my heart hurts for her again. I had resigned myself to the fact that she'd just left me without a care in the world. It was easier to resent her. But now I'm worried. Does that make sense?'

'Well I think we need to speak to your dad again Bess, and see if he can give us any more clues. We could get some names of family that you don't know. You must have dozens of aunties or uncles that you've never even heard of. We could start to do a bit of detective work ourselves. We'll sort it babe, I promise.'

'Yeah you're right, they'll be a load of them somewhere and he'll just have to give me some answers. He must know something surely. Even if he didn't love mum anymore he must wonder, worry even. It's all a bit strange.'

Bess shared out the meat she'd got from Lynn Butcher. She was right about that family, they didn't have much but at least they had each other.

I looked up at my beautiful friend who was making sure that we had food on our table. That was the great thing about our estate; people were loyal. There was a communal sense of sharing; we looked after one another, kept each other safe. I was sure there would be nowhere else on this earth where you'd get such a feeling of belonging.

'You ok Nessa?' Bess said, sensing my mood.

'It sounds trivial compared to what you've just told me but the Bailey's have done a runner. Faya told me last night. Their house is completely empty and…well…you know?'

Bess nodded, 'Si?'

'I just don't understand. Not just me, he didn't say goodbye to any of us and we were all mates. I'm just feeling sick at the moment. I know it sounds daft but I really love him. There was something going on with our souls. It was like an electric force when he was near.'

Bess looked at me seriously, 'Nessa, he was trouble and we know that. I mean he was caught sniffing glue. He broke into the local primary school and wrecked it. Come on that's our primary school, his primary school, Ness. Why would he do that? You're too good for the likes of him. You'll find better I know you will and besides he didn't even talk to you.'

She stopped while I took in her words. 'Come on let's have a beer, babe, my treat; we both need cheering up.'

I didn't like Bess telling me Si was trouble. I knew he'd been up to no good but I also knew he was misunderstood. I knew that deep down he had a good heart. I just know that behind his swagger and his hard-lined mouth that he was a beautiful person, but I suppose it was just people's perception.

We grabbed our coats both feeling pretty miserable and went to the Lion. All the locals were in there including Bess's dad. Goodness knows how they could afford to sit in here and booze every day.

As I looked around the pub, I realised I needed to get a part-time job. I had just been accepted for a place in Fielden Park College, studying psychology. I wanted to be a social worker and was determined to reach my goal. I knew it was going to be difficult but Faya convinced me and said that she would always be there to support me. This was going to be hard especially with my background. Faya had opened up over the years about my dad. I was just so grateful that I had managed to escape my father's clutches and I owed it to my sister.

Faya was a brave woman and had come out on top. She was successful at what she was doing, and ok it wasn't much in the grand scheme of things, but for us it was massive. She was raking it in. I had nothing to worry about money wise as she never let me go without. She was the best big sister in the world.

Everyone was making a fuss of Bess. It was funny because if Ella was here it would be her that they would be fussing over. I sometimes just took a back seat, but was happy to do so. It was something I never felt insecure about, it really didn't matter. I was always reasonably quiet unless I had something to say, so it suited.

I had half a lager, and enjoyed the smoky atmosphere of the bar. We were only welcome due to Bess's dad being a regular.

'What the fuck?' someone shouted making me jump. It

was Conny; he'd been approached by three lads who I didn't recognise.

'Shit,' Bess whispered. 'It's the Donohues from the Dogs.'

The 'Dogs' was so called because it was full of dangerous dogs roaming the streets to keep enemies away.

John Holland came over to us. 'Get out girls, now. Come on clear off,' he said.

It was too late, the brawl had started and we were in the middle of it. The three lads from the 'Dogs' were being thrown all over the pub by Conny. No one went in to help him, they didn't need to. He was kicking the shit out of the three of them. He had one on the floor and was stood between his shoulder blades with his steel toe caps firmly in place. Then he had another guy in a head lock, head butting him. I winced and looked at Bess's face; she didn't seem fazed at all, we were used to it.

Then a loud, harsh voice echoed across the bar.

'Fucking hell, get off him you twats. Get out. You're barred.' It was the land-lady, Lizzy. She was also Conny's mum and you didn't mess with her.

The Donohues were up like a shot. 'We'll be fucking back, you wanker,' said one of the guys snarling at Conny.

Conny just stared and said nothing.

As he turned to the door a grin spread across his face. I looked over and there she was all wanton and dreamy looking staring back at Conny. Ella Parker.

I nudged Bess and we both laughed as she walked over. 'I love him,' she mouthed. Conny had clocked it and gave her a wink as he wiped blood off his chin and carried on playing pool as though nothing had happened.

Lizzy gave her orders. 'Lock the door, Ella love, make sure the bastards don't come back in. I'll set Britta and fucking Dynamo on them if they do,' she said, referring to her two Rottweilers. I secretly thought she resembled them but wouldn't dare say it out loud.

'And where's our fucking George when you need him, eh?' she said referring to her husband. George was the absolute salt of the earth but she was the boss that was for sure. You didn't mess with Lizzy Concannon.

I sat in the corner with Ella and Bess. Things had gradually quietened down after the big flare up and we were chatting about the Bailey's moonlight flit and the mystery of Bess's mum. In the corner of my eye I spotted Peter Lawrence walking towards us.

'I see the Bailey's have fucked off,' he announced as he approached us.

The spit in the corner of his mouth made me want to retch.

'Bet you're gutted, eh Nessa?' He said menacingly. 'He didn't like you anyway, you daft cow. As if he'd like a scruffy cow like you,' he said. He looked around the bar. 'No one here to protect you now ay?' he added.

It was chilling and he meant something by it I could tell.

As Peter Lawrence came closer, there was a series of deafening bangs. Glass shattered and people were screaming. There was blood and glass everywhere and total panic in the pub. I looked around in a state of shock. Peter Lawrence was lying on the floor, he had been shot, so too had the barman. The glasses that were only ten seconds earlier stacked neatly in rows on a rack above the bar were now shards and splinters were stuck in people's faces and arms.

The place was in utter chaos. I stood and tried to take in what was going on. Bess and Ella were on the floor. Conny was hurt, he was holding his arm, and Lizzy was frantic screaming like a banshee. 'Bastards, you fucking bastards,' she bellowed.

Outside, an orange Ford Escort sped off from the pub car-park with one of the Donohues driving. Then we heard sirens.

'Everybody stay down till the old Bill gets here,' Lizzy shouted.

I stared in disbelief at the mess around me. I didn't feel scared or anything. I was just angry at the Donohues for doing this to our people. Peter Lawrence was howling in pain. I didn't care. Ella got up and moved over to Conny to see if he was ok. He laughed nervously.

'Yeah, I'm ok babe. I fucking missed the step when I ducked and landed on me arm. I think I've broke the fucker,' he said. She smiled, relieved, and he smiled back.

Bess looked at me from the floor. 'Where's my dad, Ness?' she said panic stricken.

I didn't know and I started to look around for him. I could see some casualties near the bar.

'Wait there, Bess, I'll have a look,' I said.

I saw him but it was too late, Bess had seen him first.

'Dad,' she screamed, 'Dad.'

Her natural reaction was to run over to him but Conny grabbed her back. 'Let the paramedics see to him, Bess,' he said.

'No,' she screamed, 'he's my dad.'

I covered my eyes. All I could see was the back of John Holland's head. He was on his side and there was a lot of blood.

Chapter 14

Peter Lawrence

The noise of the gun shots and bullets ricocheting off the walls had shocked me. It felt like my whole insides had left my body. It was surreal. I felt a pain in my leg but not in my wildest dreams did I think I'd been shot until I saw blood pumping out everywhere. I passed out.

I'd only gone in to tell Nessa that Bailey hated her and had fucked off. I didn't expect to get shot in my bastard leg.

I woke up in hospital, having been operated on. As usual there were no family or friends around me, nobody to give a toss and nobody to share this pain. Conny caused all this by kicking the shit out of the Donohues. Even I'd known he'd get his comeuppance. That's how it worked round our way. Thick shit, should've known better. Now half the pub was total carnage. He was a fucking idiot.

Worst part was they had all left me to it. No one came to my rescue, no one helped me. They were all too concerned about John fucking Holland. I'd already tried to sort that fucker out once before, he deserved it.

I looked at the nurse's arse as she tended to my foot. I had a mad urge to slap it hard. I grinned at the thought.

'Do you have anyone to look after you when you get home, Peter?' she said. Her eyes were dark brown and her skin olive. She looked like one of those foreigners.

I nodded my head. I wasn't going to tell her anything. The less she knew the better. I would go home and get better on my own. I'd always looked after myself and I was fine wasn't I?

Chapter 15

Ella

I had the hots for Conny, I always had. He was just so fit, so able and so fucking willing. He was ten years older than me but since our one night stand at the shabeen he'd always liked me, I could tell. There was definitely some unfinished business, that was for sure, but that Saturday afternoon in the Lion had done it for me. The way he had kicked the shit out of the Donohue boys and the way he'd been the hero in the aftermath of the shooting. He was a real man.

Following the shooting, Peter Lawrence walked with a limp which made him look more of a freak than he already was. Bess's dad had been shot in the head. Luckily the bullet had just skimmed across the top of his eyebrow taking it clean off, he was lucky to get away with just a dent above his eye which made him look quite defined in a rough sort of way.

The police had interviewed us all trying to establish what had gone on. Of course we all knew that you didn't grass, so we'd just acted dumb. We'd take care of things ourselves. They'd get theirs that was for sure, especially if Lizzy and George Concannon had their way. The police knew they were wasting their time and didn't spend much resource on it. In fact they'd been in and out in a flash and were slated for their lack of caring; they couldn't win.

'You'd better get yourself off to casualty, Conny,' his mum had said in her thick accent which seemed to be exaggerated by the drama. She looked at me. 'Go with him Ella, love, make sure he goes. He's hard our Conny. He's probably broken that arm but won't get it fixed I'll bet. Even as a kid, he'd never go to the doctor's. Go with him,' she repeated. 'Make sure he goes, alright?'

I didn't have a choice although I felt a bit daft going with him. The hospital was only half a mile away so we walked. He put his arm tightly around me. 'Come on, kid,' he grinned. 'Let's get this over with.' My stomach felt like it was doing somersaults.

I looked into his eyes and saw a softness that made me melt.

'Do you know,' he said, 'I've always wanted to say sorry about that night at Dougie's. I was bang out of order. I should never have done that to you. You just looked so vulnerable and fit.'

That was council estate romance in its entirety.

He grinned like a Cheshire cat revealing his not so perfect teeth which made him look even more rugged. I smiled back through a blush.

'I'm not a slag you know, I'd never done it before that time with you and I've never done it since,' I said. 'I'm not even sure why I did it. Think it just felt dead right. You just felt all big and strong.'

As I said it I wanted the ground to swallow me whole, cover me up and never let me out.

'Big and strong?' he repeated

He grinned again. Then he pulled me to him and kissed me hard on the mouth.

'Will you go out with me, Pamela Parker?' he said.

My legs wobbled and my insides were going crazy. 'How do you know that's my proper name?' I said, avoiding the question.

He laughed. 'Fuck that, will you go out with me or not?'

I thought for a moment about what mum and dad would say. Then I thought about what Bess and Nessa would say. Then I just thought, 'fuck it'.

'Ok yeah I will, Thomas Concannon,' I said using his full name too.

He laughed loudly and threw his good arm in the air yelling, 'Yes!' He gave me another big kiss.

I fell head over heels in love with Tommy Concannon. It didn't matter that he was so much older than me, he was amazing. It was like having my very own hero. Everywhere we went, everybody knew Conny.

He was always warring with the Donohues. I never got to the bottom of it; he never told me. There were lots of things Conny never told me, but I think I was probably better off not knowing. It was his way of protecting me from the dark side which I knew he had.

He was a grafter though and worked hard with John Holland and a few of the others from the Lion. Lizzy looked after her boys. God help anyone that said a bad word about them or got in their way. She was like a mother to all the regulars; landlady, best friend, bank of Lizzy, all rolled into one. Everyone had the utmost respect for her and looked after that pub like it was a new born baby.

My younger brothers were thrilled that I was going out with Conny. They all knew him and made out they were his mates. They were just kids but they looked up to him and aspired to be just like him.

Mum was eager to meet him. 'You know him, mum, what's your problem?' I asked.

I didn't understand the constant nagging about Conny visiting our house. Even I wasn't sure whether I wanted him to or not. He was mine and I knew my lot would just show me up. Our Josie had dreamy eyes every time his name was mentioned.

'Come on, Ella,' dad said one evening.

Mum had her apron on and was making stew in the kitchen. Stew... I'm not surprised I looked like a dumpling; it's all we ever had.

'Come on what, dad?' I said, and he went on to insist that Conny came to our house.

'It's good manners, Ella. Doesn't he want to get to know your family? If he thought anything of you he'd come and see us all,' he said.

I kept my cool. Of course he thought something of me; he worshipped the very ground I walked on. He was just a bit cool and because he was older I felt stupid asking him to come to ours. God, I couldn't handle this, what a nightmare.

'Tell you what,' dad continued. 'Ask him to come for Sunday dinner. I'll get us some nice lamb and your mum can do her famous Yorkshire pudding.'

We all laughed, mum was a brilliant cook but she had never quite mastered Yorkshire puddings.

So I had no choice. If I wanted to keep my parents happy, I was going to have to ask Conny for dinner. I cringed at the thought of it.

The girls laughed when I told them that I was inviting Conny for Sunday dinner. We were at Bess's. None of us had any money to go out so we'd gone round to hers for a smoke and a few beers.

'So come on then?' Nessa said.

'Come on what?' I grinned. I knew they were after details of my sex life.

'You know what' said Nessa.

'Well it wasn't like that dreadful night at Dougie's, that's for sure,' I said before telling them the story about our first proper night together.

We'd been in the pub. Lizzy and George were working the bar and we were sitting with all the lads in the corner. Conny had been the centre of attention as usual, making everybody laugh, toughing it out and basically clowning about. He was a bit cooler with me when we were in a crowd but occasionally he'd wink at me or I'd catch him staring and I'd feel my whole insides melt.

After everyone had left the pub he asked me to go up to the flat. Lizzy and George were too busy getting pissed with the bar staff so they didn't notice us slip through the back and upstairs. I was impressed. The flat was split in two and Conny had his own private quarters like a bedsit with his own kitchen and bathroom. It was really nice but I could feel my heart beating hard in my throat. I knew what was coming and I certainly didn't have the confidence I'd had that night at Dougie's.

'Do you want a drink or anything, babe?' he said. I loved it when he called me babe.

'Yes please,' I replied. He went downstairs to the bar and came back with two cans of Pils, straight from the fridge.

'This could have its advantages,' I said with a wink and I smiled.

We sat in his bedsit and looked through his video and music collection He had a lot of Pink Floyd, and Bob Dylan.

'What about some U2?' I said.

'Not before you've phoned your mum to let her know you're staying,' he said. He was so grown up; even though I was in my twenties he knew my mum and dad would be worried sick about me if I didn't.

We drank Pils and he rolled us a nice big joint. We sat

and listened to Pink Floyd and before I knew it we were in his bed. Even though the joint was taking effect I was still shaking when he slowly took off my clothes. I couldn't believe how different he was with me. He was gentle and he was kissing me while staring into my eyes. His pupils were huge and not for a moment did he blink. I closed my eyes tight thinking he wouldn't be able to see me.

He stopped and cupped my face in his hands. 'Open your eyes, beautiful,' he said. 'Watch me shag you.'

I couldn't take my eyes off him; it was mesmerising. Then I felt his huge, warm manhood inside me and I gasped. Waves of pleasure hit me hard. He bent his head down and pulled at my nipple with this mouth and bit gently on it, teasing it with his teeth. It was too much. I was drowning in the waves that were now surrounding me, the inside of my legs were tingling. My breathing was becoming faster and faster as I gasped and almost begged him to stop. Then I felt it; an explosion from within. I yelled as my orgasm took over my whole body.

Conny was looking very pleased and I heard him groan. 'It's here baby, it's here for my baby girl.' He let off one almighty cry and clung to me as if his life depended on it.

I felt strange, hot, shaky and breathless but oh so good. Afterwards, just like in the movies, we lay there panting and slowly getting our breath back. He lit a cigarette and passed it to me then he fell into a deep sleep and I'm sure he had a faint smile on his lips.

As I told Bess and Nessa the details they sat looking at me dreamily.

'Aw Ella, he sounds amazing,' said Nessa. She had her head to one side and had been listening intently.

'So then what happened?' said Bess.

'Well you won't fucking believe it.' I said. 'Conny was laying there fast asleep and I didn't quite know what to do with myself. I had this weird niggling feeling in my tummy which I thought was nerves. I was sitting on the edge of his bed naked, watching him sleep and I did a little fart.'

The girls burst out laughing.

'Don't say you woke him up? Ugh, did it stink?' said Bess through her giggles.

'Did it stink?' I said. 'I say it stank, I'd only shit all over his fucking bed. I had diarrhoea; I couldn't believe it, all over the fucking bed.'

As I told them I'm sure the embarrassment must have been clear to see on my face but they didn't care. They just howled with laughter. Bess rolled about on the sofa. Nessa screamed hysterically.

'Jesus Christ Ella, what did you do?' said Nessa trying to recover her breath.

'What did I do?' I repeated.

I recalled the utter shock and horror.

I think I had actually whispered out loud, 'Oh my God, I've shit. I've shit everywhere'. Then I went to the bathroom and cleaned myself up the best I could, hoping and praying that Conny wouldn't wake up. I looked around frantically for something to clean up the bed with and the best I could find was a scabby old nail brush. I found a cup and filled it with warm water and shampoo. Whilst Conny slept I scraped the mess off the bed and scrubbed it with the nail brush. Then I pulled the bed sheet as far as I could and tucked it firm under the mattress. I didn't know how long it would be before he found it but I knew I couldn't tell him that I'd shit in his bed. I lay there for the rest of the night praying for the morning to arrive so I could get out of the place.

I recounted the story to Bess and Nessa. 'Do you love him?' Bess asked through tears of laughter.

'Aw yeah,' I hugged myself, 'I love him alright.'

We talked a bit more about me and Conny and then the conversation turned to what they'd been up to.

Bess told me she had contacted all her mum's family and was getting nowhere fast in finding her mum. She'd not been up to much more. Nessa was doing well at college and was talking about some of her work experience and how she hoped to go to University.

As we talked, it occurred to me that even though I loved being with Conny, I felt a little left out. In the past I'd always known what the girls were up too, so it felt strange listening to them. It was like I'd not seen them for years.

Nessa was still missing Si but realised that she'd have to get to grips with the fact she'd probably never see him again. She said that she had let one of Conny's mates walk her home one night. They'd called in at the chippy on the way then he asked her to go back to his. I was hanging on her every word.

'Come on then, tell us what happened, Nessa?' I asked. Bess started laughing again.

'Well,' said Nessa. 'We ended up going back to his place. His mum and dad were in bed, so we snuck into the kitchen. He told me to go and take a seat in the living room and he'd put our chips out on plates.'

'Oh, ok,' I said and smiled.

'You won't smile in a minute, Ella,' Nessa exclaimed.

'Go on then,' I said, eager to hear the rest of the story.

'Well, he came out of the kitchen naked with two plates in his hand. Fucking naked with a massive, whopping big hard-on and he just said, 'chips and sausage, Ms Brown'.'

I couldn't believe what I was hearing and joined in with Bess's laughter.

'Oh my God, Nessa, what did you do?' I said.

She was laughing as she spoke. 'I almost felt obliged after all the trouble he'd gone to but I wasn't having any of it. I just told him that I wasn't hungry anymore and had to get home. Then I just left the house and ran like the wind. I'll never be able to look at him in the face again,' she said.

'Or the eye,' I added, and we fell about laughing again.

Chapter 16

Bess

The shock of the shooting had almost been too much for me. I kept getting flashbacks of my dad laid on the floor bleeding. The image was strong and I couldn't get it out of my head. When I thought about it my stomach turned and tied itself into a tight knot. What if he'd have died? I couldn't have lived without my dad, I knew I couldn't. Luckily he had got away without any real damage. His scar made him look like a bit of a gangster, a bit like Al Pacino.

I didn't know if it was because he was getting older or because of the shooting but his drinking had really eased off. He was coherent far more often than he had been before the incident. He still spent most of his time in the pub with the boys but probably because he didn't have much else going on. He was working hard, always in builders gear, steel toecaps, vests, and dusty jeans. The only time he had off was when he'd been shot in the head.

I often wondered if he ever hooked up with any of the women at the pub. He was certainly friendly enough but always came home on his own; although there were times when he didn't come home at all.

Ella and Conny getting together had got my back up. I couldn't put a finger on why, but the thought of them together gave me a feeling I didn't like. A wave of disgust would come over me when I saw them. I felt insecure around them and I was trying to fight it all the time. I kept toying with the idea of being jealous but how could I be? I only wanted the best for my friends. The girls were my life and I'd never harm them. Despite that, I couldn't even look Conny in the face at times; it was all very confusing.

Ness was dipping her toe in the water with the whole relationship thing but not getting very far. Her last escapade had been a final straw for her, and a funny final straw at that. As for me I wasn't interested. I had other priorities and I liked me the way I was.

I still had so many unanswered questions about my mum. I'd managed to track down some of her distant family by putting adverts in local papers and word soon got out that I was looking for her. I received a phone call from my mum's cousin, Richard Ellis. He didn't live too far from us and apparently I'd met him briefly at a family function when I was very young. I didn't have any recollection of him but I was pleased he'd got in touch.

He was a police sergeant based in Longsight, which was a suburb to the north of us, so I arranged to go and meet him. I was upfront with dad but he wasn't very keen on me meeting with Richard.

'I'm not sure it's a good idea Bess,' my dad said when I told him. 'Him and your mum didn't really get along. I'd steer clear if I were you. He wasn't good news when we were all kids. That's probably why he's old bill. He was always a proper rotten geezer. I can't go into the reasons but there are a few people who wouldn't be happy to see him round here so I'd rather you didn't, love.'

But I had to.

I caught the bus to Longsight. It was an interesting journey through a small subsidiary of where we lived. I enjoyed looking at the rows of shops on each side. We went through Didsbury which was a posh place with large Victorian houses, with huge old windows. If you looked hard enough you could imagine ghosts in old Victorian costume looking back at you. Then we went through Fallowfield where all the students looked scruffy but educated; the bus filled up at that point.

Dad told me to meet Richard at the Police Station. He hadn't wanted me to go but I was determined so that was the compromise. Richard was working so I didn't have much choice anyway.

Even though he was my second cousin he wanted me to call him Uncle Richard. I didn't really mind. He was a tall man with loads of hair. He had kind, warm eyes and a familiarity about him that shocked me. We hit it off immediately. I felt like I could trust him and it seemed like I'd known him for years. I suppose it just confirmed the old saying that blood is thicker than water.

I told him about mum and dad's domestic situation, about dad's boozing in the early days and how they'd had a massive row. I explained that when mum had left she had promised to come back for me but she never did. I talked a bit about how I'd become a little housewife and that Nana had helped me the best she could. I told him that most of my childhood had consisted of being home alone and helping a drunk upstairs, at the same time wondering where my mum was.

Richard listened intently and after I'd finished he put his head down.

'I feel dreadful, Bess, I really do,' he said. 'I know John was a boozer and I know our Madge was having a bad time but I didn't realise how bad it was. I knew she'd left him but me and your mum had a fall out years ago. We didn't get along at all so I just thought we'd lost touch. I feel terrible that you've been subjected to all this. You must have gone through hell.'

I couldn't help it; the tears were streaming down my face because I had gone through hell. Always wondering why mum had just left me and never came back for me, always questioning what I had done so wrong that she didn't even want me. Then there was the burden on dad. It had got easier as I got older but it was clear in the early days he had no idea what to do with me.

One thing that was confirmed during my discussion with Richard was that my mum had adored me and had no reason not to come back for me. It was what my dad had said so confusion set in again. Where the hell was my mum?

I didn't learn anything new about mum from the meeting. In fact I wondered why Richard had even contacted me in the first place as I was no further forward. He did say he was going to officially log my mum as a missing person so at least that was one thing that came from it. That really brought it home to me. That's actually what she was; missing.

Richard told me about him and his family. He was married second time around. He lived in Wilmslow, a very posh area that we on the estate didn't have much to do with. He told me he had three boys and he could see the resemblance between me and one of his sons.

'I'd like to meet them, one day,' I said.

He hesitated which surprised me a little. 'Err, well, yes we'll see,' he said.

He couldn't get me out of the police station quickly enough. As he led me to the exit, I could feel the eyes of a young policeman looking me up and down. I wasn't interested; the male attention thing never did anything for me.

During the journey home, I gazed out of the window watching the world go by, watching the students in their hippy-like outfits. Then further along the journey, the posh people getting into their big cars.

My mind was back to being preoccupied with thoughts of my mum. Perhaps she'd gone abroad, perhaps she was staying with people, perhaps she'd been kidnapped, and perhaps she just wasn't interested in me or dad. Perhaps, perhaps, perhaps!

As I got off the bus Peter Lawrence was there as if he'd been waiting all day. I looked at him and shuddered. His jet black hair was stuck to his head with grease. He had goofy teeth that made him look gormless and his mouth was coated in spit. If he had anything at all about him, it was his eyelashes which were long enough to make any girl jealous. Under the eyelashes his green eyes certainly weren't smiling; they were cold and glazed over like there wasn't any life behind them.

'Alright Bess,' he said when he saw me. 'Where you been?'

I wasn't going to tell him any of my business.

'Just out for the day, nowhere special,' I said as nonchalantly as possible.

'Where you off to?' he asked.

'Well I'm going home, Peter,' I replied, my impatience must have been obvious as his stance changed. He held his head back, his eyes penetrated mine and I had to look away. I felt my cheeks go red and a sudden urge to be as far away from him as possible. The man was a freak.

I started on my way and he grabbed my arm with such a force I thought it would come out of the socket.

'Ouch,' I yelled.

His reaction was one of shock and his head hung down in shame. 'Fuck, sorry Bess. I just wanted to walk you home,' he said.

Jesus, what a situation I found myself in. I only lived two minutes away from the bus stop but I didn't dare refuse him now, my arm was still smarting. He'd really yanked it.

Then I saw him in the distance, my Al Pacino, walking back from the pub.

'Ah there's my dad, Pete. I'm going to walk up and meet him but thanks anyway,' I smiled.

I was off before I could even take in his reaction. I could imagine it though.

That night I lay in bed going through the events of the day, my re-acquaintance with Uncle Richard and the fact that mum was now officially missing. Then there was Uncle Richard's familiarity, he really had reminded me of someone. Perhaps it was mum; it was strange. On the other hand it could be the fact that he was family and that's how it was supposed to feel. I was so used to it being just me and dad, and sometimes Nana.

I thought about Peter Lawrence and subconsciously stroked my arm. 'Bastard,' I thought, he really meant to hurt me; he nearly pulled my arm out of its socket.

The shrill ring of the phone broke my thoughts. I jumped out of bed and ran down stairs quickly to answer it.

'Hey Bess, it's me, Ella, can I come round? It's all gone mad with Conny,' she said.

My stomach lurched. 'Gone mad, what do you mean gone mad?' I asked.

She was sobbing, she wouldn't say over the phone.

'Yeah, come round, now I'm up,' I said.

Ella arrived a few minutes after her call. Her face was ashen and she looked completely distraught.

'My god, what on earth, has happened babe?' I said.

'Fucking Conny had a massive scrap in the Lion. You should have seen it, Bess. He's absolutely kicked the shit out of Bri Pendleton's dad. There was no fucking need; he jumped on his face and…' I cut her off before she could go any further.

'Slow down, Ella,' I said. 'Let's get us a brew and you can tell me,' I said, trying to get her to calm down.

'Was dad in the pub?' I said as I was filling the kettle.

Ella nodded. 'Yeah, he was trying to drag Conny off, but it was like he'd lost it.'

Seconds later Dad came in, half pissed, but fuming at what he'd just witnessed.

'Nah, he's a fucking wrong un, that Conny. Sorry Ella but I'd sort it out if I were you. You don't want a man like that in your life. Jesus Christ, our Bess, he nearly killed Billy Pendleton, the poor sod. I mean he was bang out of order but he didn't deserve that beating.'

'Do you want a brew, dad?'

I was thinking my early night plans had definitely gone right down the pan, but I didn't mind as I was with two of my favourite people. I waited for the kettle to boil and looked at them both deep in discussion about Conny and Billy Pendleton.

Apparently Billy Pendleton had asked for a tab at the bar, and Lizzy Concannon had told him to 'fucking do one.' I wasn't sure how she got away with speaking to people the way she did. She was offensive, rude and there was no need.

An argument had broken out between the two of them. By the sounds of it, Lizzy had wound Billy up good and proper. She'd called him a 'mangy bastard Pendleton'. He retaliated and called her a 'specky cunt'.

It appeared that Conny had been minding his own

business at first. He was used to the environment and his mother's abusive gob, so he just sat there. It wasn't until Billy ran at Lizzy with his pool cue. He smacked her hard across the face with it, knocking her huge glasses off and sending her reeling across the bar area. That's when Conny saw red. He'd apparently dived on Billy, grabbed him from behind by his ears and forced him to the ground. Billy had no chance. Conny threw him to the floor and stamped hard on his head and smashed his skull.

'What?' I shrieked. 'Oh my god, is he an animal?'

Ella started to cry, sobbing bitterly. There was no doubt Ella loved Conny to death, we all knew that, but there was no way she could be with anyone like that, not even Tommy Concannon.

'So where's Conny now?' I asked Ella softly.

Dad answered for her. 'He's fucked off. Ran out of the pub, so who knows, but Billy could be dead for all we know.'

I gasped. No wonder Ella looked mortified.

Dad gave us both a big hug and kiss and told Ella it'd all come out in the wash then went up to bed. I moved over to the sofa to sit closer to Ella. She'd calmed down a bit but I felt so sorry for her. Conny could go down for this.

She looked up at me with her big brown eyes, I gently moved her fringe to one side.

'I do love him you know. I love him so much, but I can't be with him, he's an animal,' she said.

'I love you Ella,' I said. I don't know why I said it. It just came out but I think it had been there for a long time.

She frowned as she looked up at me. Her face was full of confusion and I cupped it with my two hands and stared into her eyes. My heart was pounding fast. I did love Ella, not like I loved Nessa, not like I loved anyone.

She still looked confused but she wasn't moving she was staring back. Her eyes were intense, looking into my soul and I could feel them tugging at my heart. I gulped as a tear slid down her face. She was beautiful beyond belief. I couldn't control it anymore. I pressed my lips onto hers. She responded and suddenly we were kissing, hard, full passionate kissing. Her tongue darted quickly in and out of my mouth. I started to shake and my breath became more and more shallow.

Jesus what to do next?

I hadn't bought the book on 'how to shag your best friend, who is also a girl,' but I wanted her more than I'd ever wanted anything. Did she feel the same? Had she always felt like this?

I felt her hands cup my breast and I held my breath as she removed my top. I closed my eyes as her hot mouth kissed my erect nipples and I threw my head back as she sucked gently on them, sending me into a state of ecstasy. It was as though there was an invisible cord that sat behind my nipples and went down into my fanny. Then as I thought it, I felt her hand slip into my knickers, pulling them gently to one side. She started to caress me with her fingers, gently, sensuously and I couldn't take it any longer. I felt an explosion of wet, warm orgasm that left me shuddering all over.

Ella's face was a picture.

'Fuck me, I didn't see that coming,' she said and we both howled with laughter. The feeling of fulfilment for me was something I'd never ever experienced before and I didn't want it to end.

Chapter 17

Nessa

I had no studying to do so I lay on my bed in my room.

I'd started work part-time which gave me some money while I was studying at college. I had a deep desire to protect children; abuse had gone on in my own home for years as I was growing up. Luckily something had been done about it; half of us were taken away from our parents. It was a travesty that nothing had happened to them. By rights the bastards should have been locked up. The stories that came out from Faya were shocking. My elder brothers and sisters had suffered for years. Fortunately I'd been spared from the predatory animal that was my father and the weak, pathetic creature who called herself our mother.

I thought if I could prevent any harm coming to even one child my mission in life would be complete.

There was another mission in my life and that was to clear Si Bailey from my memory. He'd gone, he'd left ages ago and I hated myself for still thinking about him. He'd never been interested in me and I believed that he'd never even liked me, detested me even. The fucking weirdo had never given me the time of day. How could you grow up with someone and not even acknowledge them. I'd known him since I was a little girl and he'd shared parts of my life. I must have absolutely repulsed him. It was time to move on and build the bridges of my future.

As my Sunday morning thoughts rallied around my ever active brain, I heard it, the loudest, deafening bang. It was definitely a shot-gun and someone had definitely been hit. It was getting like Beirut around here.

Faya charged in, 'Did you hear, that? Jesus Christ,' she said as we listened to lots of screaming and then the sirens. It was close whatever had gone on.

Faya told me what Conny had done the night before. We were sharing our disbelief and disgust when it dawned on us that the shooting could be to do with that and that would not be good.

'Fuck,' Faya said. 'You don't think that fucking Conny's been shot do you?'

'Don't even say it,' I said but I felt something horrible in my gut.

I thought about Ella and Bess. Jesus Christ, where were they?'

I ran into the living room and dialled Ella's home number. Chris Parker answered; she was distraught and she went through the whole scenario.

'He's a fucking bastard Ness? You can't go around doing that, the fucking animal. I think our Ella must be with Bess or something. You know what's she's like. She wouldn't have come back here, not in that state anyway.'

'Yeah,' I said acknowledging her sentiments. 'But there's been a shooting, Christine. Have you heard anything?' I asked.

She said she hadn't so I rang off. I needed to find out exactly what was going on, my head was all over the place. I needed to get round to Bess's.

A piercing screech came from the street. I knew straight away it was Ella and something bad had happened.

I left the house and ran like the wind towards the noise. I could hear her, feel her pain. My eyes started to well up and my heart beat faster and faster until I felt like I was going to stop breathing. My mind was in turmoil; thoughts and questions I couldn't answer. What the hell had gone on? Had Billy Pendleton shot Conny? Had Conny even been shot? How was I going to face Ella?

As I ran around the corner the scene hit me like a blow to the head. There was blood everywhere and people were being pulled away. Police were trying to gain some sort of control and there was Ella Parker on the floor screaming. Bess was beside her, comforting her. As she saw me she held out her hand in desperation.

The noise that came next sounded like the wail of a banshee. The sound of pain was so great and as long as I live I'll never forget the anguish that noise sent through my soul. It was deafening and seemed to last for an eternity. It was the scream of Lizzy Concannon, a mother in despair, a mother in turmoil, a mother whose life would never be the same again. I couldn't comprehend the scene. I couldn't take it in. I saw his legs and the paramedics trying to do their bit but it was clear; Conny was dead.

Peter Lawrence, as ever, was nearby. I swear he had a smile on his face. I wanted to punch him right between the eyes and I walked over to him. I wasn't sure what I was going to say, but how dare he smile, how fucking dare he look on as though this was a good thing happening.

'What are you laughing at, you sick bastard?' I said, but before I could say anymore I felt his fist hard in my face. The tension of the situation seemed to snap and it kicked off. The whole town seemed to be in some mad sadistic brawl, fighting for Conny, fighting for Ella, fighting for Lizzy. A riot had erupted. It was total hysteria and it didn't stop until late that Sunday evening. Then the tears came.

Chapter 18

Ella

I couldn't think straight, the whole thing was surreal. It felt like I was dreaming but it wasn't a dream. It was as real as the daylight and as scary as the night time. People thought Conny was bad but it was just his temper. It was in his build, in his makeup, in his DNA, but he was never bad to me. Lots of people loved him and I loved him.

I thought about his face, about the night at the shabeen. I thought about every expression, every smile and every frown. I couldn't control the tears that built up inside me. I lost it; completely lost it. I screamed, I cried, I punched the walls. I pulled the curtains off my bedroom windows. I wanted the horrible feeling in the pit of my stomach to go away. It felt like someone had punched me in the stomach and it hurt, it really hurt. I actually felt like my heart was physically breaking.

My mum came into my room, her eyes were swollen; that made me cry harder. She cried at anything. She looked awkward. What could she say? What could she do? Absolutely nothing, nobody could. It was horrible. She just stared at me. I felt her love; her motherly power. My mum only ever wanted for me to be ok. She'd do anything to make the pain go away but she couldn't do anything about this. She couldn't turn back the clock. She couldn't bring Conny back, nobody could.

I think my brothers and sisters had been told to steer clear of me as I seemed to be alone in my room for what seemed like days. I remember mum phoning the doctor and he came and prescribed me some Diazepam. I could hear the worry in my mum's voice as she closed my bedroom door and told the doctor I'd not eaten anything or spoken to anyone. I heard him tell her to go with it for now and that sleep was the best medicine. I looked down at the tablets in my hand. I wanted to take the lot. I wanted to go to sleep and not wake up. I wanted this pain to leave me alone. I wanted my life back as it was. I wanted to feel normal again. I couldn't cope with this pain.

Every emotion was running through my body right now but the biggest was guilt. What I had done with Bess was eating away at me, on top of everything else. It was making me hate her. I didn't want to see her, even though she'd been around. I'd told mum not to let her in. I knew it would be hurting her but I didn't care. I just wanted Conny back and didn't care if I never saw anyone again, ever.

Chapter 19

Bess

I just didn't know what to do. Why on earth did this have to happen? I knew Ella well enough to know that she would blame me. This was it now. I knew things would be difficult between us and that our lives had turned a corner.

I don't know what she had thought after we had sex that night. I realised I'd had those feelings all my life but I had been wrong to push things with her. She'd been vulnerable and I had no right. I realised this afterward. It was hasty but I hadn't been able to control myself any longer. I'd ached for her all my life. I knew that now.

I thought about the whole thing and remembered looking at Ella's beautiful face as she slept so peacefully on the settee. It had been a very traumatic night for her but as she lay there, I couldn't help thinking it was just so right what happened between us.

While Ella slept Conny had knocked on our front door. He stood there, a frightened mess in a dishevelled state, clearly petrified of the repercussions of what he had done. He wasn't daft, he knew you couldn't do such things and get away with it. If it wasn't the police, it'd be the family themselves who would take the law into their own hands. The family in question were old school bare-knuckle fighting gypsies so Conny knew the future didn't look rosy.

He stood there panting and out of breath.

'I need your help Bess, have you seen Ella? I can't find her anywhere. Please help me. I'm fucked Bess, I really am. I've done a bad thing for fuck sake. I need to fuck off away from here,' he said, somewhat pathetically.

I immediately felt protective and territorial over Ella and wanted him to go away. I wasn't thinking straight. I wasn't thinking about the fact that it was Conny who I'd grown up with, my dad's mate and boozing partner, who had been loyal to us all. I just wanted to get rid of him. Had it been a few hours earlier, I would have helped Conny. He was like family to us and I knew Ella loved him and I loved Ella. I would never do anything to upset or betray her but my mind wasn't thinking clearly.

I lied to Conny, told him I'd not seen her. I'll always regret that. I regret not sheltering him that night like loyal estate people would do, even though he'd done wrong. I could have helped Conny but instead I left him, deserted him, allowed him to go off into the early hours and be shot in cold blood, shot down in the street. He was dead, gone forever and no one would ever know that it was my fault.

I lay awake all night thinking about what had happened between me and Ella. It had been beautiful and everything I'd ever wanted but my heart felt heavier by the minute. I was dreading her waking up. How would she react on reflection?

I knew that even though she was furious with Conny, she loved him dearly. Life wasn't so straightforward that we'd both get up and be a couple who were in love. The thought filled me with questions. Was I a lesbian or did I just love Ella because she was Ella? Did I like men at all or just women?

I got up and found one of dad's newspapers. I turned quickly to the naked girl on page three to see if it gave me a tingle between my legs. It did. I started to rip up the paper in anger and frustration. I was a lesbian, I was convinced. I didn't like men. How on earth had this happened? I didn't want to be a fucking lesbian. I wanted to be normal, like the girls. Or was Ella a lesbian too? Maybe she was. What a mess.

That night was one of the best and worst nights of my life.

I was upstairs in the bathroom when I heard it. Bang. Bang. Bang.

'Bess, Bess,' Ella was shouting from downstairs. The pains in my stomach subsided and I ran down to see what was happening. She was pacing the living room.

'Did you hear those bangs?' she said and looked at me strangely.

Dad came in. 'What the fuck?' he said. 'That was a shotgun and it was close by.'

We all ran outside and headed toward the Lion. Police Cars and Ambulances had beaten us to it but there he was, lying face down on the pavement. Conny was dead.

Ella lost it completely, screaming uncontrollably and trying to get near him, but the police were pushing her back. I saw my dad run into the pub to alert Lizzy and George. It was carnage. The sight of Conny lying there would never leave me; it was horrific. I felt the bile rise to the back of my throat and I threw up into a neighbour's bush. Everything escalated around me.

I felt like my insides had left my body. I looked up to see where I had gone. My inside couldn't cope. She'd left me and was watching from afar with one hand covering her mouth. My body was looking hopelessly at my beautiful Ella, whose face was pained whose heart was at that moment being ripped to shreds in a slow and barbaric way.

I tried to gather my senses. I had to go to her. I had to be there for her. This was my fault. She was looking around helplessly, her tears coming fast. It was like a silent movie being run in slow motion. The next thing I saw was Lizzy reaching her son, screaming a high pitched scream that I would never forget.

I couldn't bear it anymore. I ran to Ella to hold her, comfort her and try to stop her from shaking. My guilt was eating away at me. Then I heard Nessa running towards me and Ella. I handed Ella to her. We made eye contact which said a thousand words. We didn't need words. We both knew what the other was thinking; our girl needed us.

Chapter 20

Nessa

It took twelve months for things to settle down after Conny's death. It was an emotional roller coaster. Everyone and anyone who knew Conny had been affected by his death but it was Ella who had the most difficulty coming to terms with it. I think Conny took a part of her when he died and she never fully recovered. It was a whole year before she even came close to being back to her old self.

Bess also took it badly and in some respects she was worse than Ella. She became distant, too distant. She got her head down into her hairdressing and never came up for air. I saw her as often as I had done before, but she rarely made eye contact. She became withdrawn and she and Ella hardly spent any time together. In fact the whole episode had destroyed the very thing that should have brought us together; friendship. I didn't get it.

I read a lot over that year. Reading was my way of escaping.

In primary school one of my teachers had asked me why I was always yawning. 'I can't sleep at night,' I replied.

'Have you tried reading a book?' she asked.

'We don't have any books,' I said, almost ashamed.

The next day she brought in a sack full of Enid Blyton books. I was ecstatic. I was always grateful that she had brought in those books because if she hadn't I would have missed out on so many fabulous stories from which I had gained so much.

From that day forward I read whenever I couldn't sleep

or wanted to relax or needed to escape from reality just for a while.

After Conny died I had a lot of sleepless nights. When I wasn't reading I was thinking. I thought about Ella and Bess and this sudden change in our relationship.

I thought about Si Bailey.

Why did he still come into my head? I really needed to move on from it all. I had tried. I had been with other men but I hated them all. They were all the same and no-one stood out. They never had that 'thing', that spark that made my soul ignite, that boisterous wild look about them that I loved.

There was one guy at college who I found interesting. He drank in bars on the outskirts of Manchester. To me this meant he was worldly. For any of us to know someone outside the estate was massive. Whilst I loved being part of the close-knit community, sometimes it could be suffocating. You couldn't do anything without someone knowing your business.

Faya said I needed to get a grip. If something was meant to be it would happen. She believed that there was someone for everyone; there wasn't any rush. I didn't have too much faith in that theory based on the string of undesirables that she had chasing after her. I wouldn't touch any of them with a barge pole.

I resigned myself to the fact that there would never be a chance of me being with that person. He'd disappeared off the face of the earth and he clearly couldn't stand the sight of me anyway. So she was right, I really did need to get a grip.

I needed a plan. I needed to get my girls back, needed to laugh with them again, smile with them and just be in the same room as them. I felt like our bond was disappearing.

Without them I didn't feel whole and I was sure they must feel the same. We needed to sort this out and I was going to do it. We'd been through too much together. I got off my bed, went to the phone and invited my two best friends over to mine.

'Why don't we all go on holiday, just the three of us?' I suggested when they came over that night.

I couldn't believe how nonplussed they were. They weren't even looking at each other, Ella and Bess. It was then that it dawned on me that something was seriously wrong. How had I missed it? What had happened? What didn't I know?

I looked at one and then the other and they were both staring into space. This couldn't just be about Conny, surely. It was no good, I had to ask outright; there was no other way.

'What's going on girls?' I asked calmly. No response. 'Please girls, something's not right between us. What is it, Ella?' I said.

I asked Ella first because she was the most outspoken of all of us and surely if anyone was going to say anything she was, but she didn't. I asked the same question to Bess. 'Bess, what is wrong, please babe, tell me, what's happened?' She just stared into space.

'Fucking hell. For fuck sake, you look like a married couple who have just had a row. What the fuck is going on?' I yelled at them, my frustration was real now. They were pissing me off.

They'd clearly had some kind of spat. I realised that they'd not spoken properly in the last twelve months. Maybe it was because Bess didn't go to Conny's funeral. Maybe that was it.

Then Bess spoke, it was like an explosion; she didn't stop. Ella just listened, gobsmacked, but not as gobsmacked as

I was. They'd slept together. Fucking hell, these two been licking each other's fannies and there I was trying to arrange a holiday for the three of us.

Jesus Christ, I didn't know what to make of it. I didn't understand where it had come from. Suddenly I felt a bit left out. Why these two and not me? Where did I stand in all this? I stood to lose my two best friends. We were supposed to be mates, best friends, not a bunch of lesbians who have debauched sex with one another. I'd never do such a thing. How could they? My stomach turned and I felt a bit sick.

I remained calm. I tried to think of what to say then I looked at their faces. Ella was clearly mortified and afraid of my reaction. Bess was devastated but relieved. The guilt was dropping away from her like she was shedding skin. I could see she was in love with Ella and was probably the one who had instigated it.

It had happened the night that Conny had been killed, so while the poor bastard was getting shot, Ella had her legs wrapped round Bess's neck. The vision appalled me, but the guilt must have been overwhelming for her. It must have been eating away at her, at both of them.

Bess stood up to go. 'I need to get out of here,' she muttered.

'No way, lady,' I said. 'You're going nowhere. We're best friends and no matter what you've done and no matter how disgusting it is we need to sort this out.' They both shot me a look then looked at each other. I continued, 'So what's next? You two want to set up home together or what?'

They both shook their heads and then, out of nowhere, the laughter started. I couldn't help it. I think it was the shock. I wasn't laughing at them. I just didn't know nor could I imagine how this had come about. They both started laughing too and the tension eased. It was obvious a serious talk was needed to get it all off their chests. As long as they didn't touch my chest, I wasn't bothered. I still loved them both the same.

'So where shall we go?' I asked and we got excited as we started planning our first ever holiday abroad.

Chapter 21

Ella

'We're going to Benelmadena, mum,' I shouted as I ran into the house after the incident at Nessa's.

I was relieved that Ness knew our little secret and I felt better for talking it through, just the three of us. I still felt sick about what we had done, but that was something that couldn't be changed; it had happened. It wasn't really my fault, my emotions had been all over the place at the time; Conny had just stamped on someone's head. It was only after the talk at Nessa's that I felt the guilt and stress of it all start to ease.

Mum rolled her eyes at my announcement but I'm sure there was a little smile there too. I think she was pleased that things were finally moving forward after Conny. I had been numb for a year. He never should have been snatched away from us like that but if you live by the sword you may well die by the sword.

I needed to get some new clothes for my holiday but I didn't even know how I was going to pay for the trip let alone new outfits. I wasn't working because I'd been laid off. I wasn't surprised when they let me go. My head wasn't really in it after Conny died.

The flight was only £80. Ness had booked them and said I could pay her back after the holiday. That meant I only needed cover my share of the apartment and spending money. I thought about Conny and smiled. I could hear him telling me to go and have a good time. He would definitely want that for me.

I decided to get a loan off Norman; one hundred and fifty quid for my spending money. Conny's mum kindly offered to give me the money for the apartment. A girl I used to work with offered to lend me a load of her summer gear so I'd have some nice stuff to wear while we were away. That's how it was done in those days; that's how you got by.

Of course Bess had been shopping and bought all new. From being a little girl, she always had the best, always looked immaculate. It was a contrast to my shabby self, but maybe that's how it was meant to be. She was lucky in that respect but then I suppose I was lucky in other respects. She treated me to a pair of espadrilles, a new lilo and a Madonna T-shirt that she'd been given by one of her punters.

We were so excited but we were nervous as well. We flew from Stanstead which had been a bit of a trek for us. Our flight was early in the morning so we'd had to travel through the night to get to the airport on time. As we landed in Malaga we were all feeling giddy. Tiredness was cancelled out by excitement. The heat hit us as we stepped off the plane and we started stripping off layers.

The taxi ride to the apartments was shocking. The Spanish driver was practically trying to shag all of us. He couldn't keep his hands or eyes to himself. If this was what it was going to be like then we might be in for a good fortnight, I giggled to myself.

The view was something we'd not seen before. None of us had really been off the estate other than the odd trip to Manchester. A day at Manchester Airport would be the extent of our summer holidays, watching the planes coming in and taking off.

So there we were, the three of us, mesmerised by the long, wide road that ran through the Costa Del Sol. The heat was bouncing off the cars, the sun was shining, music played everywhere, people were speaking in a different language; it was just beautiful.

As the taxi turned the corner down a really steep hill, we got our first view if the sea. It took my breath away.

'My god,' I screamed. 'Hurry up I want to get on that beach.'

We finally arrived at our apartment and got our key from the receptionist. We looked a bit out of place with our scruffy cases and the way we were dressed, even though we'd all made an effort with new clothes. We reeked of council estate scum, but we didn't care, we were proud of it.

The apartment was ok, nothing special. It had a balcony that looked out to sea and down stairs in the piazza you could hear a piano being played.

'I feel like I'm in Heaven,' Nessa gushed. I agreed; it was beautiful.

'I'm not going home,' Bess replied and we all started laughing.

Bess and Nessa were unpacking their clothes but my impatience was getting the better of me. I was pacing around in my borrowed stripy bikini. I'd blown up my lilo, put on my espadrilles, and placed a cap on my head which my mum had made me promise I would wear. Even at twenty I was still under Christine Parker's thumb; it was a case of do it or die in our house.

'Jesus, Ella, why don't you get a white handkerchief and tie four knots in the corner? You might look like a proper tourist then,' Nessa said.

She always made me laugh but I was just so excited. They finally got around to getting changed. The sight of Bess's body made me do a sharp intake of breath, and she noticed.

Her eyes lingered a bit too long on mine but we got over it quickly.

'Have you brought some cream?' Bess asked us both.

'Erm,' I hesitated.

I hadn't thought about it, neither had Nessa, but sensible Bess had, so she rubbed it all over us before we set off.

We looked a right load of twats; me with a lilo under my arm, Bess with her huge bag, and Nessa lugging her radio cassette player. She couldn't go anywhere without her music.

We lay on the beach all day, watching the world go by in Benelmadena. I listened to the dulcet tones of a man selling ice cream then a woman selling watermelon. Black men tried to sell us purses and belts. I wanted to buy all my family presents but the girls stopped me.

'For fuck sake we're here for two weeks, there's no rush,' said Nessa.

It was just amazing, I loved every second of it. I felt a million miles away from home and all my problems. The girls looked happy too.

We lay there and we lay there, almost in a state of hypnosis. We could feel the heat on our faces and hear the waves as they lapped the sand. Children were playing everywhere. Every so often we'd sit up and have a cigarette. We talked, laughed and relaxed. When we got too hot we went in the sea to cool off.

As dusk set in we decided we'd better get some tea. I couldn't believe we were on marble floors in our bare feet getting something to eat. We went to an all you can eat buffet. It only cost us the equivalent of about two pound fifty. We absolutely stuffed our faces, plateful after plateful, we ate, and we ate.

We headed back to the apartment. I started to feel rough.

It wasn't the food it was something I couldn't quite place. My body felt like it was on fire. I looked at the others. They weren't looking so good either.

I couldn't believe my face when I looked in the mirror. I looked like a great big tomato. I went to sit down in despair and screamed. My arse was on fire; so were my legs and my back. I looked at Nessa who was spread-eagled on the bed.

'I can't touch my skin, oh my god,' she yelled, and Bess lay naked on the marbled floor, in total agony. We'd managed to completely burn ourselves and the sun stroke had started to set in. Yep definitely a load of council estate idiots; I would have laughed if I wasn't in so much pain.

I don't know how we managed it but we took it in turns to shower, all screaming in agony. We put on some loose clothes and went into the town.

We could barely walk; we must have looked like zombies as we approached the main square. We went in to a bar and ordered a round of Bacardi and cokes. We were shocked at the amount of Bacardi they put in; no half measures here. Conny and Lizzy flashed through my mind momentarily, but I let them lay to rest and got absolutely slaughtered. We danced until the sun came up. It was amazing.

Chapter 22

Bess

We all needed a holiday and it did us the world of good. Nessa had been right. We came back feeling bright and refreshed.

I don't think we'd ever laughed so much in our lives. The stuff Ella and Nessa got up to wasn't for common knowledge. It would stay between the three of us.

One night they'd managed to get a spliff off a black lad by the pool. We'd smoked it the next day then gone to Tivoli Land, a massive water and fairground near Torremolinos. We were on one of the rides when Nessa started to get the giggles and nearly fell off, only just managing to hang onto our legs. It was pretty frightening really but we found it hilarious because we were stoned. She laughed so hard she started to piss which went all over the revellers below. They were not happy.

Ella and Nessa were enjoying all the male attention. I enjoyed watching them both have fun with the lads, observing them preening themselves. The way their body language changed when they saw someone they fancied. It was like they were a pair of bitches on heat.

They almost had a fight over one lad. His name was Juan and he had a moustache that looked like there was a dead beaver on his lip. I didn't see what all the fuss was about but he was certainly playing them off against one another. It was amusing at first but in the end I had to tell them to get a grip and take stock of the situation. Were they really about to give up twenty years of friendship for a lad they'd known ten minutes. It turned out they'd both shagged him. They were mortified when they found out. I found it hilarious and eventually they both did too.

I realised that I definitely only liked women and the night with Ella hadn't been a one off for me like it was for her. We had the conversation. I think Ella found it a bit distressing but I needed them to know the truth. I was a lesbian.

I wasn't going to find anyone here on holiday, in a small part of Spain where sex was about the opposite sex and no more. I'd probably be alone for the rest of my life, but right now that wasn't such a bad idea. I liked myself and was happy with my own company. I certainly didn't need idiots like Juan in my life.

The whole holiday was a great experience. By the time we landed back in England the third degree burns had been replaced with gorgeous golden tans. I couldn't wait to see my dad, I'd really missed him. He was dead excited when I got in the house. He'd made me some boiled potatoes, onions and bacon, with loads of butter on. I'd definitely missed that.

He filled me in on all the gossip and I smiled as I watched him gabbing away. I loved that man more than anything and anyone. He would probably be the only man I ever loved. I wondered what he would think of me if he knew I was a lesbian.

I couldn't even bear to say the word in my head, never mind out loud. I put it back in the little box with all my other denials, secrets and things I didn't want to deal with right now, and shut the door firmly.

After tea, dad asked if I wanted to go to the Lion for a drink so I rang the girls to see what they were doing. I was missing them both already. Ness was up for it but Ella was skint as usual. I offered to buy her a couple of lager and blacks and she soon changed her mind. I was so lucky to have such beautiful friends. Even through the confusion I was experiencing, they were there. They knew and they stood by me.

Peter Lawrence was propping up the bar. He looked at us all one by one as we walked in. He seemed to have pure hate on his face. Today it was Nessa he didn't like. I felt a bit intimidated as he walked towards us dragging his dodgy leg. I was hoping he wouldn't start anything; enough had gone on over the last twelve months and surely it was time for some peace.

'Did you enjoy you holiday, girls? Did you all get fucked?' he drawled.

Before anybody could answer, Lizzy jumped in, 'Don't fucking start, Lawrence. I fucking mean it; you'll be out on your arse. I'm not fucking having it, you cheeky bastard. Take your pint and go and sit in the corner and shut the fuck up, or get the fuck out. It's your choice,' she said.

If that didn't shut him up, nothing would.

Lizzy winked at us as she continued to slag him off. He deserved it; the man was vile and I wondered why he even existed. He was like a single cell amoeba, a nothing, with no-one. He'd never been a nice person, always a pain, always there, tormenting the three of us.

I had finally started to come to terms with what had happened to Conny and blamed myself less and less. It was a fact that when someone on the estate wants your blood, they get it, one way or another. There was really nothing I could have done about it. I mean, I hadn't caused any damage to that poor guys face, Conny had.

I still loved Ella but it was clear she was very much into men and I had to accept that she would never be mine. I was just happy she was still part of my life even if my body ached for her every day. It could have destroyed us but it didn't and I was grateful for that.

Chapter 23

Nessa

I was feeling a bit deflated after having such a fantastic time in Spain. Not that I wasn't happy to see Faya, I'd missed her incredibly. She loved the leather purse I bought for her. It was from a little shop on the front of the Costa Del Sol; not the fake rubbish from the guys trying to flog it on the beach.

When Bess called to see if I wanted to go to the Lion I jumped at the chance. I asked Faya if she fancied a night out too and she was made up. I could tell she had really missed me. I felt flattered. I went to get changed.

The phone rang again. Jesus, Bess was so impatient at times. Faya answered it and then came into my room grinning.

'What?' I asked.

She looked bloody gormless. 'Someone called Tony's on the phone asking for you?' she said.

My stomach did a somersault. 'You're joking?' I said.

She shook her head, she wasn't joking. I ran to the phone in the hallway of our flat.

'Hello,' I said in my sexiest telephone voice which made me sound like a cross between Vera Duckworth and Jimmy Cranky. I looked up to see Faya howling with laughter at my attempt to sound sophisticated. I picked up the big telephone directory next to the phone and launched it at her and we both shared a giggle.

'Hi, is that Nessa?' said the husky voice at the end of the phone. It made me shudder.

It was Tony from College. I knew he liked me, but I hadn't

been bothered enough to do anything about it. The more he spoke to me, the more I found myself thinking he was nice. He was a bit different. He seemed smart and really wanted to go places, which was more than could be said about the lads from round our way.

He'd called to ask me if I fancied a drink in Didsbury. I did but I'd already arranged to meet up with the girls and Faya was coming so I wasn't sure what to say. I could see Faya mouthing, 'ask him to come. Get him to come to the Lion'. So I explained the situation and he said yes. Oh my god what had I done?

I was really nervous. What had supposed to be a quiet drink with the gang was turning out to be a date. I couldn't believe I had got myself into this situation. It was like taking him to the Lion's den. Oh well, it would probably be the one and only date I'd have with him.

After much deliberation about what I was wearing and how I should wear my hair, we finally made it to the pub. The poor guy was among the riff-raff in the pub. I felt dreadful. I walked over to him and could feel everyone's eyes on me. I wanted the floor to swallow me up. I wanted to die.

'Hiya,' I said nervously. 'I'm so sorry I'm late.'

He smiled. 'What would you like to drink?' he said.

I smiled back. He spoke properly not like us lot.

'Half a lager, please,' I said.

'Hmmm, classy chick,' he said.

I was mildly offended but laughed anyway. Ella and Bess's eyes were boring holes in the back of my head.

'We'd better go and sit with the girls,' I said and nodded over to them.

We went over and sat down and I introduced him to everyone. He didn't fit in, he just didn't belong, but that was ok. He was different, so why would he fit in. I felt a bit awkward but the girls were on form, telling everyone funny stories about our holiday, and we all had a good laugh.

I could tell that Tony wasn't impressed but he smiled occasionally. I'm not sure what his problem was. Perhaps he was shy. He was in a strange environment with different types of people, different class of people even. He came from a very well-to-do background. His parents had several businesses and their own house. We could only just manage to own a pair of shoes.

It got late and Tony asked if I wanted to go back to his. I was a bit surprised that he'd driven and had a drink but I thought, why not. So we jumped in his car.

'Are you ok to drive?' I asked him.

'Shit yes,' he said. 'I've only had a couple.'

He took me to a beautiful old-style house which had been converted into flats for students. I was impressed.

'My god,' I gasped. 'I love it here, it's gorgeous.'

'I love you, Nessa Brown', he said very seriously.

I nearly laughed but could see he meant it. Freak alert, I thought.

'Do you heck,' I giggled. 'You hardly know me.'

'But I do. I understand the dynamics of love and how it works. I am fascinated by you. The way you are with people, the way the room lights up when you walk in, the way everyone is drawn to you, and the way you can talk with your eyes. You're charismatic and have people eating out of the palm of your hand,' he said dramatically.

I felt overwhelmed by him. I couldn't believe he noticed so much and knew me so well. I was touched and didn't really know what to do so I kissed him straight on the lips.

'Thank you, Tony,' I said. 'That's beautiful,'

Seconds later we were rolling about on his unmade bed. His room was an absolute tip, full of beer cans and overflowing ashtrays, but it didn't matter. I wanted him, him and his poetry. I wanted him and his intelligent words of wisdom. It made me wet between my legs.

He was attentive, stroking my hair and face. He was soft and gentle as he held me tight, pulling me towards him, kissing me. As he entered me, he stared intensely into my eyes and stopped as though he was letting me savour the moment, the moment of him and me being one. It took my breath away. He continued to kiss me all over as he made strong passionate love to me and just for a moment, because of the intensity and the way he was holding me, I actually believed that he did love me.

I was gasping with every thrust and clenched his shoulders hard. Then suddenly he stopped. I could feel a difference in him, like a panic or a moment of realisation. He rolled off me, just like that.

I could see that his cock was no longer hard. He just lay there, panting and looking at the ceiling. I wasn't quite sure what to do, I was in shock. I felt so embarrassed. It had been beautiful while we were doing it. What had happened? Was I a bad lover? Did turn him off? Maybe he hadn't been enjoying it.

I actually started to feel sick. Then my stomach started turning in knots. I was so uncomfortable.

He turned onto his side and started to stroke my face.

'You're so beautiful. I've never seen a face like yours,' he said.

'Yeah, it was my fanny you didn't like,' I wanted to say. I didn't say anything, just smiled back at him, studying his face. He had a nice face but no colour to his eyes. He had nice eyelashes and I really liked his mouth and his wide smile.

I drifted off into a confused sleep and dreamt Si Bailey was shafting me up the arse, tearing the shirt off my back as he did. I woke up shuddering; a hot sticky mess.

The next day I met up with Bess and Ella at Ella's house. It was a mad house; it always was. Her mum, Chris, was as loud as ever.

'Want a brew Ness, love? Have you had any dinner? Just doing a roast if you want some?' she said.

For a minute I felt a bit guilty about Faya who was stuck at home, but it soon passed.

'Oh yeah I'm definitely up for some of that,' I said with a big smile then I ran upstairs to where Bess and Ella were waiting for me.

'I don't like him,' Ella said, always the spokeswoman.

'Oh,' was all I could say. I felt disappointed. 'Why?' I asked. I wanted to tell them to give him a fucking chance but I stayed calm.

'I don't know, I can't put my finger on it,' Ella continued, as she picked at the cotton on her pillow.

I looked to Bess for some support.

'He's ok,' she said but she went a bit red as though she'd betrayed Ella. 'He looked down on us all a little bit. He looked like he thought he was too good for us,' she said getting braver.

As she said it, I half agreed with her. I could understand where they were coming from, but he could have just been nervous. After all, who wouldn't have felt intimidated and a bit out of place in the Lion? It was full of locals, a load of uneducated bastards with no idea how to treat a person who was a bit different.

Bess could clearly see I was getting agitated so she backed off. 'What happened after the pub?' she asked.

I told them about how intense he was and that it was like he adored me.

'He doesn't even know you,' Ella piped up.

'We do go college together every day,' I said defensively.

What was their fucking problem? They'd licked each other's fannies for god sake but I didn't slate them.

I didn't tell them about Tony's flop. I felt like it would be disloyal to Tony and I didn't want to give them any more ammunition. I kept it to myself and that's how it would be. They would clearly never like him but for some reason I felt loyal to him and wanted to protect him.

Chapter 24

Ella

It had taken time but eventually Conny's murderers had been caught, brought to trial and sent down. I was glad but not as glad as Lizzy, she was ecstatic.

I'd started working at the Lion, it was easy work and it felt comfortable. It was a bit of extra cash and I felt close to Conny. As time passed by it got easier but I still felt lost.

I listened to Lizzy go on about the bastards who killed her son. I looked at her, her face lined with anger. She had a permanent frown etched on her brow. Even though I was still grieving I couldn't imagine how she was feeling. She was his mother and she'd given birth to him. I felt the tears stinging the corners of my eyes. I didn't want to feel like this; I wanted to move on, it's what I needed to do.

I looked around the pub and felt such a strong sense of belonging but what was I really doing? I suddenly felt the urge to get away. The thing with Bess didn't help. It was always going to be there just hanging between us. It had made things different no matter how hard we had tried to go back to how we were before. We'd overstepped the mark and for me it was something that should never have happened. I'd loved it at the time but I had no inclination to do it again. I didn't like the fact that I'd slept with another woman and I knew I never wanted to repeat it.

Lizzy was planning a big event night to celebrate the Pendleton's comeuppance. They'd murdered her boy and they were paying for it. Typical Lizzy, she wanted the world to know her boy had been right and hadn't deserved to die in cold blood. I understood why she felt it was something to celebrate but Billy Pendleton had only half a face left by the time Conny had finished with him. She seemed to have forgotten that part.

She chucked me a big black diary from behind the bar.

'Get phoning some bands,' she said. 'We'll put on some food and invite the world. We'll have the best night this place has ever seen. Let's do it Ella,' she said.

By the end of the day we'd organised a big bash to take place at the pub. George would put some food on and we'd managed to get a band called North West Soul, who did covers of U2 and various other rock bands. We'd got some football scratch cards which would help cover the cost and we'd booked a DJ to MC. It was all very exciting. Conny had loved North West Soul so I was glad they were available that night.

I heard the familiar sound of the dray truck and the clanging of the cellar doors opening. I picked up a copy of the Evening News which had been left on the bar. I was feeling claustrophobic. I knew I'd never amount to anything if I stayed around here. I was really getting a strong sense of itchy feet.

Suddenly I saw the answer. It was there in the newspaper in big bold capitals; an advert for various vacancies on a cruise liner. Chambermaids, hairdressers, couriers, bag carriers; they were looking for people to fill all kinds of roles. They were holding an open day in Manchester. This was it, I was going; it was fate.

The next day I told mum and dad I was going to apply. They were not happy. I explained that I'd been through enough with Conny and I didn't want to live on a council estate for the rest of my life. That didn't go down well since they'd lived on a council estate all of their lives. I convinced them that I was only going to find out what all the fuss was about and it was unlikely I'd even get accepted anyway. They soon came round to the idea.

I spoke to Bess and Ness about it. Ness had become so engrossed with Tony that I wasn't sure if she'd even heard me. I didn't know what was going on with her. She was infatuated with someone who thought he was so much better than us.

Bess took the day off to come with me to the open day. We got the bus to Manchester and walked from the bus station to the Britannia Hotel where the open day was taking place.

When we arrived they had stalls set up with people answering questions about each particular role. They had big posters behind them of the cruise ships and the countries they visited. It looked absolutely amazing. We spoke to all of the people, just for the heck of it. They explained that the shifts were long, fifteen hours, but it was worth it. On the few days they got off each month they were able to disembark and see the sites wherever they were at the time. The wages were low but accommodation and food was paid for so they spent very little.

It was like a dream. It sounded too far out of my reach, almost beyond reality.

'I want it more than I've wanted anything,' I said and stared into Bess's eyes.

'Because of me?' she asked. I shook my head. It wasn't just because of her. I needed out. I wanted to see the world, or at least see somewhere beyond the Lion.

The woman who was in charge of recruitment held a group session then asked anyone who was interested to stay behind for an informal chat. I stayed back.

She liked me, I could tell. She gave me all the details. I couldn't get my breath it was absolutely amazing. There would be a thousand crew members looking after nearly three thousand passengers.

We spoke about my experience. I didn't really have any but filled in the gaps where I could. The only job that I would be eligible for was cleaner or chambermaid but that was fine by me. I filled out an application form and she said she would let me know.

Afterward we went for a burger and Bess grilled me about the interview. I could tell she was gutted that I wanted to leave so badly.

When I got home my mum was waiting with a huge smile on her face.

'You got it Ella, she shouted as I walked in, 'my clever girl. They phoned already to say you got it. You're going to work on a cruise ship.'

I screamed my head off. I'd never felt so happy.

Chapter 25

Bess

I left Ella at her front door but when I heard the screams seconds later I ran back in. I knew she'd got it. I gave her the biggest hug ever, I was so proud of her. Deep down my heart ached. Even though I knew there'd never be a future for us as a couple, I was going to miss my friend, my longest dearest beautiful friend.

Chris Parker looked at me. She had always taken a motherly interest in me and knew me well enough, but she had no idea what was really going on. She put her hand on my shoulder in a protective way.

'Don't be sad, it's only for a year. She'll be back before you know it,' she said.

She was right the contract was only for a year but I knew it would open up massive opportunities for Ella and she'd probably never come back. I didn't want to say that to her mum though so I just nodded and said, 'yeah I know.'

I decided to leave them to it. The boys and Josie were asking Ella a multitude of questions. Her parents were proud as punch. I walked the half a mile to my house thinking about how in two weeks she would be gone.

I thought about Nessa and I was worried. I wasn't sure that Tony was the right person for her and I made a mental note to talk to her more about it. She may be just getting on with it but I wasn't sure whether she was getting on with it in a good way.

As I got near my house I could see a really nice car parked outside. I took a closer look. It was a Sierra Cosworth, a pale metallic blue with a big wing on the back, proper smart. I wondered whose it was.

I could see dad's silhouette through the window talking to a very tall man. I opened the front door quietly and listened. Even though their voices were muffled I could hear dad clearly.

'You're taking a fucking risk coming round here mate,' he said.

I opened the living room door and instantly recognised the tall figure. It was Uncle Richard.

'Hey, Bess' he cried and opened his arms.

I went over and he embraced me in a big bear hug. He was related to my mum and this made me feel so close to her.

I stepped back and looked at him in expectation. 'Do you have news about mum?' I asked with such desperation in my voice. I could have sworn dad had a tear in his eye. I waited anxiously for Richard to tell us what he had to say. For me it meant one of two things, either she was here nearby, or she was dead. I just needed to know.

Richard had been doing some digging since we last met up. He told us there was no evidence that she'd left the area. He'd gone through the taxi ranks and checked all the bookings to the local train stations. He even had the airport provide a report on all outgoing passengers for that year, but had drawn a blank. Unfortunately it was so long ago that there wasn't that much on record. There had been no log of her passport being used during that time so it didn't appear she had left the country. It was useful being a police sergeant.

Dad looked at me and I looked at Richard

'So does that mean she is still in this area?' I asked.

'Well, she could be,' he said, 'unless she got a lift

somewhere with someone. I've asked around all her friends and family, or at least the ones I could track down, but nobody seems to know anything. It really is a mystery.' He turned to my dad, 'John, I need to ask you, are you sure you can't think of anything mate?'

Dad just put his head down and shook it solemnly.

'I've been over it and over it in my mind and I can't think for a minute what's happened. I'm gutted I didn't do more about it at the time but I just thought she'd be back. She was always threatening to up and leave but she never did and you know what she was like about our Bess. I mean, she'd have never have left her baby girl.'

He stared at me with his beautiful blue eyes. 'I know it sounds strange,' he said 'but in a way I'm glad she didn't come back for Bess.' I smiled back at him. I knew what he meant. We were each other's rock. Even though it had been hard when I was young I couldn't imagine not having my dad in my life.

Dad and I spoke at length after Richard had left. I was dying to ask what he meant about Richard taking a risk coming round here but I didn't want to pry, he'd tell me if he wanted to.

I went to bed that night and as I had done many a night I cried over my mum. Where the hell was she? Was she dead? She must be. But if that was the case, I just wanted to know so I could have closure.

I drifted off into a difficult sleep. I dreamt I was on a big ship looking for Ella. I was shouting her name and running from deck to deck. I asked a lady to show me the way and she grabbed my hand warmly. I smelt the familiar smell of her; my mother.

Chapter 26

Nessa

I was taken in by his looks, his eyes his messy hair and his student image. I was taken in by his intelligence, his thirst for knowledge and his awareness about everything and everyone. He didn't compare to Si Bailey but Si had left and was becoming a distant memory to me. So I'd fallen for Tony instead.

Tony was hard work. He was becoming more and more difficult by the day. At least he didn't have a police record as long as your arm, or aspirations that were confined to signing on every other week.

I spent most of my weekends getting pissed up in student pubs around Fallowfield. We all liked a drink now and again, but he seemed to like it more than anyone. He loved to booze which meant when it came to bed time he could hardly perform. I seemed to spend a lot of my time with my hands between my legs as he snored next to me.

The news about Ella made me cling to Tony even more. I knew that when she went I would still have Bess but I would miss Ella dearly. I knew we'd cope but I needed to keep busy. What were we going to do without her for a year?

Tony had taught me to drive and I passed my test first time. I was ecstatic when he had me insured on his Vauxhall Nova. It wasn't until later I realised he'd only done that for me so I could be at his beck and call. He was constantly calling me to pick him up from a bar or club. He'd be pissed out of his skull and unable to walk. Half the time I wondered how he'd even managed to call me.

This particular occasion was no different; it was two in the morning and I was fast asleep. The house phone was ringing for ages and in the end I dived out of bed wondering who it could be. Faya had beaten me to it and was glaring at me until my blood felt cold. 'Tony's pissed,' was all she had to say.

His slurring made me feel sick but when he adored me, he really adored me and I hung on to that side of him. Maybe it was because of the start I'd had as a kid or maybe it was that constant craving for a boy who was never interested, I don't know.

I got dressed and went to pick him up. I couldn't believe the state he was in when I got there. He instantly attacked me for making him wait. He wasn't telling me how beautiful I was or how I was his life. Instead he told me I was vile, disgusting and a fucking idiot. He leant over and spat in my face.

He got in the car and we drove for a few minutes while he screamed at me. I was horrified. Then he told me to get out of the car. He was so aggressive and so adamant that he wanted me to get out that I did as he said. Like an idiot, I got out of the car in the middle of Didsbury village. Without hesitation he jumped into the driver's seat and drove off into the dark, absolutely out of his head. He nearly hit the oncoming traffic and other revellers who were falling out of parties and walking about to find their next beer. The irresponsibility of such actions never hit me at the time. The very fact that he could have hit any innocent bystander barely entered my head. All I could think about was what a twat he was.

I stood there open-mouthed, cold and totally pissed off; pissed off at myself more than anything. I had no money on me so I had no choice but to start the hike home. Hot tears of fury were streaming down my face and I slapped them away like an irritating fly. To make matters worse the keys to my flat were on the car keys that Tony had just driven off with.

I was shaking now with frustration and actually wanted to throw myself in front of a car so I wouldn't have to own up to such humiliation. I carried on crying and I carried on walking.

I heard a horn and I looked around. There he was driving towards me like a mad man. He hit the kerb as he pulled up right next to me.

'Let me drive,' I demanded. 'You're pissed out of your face.'

Like a baby kitten, he just rolled onto the back seat looking all forlorn and lost, vulnerable and definitely fucked up.

I drove him back to his luxurious pad and dumped him on the doorstep,

'Come in Ness,' he shrieked.

'No,' I said.

I wanted to fight him, wanted to kick him in the face, but I didn't. I knew when he woke up in the morning that he'd be full of remorse. I'd speak to him then and make his fucking life hell.

I got back into the car and drove to the safe haven of my flat. I just hoped and prayed that Faya would be asleep when I got in.

These were the things that I never shared with Ella or Bess, although they could tell that something wasn't right about Tony.

I managed to get in without waking Faya, although I felt like getting in her bed and cuddling up to her, burying myself in that familiar smell that was my big sister. She would go mad if she knew what had happened and she'd probably kill

Tony. Fuck it; I'd sort him out myself.

I was awakened the next morning by someone hammering on the flat door as though we owed them money. I staggered towards it, banging my toe on the phone stand in the hall. I winced then cursed as I wondered who it could be.

It was Tony, hung-over with a cheeky grin and a bunch of shit flowers. It almost made me laugh but I let him in and led him to my room, away from Faya. When we got to my room he grabbed me and held me tightly in the intense way only he could. He stared at me hard as he pulled me towards him. I could smell the stench of stale beer on his breath which made me want to gag but I got over it. We fumbled and tugged at each other's clothes. I was knackered and I looked a mess but I didn't care. I needed him close. He threw me on the bed and got on top of me and I rocked backwards and forwards with him. I closed my eyes tight and tried to focus on him and the moment.

Chapter 27

Ella

I couldn't believe that I'd got the job. Ok, I was only going to be changing bedding but I was going to be doing it on a cruise ship halfway around the world. I couldn't believe this was going to happen and I only had a few weeks left to sort everything out.

When I thought about it my stomach did a flip and jumped right up to my throat. I felt tightness around my neck. I was frightened half to death at the thought of leaving my mum and dad, and my brothers and sister. I was frightened of leaving Lizzy and George. I was frightened of leaving the pub, of leaving our road, leaving my surroundings and I was frightened of not seeing my girls for ages, my dearest friends, my soul sisters.

I was frightened of being on a big ship surrounded by people I didn't know. I was frightened of failing at a job I'd never done before. I couldn't sleep. I could have easily talked myself out of going but I knew I'd get lynched if I did that.

I was worried about Ness. This Tony was an absolute idiot and was taking the piss out of her good nature, taking her kindness for granted. She thought we didn't know but Faya was keeping a close eye on her and then speaking to me and Bess about it. She was concerned. Ness had definitely changed since she'd met him and she got angry if we even mentioned his name. He definitely had some kind of hold on her.

One night when I was struggling to sleep, I got up and

made a brew. I sat in our living room thinking about Bess. The curtains were open. Although it was dark outside, the cosy orange glow of the street lamp lit the room enough for me to see. Suddenly, I thought I heard a sound coming from outside, close to the living room window. My heart stopped for a second and I put my brew on the floor.

I started shaking. I sensed that someone was there looking into the living room. I was certain; I could almost see the white of their eyes. A heat enveloped my whole body. Someone was standing there. My gut instinct was to shout for my dad as loud as I could, but what if this person was armed?

A sudden surge of strength rushed through my body. The thought of anything happening to my family suddenly made me grow a pair of iron steel balls. I jumped up from the chair and looked right at him. Peter fucking Lawrence stood there as bold as brass with his nose on the glass and his cock in his hand. Then I did scream for my dad.

The next hour was chaos. Lawrence claimed he had come looking for our Josie, which set the guns blazing. My brothers and dad were fuming.

'What does that even mean?' said dad furiously. His temper was like I'd never seen it before. 'It's two o'clock in the morning, what would you want with our Josie?'

'I wanted to ask her out,' said Peter in his thick accent. Mixed with saliva and spittle it made everything sound worse.

'No way she's fucking going out with you, you thick twat. She's a little girl,' said Henry and head butted him in a complete rage.

The crack of the two heads locking and banging together went through me and I screamed. 'Just get him out of here.'

The boys dragged him out and threw him onto the road. I heard Peter scream so I'm not sure what else they did to him.

My mum and Josie came downstairs and we all sat drinking cups of tea, snuggled up on the settee. We didn't talk about what happened because the boys were making enough noise about it in the kitchen; the air was blue.

'What was you doing up anyway Ella?' my mum asked.

I explained that I couldn't sleep and that I was worried about going on the ships and leaving them all. She told me I was going on the ships and that was that. I smiled. None of us went back to bed; we were knackered the next day. Peter Lawrence was going to get it when I saw him, the fucking weirdo.

Chapter 28

Peter Lawrence

He had told me to watch every movement Josie made. He told me to track down her day, her night and her every breath. I'd taken it literally. I was thick as pig shit sometimes. I had been there trying to watch every move she made. I thought she might have been moving about the house, sometimes she did. It was all so confusing. I was out of breath as I ran up the road, away from the Parkers' house.

I didn't know where to run. The fuckers had caught me red handed. Ella Nosey Parker had spotted me while she was sneaking about on her own in her living room.

He'd said it'd be alright. He wanted something to happen to the Parkers and he said he'd sort me out. I think he meant he'd give me some money, a lot of money.

The brothers had twatted me in the face. It was nothing; I was always getting twatted in the face, so it didn't matter. Tears stung my eyes. Why was I crying? I punched myself hard in the eye. I was annoyed with myself for fucking crying. I hated the lot of them round here.

My thoughts changed. I had enjoyed watching Ella through the curtains. I'd thought of her jumping Conny years ago. I hadn't meant to get hard but I got over excited and fucked up.

I always fuck up but I'd come through in the end, that's one thing I knew for sure.

Chapter 29

Bess

Restless nights, bad dreams and deep thoughts were making me tired. I kept wondering why dad told Richard it was a risk him coming round here. I'd come to the conclusion it was because he was police, old bill, a copper, the fuzz, whatever you wanted to call him. Police weren't exactly welcomed with open arms on the estate.

I heard the phone ringing. I was tempted to ignore it but the caller seemed determined to get through so I dived out of bed and ran to answer it. It was Ella, phoning to tell me about an incident with my 'lovely' neighbour, Peter. What the hell was it with that man? We both came to the conclusion that something needed to be done. Where was his family? What had happened to his dad? We hadn't seen him for years. We had him dead and buried in some sordid episode of Peter Lawrence madness.

It wasn't a question of phoning the police. It didn't work like that round here; we often took the law into our own hands. Not right I know, but it was the only way we knew. The police couldn't be trusted and didn't much care about what happened on the estate; as long as it stayed on the estate.

We talked about Nessa too; about our concerns for our beautiful, easy going friend. I suggested maybe we let Peter loose on Tony and just see what happened. Ella said perhaps he could bum him. 'Yeah if Tony could keep it up long enough,' I snorted. I couldn't breathe through laughing.

After I hung up the phone I decided to confront Peter. I

got dressed and headed round to his house. I'd never been in his garden or his house in all the years I'd lived next door to him. The house was dark and dingy, it looked untidy. It still had the old steel window frames. To me, each window looked like a great big face, but none of them smiled at me. They looked like they were frowning, telling me to go away.

The grass had grown so tall that it was up to my waist. The garden was large and the walk up to the front door seemed to go on for miles. I could have done with a scythe to make my passage easier. I felt drawn to the house but it wasn't pleasant, my heart was thumping hard in my chest and I was finding it hard to get my breath.

I had to speak to Peter, reason with him and explain that what he was doing was wrong and that he needed to sort himself out. He was thirty at least but probably a lot younger in his head. I didn't care about him but I did feel sorry for him. Maybe with a different start in life he might have been a different boy, who grew into a different man. Maybe he could have been our friend. As it was he had no one; no one who loved and cared for him. He'd been left like a dog to fend for himself and he wasn't right in the head that was for sure. It was a real shame.

The stench from the house was dire like there was a cadaver lying in wait for me. I knocked on the door and it swung straight off its hinges and smashed onto the path. Peter Lawrence appeared from nowhere screaming in a blind panic.

'What do you fucking want, you cheeky fucking slag? Fuck off,' he yelled at me.

My nerves got the better of me and I almost laughed. I had no idea where it came from. He started to walk towards me. I flew up the path back to my house next door as fast as my legs would carry me. I stood for a moment rummaging for my keys. 'Come on, come on,' I said out loud, trying to aim the key into the lock. I daren't look back. The door opened and I dived inside, slammed it shut and locked it. I slid down the door panting heavily. What was I thinking? What did I even intend to say to him? Fuck it, leave him to it.

I made myself a brew and put plenty of sugar in it. I felt dizzy and a bit sick. I sat still for quite a while but I could feel him listening through the walls. I could feel my pulse strong in my neck. He'd lived there all my life why did I now feel so scared? I had no idea what he was capable of but he was a wrong-un, a definite wrong-un.

Later that day, when my nerves had settled back down, I decided to go and see Nessa. I needed to see how she was. On the last few occasions I had seen her she looked absolutely knackered. Her appearance had been dishevelled and she seemed subdued, almost withdrawn. I was concerned it was something to do with how that knob head, Tony was treating her and I wanted to make sure she was ok.

When I arrived at the flat, Nessa wasn't in but Faya was in an absolute rage. She was throwing stuff around Nessa's room. I felt uncomfortable. Even though they were sisters, I wouldn't like the idea of anyone going through my stuff so I was sure Nessa wouldn't be happy about it.

'What's going on?' I asked.

'The man's an absolute idiot Bess, he's a boozer, a dirty fucking drunk,' she said.

I put my head down. I thought of my dad who'd been a boozer all his life. She picked up on it straight away and apologised.

'Sorry Bess but it's different. He's sly and manipulating and he's no good to her especially with drink,' she said.

'Here, look at this.'

She picked up a box from the table and showed it to me. It was full of pictures that he'd taken and developed of some girl. She was naked and he was naked.

'Why has Nessa got these? What's this man doing to her?' said Faya.

There were pictures of a little boy too. She showed them to me. 'I think he's got a kid,' she said. I was shocked.

Faya looked really concerned and I could tell she was at the end of her tether with it all.

'There's something else too,' Faya said, 'Pat and Kenny gave each of us some money when we reached eighteen. Ness kept hers in the post office and it's gone. She had nearly a grand in there Bess and it's all gone. And I found some receipts from Norman in her drawers. She's had about three or four loans off him, nothing major, but why would she need them? She hasn't bought anything new that I've seen and she's always been good with her money. It must be something to do with him.'

We were both as perplexed as each other. Nessa was definitely being taken for a ride here. She was clearly blinded to the situation. As we stood there trying to take it all in, the flat door opened and was slammed shut. Clearly someone wasn't too happy.

We both jumped out of our skin and stared at each other in shock and disbelief for what seemed like ages. I didn't know what to do and nor did Faya. She had more or less ransacked Nessa's bedroom and it looked like I'd had a hand in it too. We both started to move stuff about but we had no idea where things were supposed to be. There was mini chaos for a moment until we both looked up.

Nessa stood looking at us both with despair in her eyes.

'What do you think you are doing?' she said calmly.

I looked at Faya. She loved her sister dearly and wanted to protect her. She could see things were wrong but, instead of calmly explaining, she lost it.

It didn't go down well and before I knew it the two sisters were rolling about on the bed kicking each other. I'd never ever seen Nessa lose her temper before. She was the calmest, gentlest person I knew. It was soul destroying watching the two of them fighting.

Faya's legs were wrapped tightly around Nessa's neck whilst Nessa clawed at them like an animal. I screamed at them both to stop and they did.

'You need to talk, for god's sake, not fight,' I shouted. 'Nessa, Faya is worried about you, we all are. We're worried about the way Tony's treating you. Tell us what's going on? Be honest, what the hell is going on?'

She burst into tears. 'I don't know what's going on. Most of the time he's lovely to me, treats me like I'm a princess. He loves and adores me but I think he's having some sort of mental break down,' she said.

She ignored the glances Faya and I were throwing each other. I couldn't believe what I was hearing. I mean, I wasn't exactly sure what was going on, but this fella had our girl right under his thumb.

Faya was exasperated. 'He loves and adores you? So what's with all the boozing? What's with the abuse and arguments? I hear you on the phone. You look shit, you've complained about the sex. He's spent all your money and you've got loans for him. I've seen your bank book and the receipts. I'm sorry I know I shouldn't have looked, but I'm worried sick. Is he on drugs? Are you paying for his habit?' she stopped to draw breath and her eyes filled up. 'I want my

Nessa back, my beautiful happy-go-lucky sister,' she said. Then we all lost it; we started crying and hugging each other.

Ella's entrance calmed us all down. 'What the fuck?' she said in shock at seeing us all in a pile of hugs on the bed. 'Is this about that bastard?' she said.

I shook my head at her to let her know not to push. It was a delicate situation.

'Put the kettle on El, let's have a brew', I said with a smile.

She did as she was told and we all had a good chat.

It was clear that Tony had a hold over Nessa. She didn't stop harping on about his intelligence, his potential, how good he was at what he did, how different he was from the lads on the estate.

She was clearly smitten and we let her talk. There was definitely stuff that needed sorting out. We didn't fully understand how the mind worked because we weren't fucking psychiatrists but even we knew something wasn't right.

'Ah Ness, come on babe, this is stupid,' I said. 'He's nothing special. Ok, so he's had a private education but he spends most of his time pissed up. He's destructive that much I do know. Just because he's intelligent and knows a few big words doesn't mean he's good for you. You've said yourself he wouldn't know what to do if there was a crisis. We'd fight hell and earth for each other, wouldn't we? Would he for you?'

'What about these pics?' Faya said. She had them in front of her. 'It's him and some other woman. What's that all about?'

'Ah, I know, I was pissed off when I found them,' Nessa said.

She started explaining how he'd had to pop out one

evening as his son was poorly. As soon as she said it she realised she had let the cat out of the bag.

'So that is his kid.' Faya shouted. 'He's got a kid? So when were you going to tell us this? God Ness, what else are you hiding?'

'The girl in the pictures is his ex, the kid's mum, and he was going to use those pics for an album cover. His mate's in a band,' Ness said avoiding the question about his son.

'He's a knob,' said Ella. Her sharp tongue couldn't help itself. 'And I don't like him.' she added.

And that was that; back to square one.

Chapter 30

Nessa

I couldn't handle the girls' reactions to Tony having a son even though I knew that everything they were saying was right. It was how it must have looked from the outside but they didn't know the half of it. My poor man hadn't seen his son for months because he was seeing me. His ex-girlfriend had gone mad and decided that she didn't want her child to meet another woman. I wasn't too bothered about that. I wasn't ready to become a step mum. He was a little twat from what I'd heard anyway so I really didn't want to get involved.

Nevertheless, I hated the impact it had on Tony. He was always down and didn't have much in the way of motivation. The mum had said that she wanted money for her son as Tony hadn't given her a penny towards his upbringing. Tony told me that she had been violent towards him. He'd known her a long time and had spent a couple of years with her from eighteen onwards. He said that they'd actually split up before he had found out she was pregnant.

They had agreed on an amount of money. I think she worked out so much a week from when the kid had been born and it came to a hefty sum. The whole episode really got to him. For weeks he just lay on his bed staring at the ceiling of his luxurious pad, which I had discovered, was paid for by his parents.

When I went round to see him, he cried for his son. He cried because of the impact it was having on us, and he cried because he didn't have any money. If he could just get the money he could see his boy.

I left him that day feeling so sorry and sad for him. That woman was ruining his life and using his child to do so. I thought about the money Pat and Kenny had given to me when I'd turned eighteen. It was just under a grand and if I got a loan off Norman I could give Tony the money he needed.

I knew Tony would eventually do well. He had the world at his feet in terms of his career. His intelligence and qualifications would allow him to do anything he wanted and earn a fortune. I knew that one day he would repay me.

I was excited that I could make it right for him. He would be so grateful and love me even more than he already did. He would think I was the most beautiful person in the whole world. I couldn't wait to hear his words and expressions of thanks. They would be poetic, romantic and would make my heart melt.

I got the money together that this pathetic woman wanted so that Tony could see his son. I thought his face would light up when I threw it on the bed in an envelope with 'Tony' scrawled on it. He sat up immediately and stared at the envelope for ages.

'What's this?' he asked.

'It's for you,' I said shyly looking for some sort of light in his eyes which had lately seemed to appear so dull and lifeless.

'What do you mean, it's for me?' he said.

He looked horrified, I cringed.

'It's for you, so you can get your little boy back. At least now she'll let you see him occasionally,' I said.

'I don't want crumbs,' he said. 'I want to be a dad. I want to wake up with him every morning and put him to bed each night. I want to be responsible for his upbringing and his education and be there for him.'

I wanted to scream at him, 'well you can't do that laying on your arse all day staring at the ceiling,' but I didn't. He couldn't help it, he was depressed. It wasn't his fault.

He took the money and told me he was eternally grateful.

'Come here, beautiful,' he said. 'You're an angel sent to me from heaven. You know that, don't you?'

It was good to see him smile and felt good to be in his arms despite the stench of stale beer on his breath. We lay there for hours and I wondered if we would have sex. It had been so long since we'd last done it and I needed it, I wanted it and I wanted it with him. But no, I lay with him staring at the ceiling wondering if the couple of words of gratitude were worth me racing about trying to get the money together so he could get his son. I wasn't looking for anything in return. I just wanted him to be ok.

A couple of days later he walked into college looking more chipper and smarter than usual. He was wearing a jacket that I'd never seen before. He nodded across the canteen and gave me a wry smile, which I didn't know how to interpret. I smiled back and continued to eat lunch with my college mates, mates that Tony said were stagnant idiots. I wondered if that's why the smile had seemed so disapproving. I'd better get away from them, I thought. He clearly didn't approve. So I grabbed my tray and went to sit with him instead.

'Hiya', I said cheerfully. 'Good to see you out and about, you look nice.' I meant it.

'Thanks angel,' he replied. His words melted me.

'Is that a new jacket?' I asked, almost afraid of the answer.

'Yeah,' he didn't flinch. 'I treated myself. She wouldn't have expected all that money all at once. She knows I don't have any. So I gave her some of it and then went into Manchester to buy a few bits. I haven't had a decent coat in years. This one will last forever, so it's an investment, really. You don't mind do you?' he said.

My stomach felt like it had been replaced with lead. I went all hot and didn't quite know what to say. That was my life savings and I was still going to have to pay Norman back the money I'd borrowed. There he was in a brand new coat without a second thought for me. Did I mind? I thought back to our struggles as kids and how I used to nick my brothers clothes to keep warm, a long, long time ago now, but the memories all fresh. I bet Tony never had to do that. He hadn't lived, hadn't struggled and he'd never been hungry.

He interrupted my thoughts. 'Good news, though, I get to pick up my beautiful little boy on Friday. She's letting me have him Friday and Saturday night. I was going to stay at my parent's house with him. You're more than welcome to come,' he said.

Why did it make me feel sick?

I couldn't endure another hour of college. I needed to get away. I felt such a fool, him sat there in his new clobber, me with nothing in the cupboard at home and nothing in the post office and nothing to pay Norman back. Tony was happy. Happy he was going to see his kid at the weekend and all because of me. And I bet she was happy too with half my money or whatever he had given her. I was mad.

I stood up. 'I'm off home, Tony. Have you got the car keys, please?' I said.

He said I'd have to walk as he needed the car. He also said it'd do me good as I'd put on a bit of weight. My anger nearly reached boiling point. I'd never experienced much anger before I met Tony because I was usually so happy to please but it was an emotion I was getting quite used to.

I stormed out of college and set off towards home. I heard someone shouting me, 'Ness, Ness.'

I looked back and there was Tony, all handsome and aloof. He came running towards me. I was shocked he could run, as he barely moved usually.

'Are you my friend?' he said.

'Why wouldn't I be?' I said.

Was there going to be some recognition of his wrong doing, squandering all my money on clothes and stuff?

'No reason, you just got off pretty quickly,' he said, then grabbed my face with two hands. 'Please come at the weekend. My folks have a big holiday home in Yorkshire. It's beautiful and you can meet little Sammy, he's beautiful. He'll love you just like I do. I adore you, Ness. You're my angel and the best thing that's ever happened to me. You know that don't you?'

I was beautiful. I was also kind. I was an angel but I wasn't sure I believed he really thought that. I eventually agreed to go to his parents and meet Sammy, a thought that filled me with dread.

Later that evening, I lay alone in my bed where I very much wanted to be. I didn't want to be with anyone else. My mood was at an all-time low. I kept going over what had happened. I thought about what the girls would say if they knew. I tried to reach into my soul to see what my feelings were for Tony. Did I love him or did I feel responsible for him? Why did I feel responsible for him? The turmoil in my head kept me awake. I was starting to dislike myself for being so nice to this man. My kindness was to my own detriment and I knew it.

The phone rang. I turned over and ignored it, but that made

me feel worse. What if he was upset or having a moment? What if he needed me? The phone stopped and I drifted off into a deep sleep where my mind played tricks in the depth of despair. I didn't love him. I did love him. I loved him but not how I should love him. Did he love me?

Chapter 31

Ella

I sat in the kitchen talking to my mum about Nessa. I told her what a state she was in and about what had happened the other day, that we'd all had a go at her. She needed to be rid of this freak who she thought was the dog's bollocks. It was insane. Mum listened and explained that none of us knew what went on behind closed doors.

'It might seem bad from the outside but you don't know what he's like when they're alone together,' she said. 'He probably tells her everything a girl wants to hear. Then when he treats her like shit she's just blinded by all the good stuff.'

'Mum, they don't even really sleep together. She told me the other night. She said she even wore a really low cut top and more or less shoved her breasts in his face, and he hardly even noticed. I don't remember Conny ever being like that mum.'

I couldn't go into too much detail about my sexual encounters. It wasn't that sort of relationship, but I wanted to know what she thought about it.

'He's a fucking queer,' she yelled.

I laughed. Well at least I understood loud and clear what she thought about it. I bet he was; it made sense. He was a fucking queer. I bet he took it up the arse and he was using her as his leaning post. She was his emotional rag to oil himself when needed and then toss to one side when he'd had enough.

Tony was impacting on all our lives. Bess said she couldn't stop thinking about him and Nessa either. Faya was in a right state, but what could we do? Nessa was a big girl and she knew what she was doing. I decided I would have one more talk with her about it and if that didn't work, I would stop wasting my breath. I had my future to think of and I had to get organised for my new life but first I had to get ready for The Stone Roses.

Ness, Bess and me were off to Spike Island to see them live. We'd been looking forward to this gig for ages and I was so excited. Their album had come out the year before and we were all smitten. Bess had it on a cassette tape in the car and we played it constantly. We'd rewind it, pause it and write down the lyrics.

Their sound was something we'd never heard before; music with a difference. There was a whole new vibe around the music scene in Manchester. It was mad. In fact, it was so mad they named it 'Madchester' and it was amazing to be part of it.

In the eighties, The Hacienda in Manchester was the place to be. It had bands such as New Order, The Happy Mondays, 808 State, the Charlatans, James and many others. We all loved it and we'd go as often we could. In the late eighties and early nineties, Manchester was definitely the place to be for music and we were in our element. Now we were off to see The Stone Roses live and we were expecting it to be the best day ever.

Bess packed up her little car. I ran up to her house, something I hadn't done since I was a little girl but I was so excited. I loved going to gigs, we all did, but we'd never been to anything as big as this. This was massive and she was just as excited as me. As I stormed into her house I was met by someone I didn't recognise. A man, who wasn't her dad, a man who immediately gave me butterflies.

'This is Uncle Richard,' Bess said and smiled.

As Uncle Richard extended his huge hand to shake my tiny one, John Holland barged into the living room and almost knocked us both over.

'Right girls, have a top day, it's going to be belting,' he said whilst pushing us towards the door.

We both stood on the doorstep and looked at each other in shock.

'He's off his head,' Bess said and smiled, full of adoration for her dad. He'd turned out to be a pretty good dad in the end. Despite his early mistakes he'd certainly turned things around for his daughter and you couldn't help but love him.

'Come on let's get Ness,' I said. We were about to drive off when Uncle Richard came out of the house and walked up to our car.

'Your dad said you were going to the Spike Island gig? Have a brilliant time ladies. I hope Ian does you proud. If you need anything give me a ring,' he said as he handed me his business card with a mobile number on it.

'Ooooh,' I said cheekily. 'You've got a mobile phone?'

He grinned and pulled out what looked like a brick with a massive aerial on it. Bess and I burst out laughing.

'Cool,' we giggled.

'Better than yours,' he said.

'Good point, Sergeant,' I said, half taking the piss, but half impressed by his title.

Bess looked at me, and then back at him. She had a strange look on her face. I put it down to jealousy; she was in love with me. She had no need to be jealous. Richard was old enough to be my dad. I did feel a strange connection to him though. He made me feel very comfortable. As I looked at his eyes, they bore into my soul and I shuddered.

'Hey you want to sort that cretin out,' I said as I spotted Peter Lawrence spying on us behind his manky net curtains.

Richard didn't bat an eye lid. 'Don't worry, he'll get his,' he said, and with that he winked and walked over to his cool Sierra Cosworth.

'Ah, your uncle seems nice,' I said.

Bess frowned. 'Come on let's get Nessa.' she said.

Chapter 32

Ness

I was on my way to Yorkshire with Tony and his child Sammy, a one year old mass of blonde curls. He had the brightest blue eyes and was utterly adorable. I wasn't sure of my position so I kept quiet. Tony introduced us, not that Sammy had a clue what he was saying, but he did acknowledge me with his gorgeous eyes.

I'm not sure why the pit of my stomach felt like it contained a mini chainsaw, but I did always get a dull ache being around Tony. I couldn't explain it; his presence unnerved me. It wasn't quite right but there was also a definite feeling of warmth at times and I admired his intelligence. He was so pleasant to speak to, so different from the others, and judging by his intellect and qualifications, he was definitely going places. I'd be mad not to be in it for the long-haul.

I looked across at him and my thoughts very quickly switched. It was the stench of stale ale that jolted me. I asked him if it would be better if I drove.

'No angel, I'm fine,' he said. I wasn't sure but I let it go.

'Don't forget we need to leave on time tomorrow,' I said and smiled.

'Yes I know,' he snapped.

'I'm going to see the Stone Roses,' I said and grinned.

'Yes I know,' he replied. His cheerful demeanour had disappeared.

What was I doing with this miserable bastard? Mentioning leaving early seemed to have really pissed him off and we were silent for most of the journey. I was worried. I didn't want anything upsetting this weekend. I was going to meet his parents and really needed to be in the right mind-set.

After a couple of hours we pulled onto a camp site, full of tents and mobile homes.

'My folks own this,' he said. 'I've asked them to set a tent up for us, you'll love it.'

Wow, I was thrilled. I jumped out of the car and breathed in the beautiful Yorkshire air. The views were stunning, we were on moorland and a drystone wall surrounded the campsite. There were sheep everywhere which freaked me out slightly but I would cope.

Tony took me to our tent. There were a few other campers on the site but it wasn't packed, just nice and relaxed. The tent was nothing brilliant but there were airbeds and sleeping bags in it. There was a little camping cooker with tiny bottles of gas, a few plates and stuff to make a brew. I'd never been camping before, so I was excited.

We unpacked the car and started to put our own stamp on what was our home for the weekend. Sammy started to cry and get distressed for what seemed like no reason. Tony became very upset too. For the next two hours it was non-stop crying whilst Tony paced around getting more and more worked up.

I was more than stressed. I took Sammy from him and tried to calm them both but the kid wanted his mummy, or at least that's what I thought he was saying.

Tony was distraught. 'He always wants his mum. He doesn't know me,' he said.

'Come on,' I said, 'he'll calm down. Let's get his trolley and take him for a walk.'

We walked along the dales. It was beautiful. As we headed back to the tent dusk started to set in.

'Are we going to see your parents?' I asked.

He shrugged and sat down. 'I'm starving,' he said and just smiled.

'Is there a chippy around here?' I asked.

He mumbled something about a chippy just outside the site and tried to give me directions but it was hard work as ever.

I realised I'd just have to find the chippy by myself so I headed off down the lane with Sammy in his trolley. My stomach was rumbling, but not as much as my blood was boiling. It really was like getting blood out of a stone out of Tony.

I was starting to realise that his negativity was really getting me down. I thought about the long haul and wasn't really sure that I even wanted it. What was wrong with him? He had the world at this finger tips, he had me and he had this beautiful child. He'd had a fantastic education and a wealth of opportunities handed to him on a plate. Yet he seemed so unhappy. I looked down at Sammy and thought about his mum and wondered what her relationship with Tony was like. He had made out that she was lunatic, a nightmare, always in the wrong and even violent. He'd explained how she'd once broken both her wrists by hitting him on the head. Another time she'd kicked him down the stairs. I could understand that, there were times when I'd like to kick the fucker down some stairs myself. Unfortunately, I was laid back, easy going and too simple to create complications so I could only empathise with her. She was willing to snap her wrists on his head out of pure frustration. I could identify with that. She was clearly feistier than I was.

We found the quaintest chippy that I'd ever set eyes on. The little building was made of stone, it made a change from the usual red council brick that I saw on a daily basis. The entrance was arched with a big porch and a great big wooden door which you couldn't see through. There were two little tables in the corner. I decided it would be better if me and Sammy ate in and took back some chips for Tony. I ordered a plate of chips, meat and potato pie, peas and gravy with bread and butter. I had a coke and Sammy had his bottle.

After we'd finished I was stuffed. Sammy was looking knackered and I was betting Tony was starving. I gathered our stuff together, paid the lady and headed back to the camp site.

As I was trying to remember where our tent was I saw Tony walking towards us. He was staggering all over the place. He was out of his head, again. My heart sunk; once more no sex for me.

I approached him. He gave me a big smile and stared right into my eyes.

'You took him out, my Sammy, and he loves you. Sammy, tell Nessa, I love her,' he said looking at his son. Sammy gurgled.

'Come on let's get back to the tent,' I said.

I had to get Sammy ready for bed since Tony was in no fit state. I didn't have a clue what I was doing and he knew it. He wasn't shy in letting me know either. He wailed, he sobbed, he screamed, nothing I could do would console him and all the time Tony stood staring at me, just fucking staring.

I was exasperated. 'You need to sort him out, babe. He's your kid,' I said. I tried to keep my tone patient and gentle so as not to wind him up.

He took Sammy off me and tried to soothe him. He lay him down, shook him gently, then he stood up and carried him, pacing up and down. Sammy wouldn't let up. My nerves were shattering under the strain and I could have cried myself. I just wanted to go home but there was no way out.

'I'll have to take him to my parent's house. He really won't settle. I'm not sure what's wrong with him,' Tony said.

The parents, I thought, I wondered when they were going to get brought up. I stood up ready to go but he stopped me.

'You wait here sweetheart,' he said. 'I won't be long, it'll be easier. I can't be bothered with the introductions right now not while Sammy's like this. I'll come back for you in a bit, don't worry.'

With that, he jumped in the car. He was half-cut but this time he had that little boy in the back and was putting him at risk too. This was everything I was against. It was what I was learning at college, how to protect children. But it was too late, he was gone, driving down the makeshift road towards goodness knows where. I was dumbstruck, lost for words and my breathing was shallow.

I went to my bag and fished out a joint I'd made earlier. I made a makeshift chair and placed it outside the tent. The air was cool, but not cold and I was wearing a thick sweater. I lit the joint, and welcomed the heat on my lungs allowing the sensation to take over my body. I closed my eyes and relaxed for a moment, grateful for the brief respite from Tony. Gradually I started to panic. I didn't know how far away Tony's parents lived but he seemed to be taking an awful long time to come back. Before I knew it, it was midnight. I was stoned out of my brains and I was deserted on a camp site somewhere in the middle of Yorkshire all by my fucking self.

Chapter 33

Bess

As we pulled up outside Nessa's flat we could hear the Stone Roses blaring out from inside. We were excited to see our fellow rock chick again. Faya opened the door looking ashen. My heart stopped beating for a minute.

I wound down the window and shouted. 'What is it Faya? What on earth's wrong?' She looked like she'd seen a ghost.

Ella and me dived out of the car and ran over to her.

'What's up? Where's Nessa?' I asked concerned.

Faya explained that Nessa had gone with Tony, the fucking manic depressive, to see his family, with his little bastard of a kid. We already knew that.

I was getting impatient, 'And?' I asked in frustration.

'And she's not fucking back,' Faya screamed. 'She knew what time you were leaving and I've not heard from her all weekend. I'm worried sick.'

I wasn't worried, I was pissed off. It was typical of Nessa not to call, typical of her not to be on time, she was never on time, and I knew today would be no different. I felt like driving off and going without her.

Ella was quiet. 'God do you think she's alright?' she said. 'I mean, we don't really know this geezer and we haven't a clue where they've gone.'

'She'll be back any minute,' I said, still pissed that she was late. 'It was her idea, she got the tickets. She wouldn't miss it for the world. Let's chill out, go in and wait for her.'

We waited for nearly three hours but she didn't come back or even call to let us know where she was. We concluded that because she was so smitten with that bastard, she'd fucked us all off and decided to stay playing happy families.

I was fuming, we all were. Faya said she'd come in Nessa's place so that brightened the mood slightly.

After we'd gone over it again, we convinced ourselves that she was safe and just being idiots yet again. We decided that we weren't going to let it spoil our day. It was the day we'd all been waiting for, the legendary gig at Spike Island by the Stone Roses.

I drove like a lunatic all the way. We were already three hours late and had missed the whole build up to one of the biggest gigs to be played outdoors for a long time. When we got there, however, we soon caught up. The crowd was huge and the noise and atmosphere was exciting and wild. Everyone was out of their heads, drugs were rife. I was offered more white powder than I knew existed. I licked my finger and took up the offer of a bit of whizz.

It wasn't often I let my hair down but I couldn't wait to hear the band. I was really getting into the mood of it all and it felt good. Ella looked good too. I groaned inside my head, but no sooner had the thought appeared, it disappeared, it had to, it was wrong.

We sat in the sunshine, it was a gorgeous day. The support bands played in the distance as we lolled in the hazy heat. We laughed along with other groups of revellers, enjoyed their stories and shared ours. When The Stone Roses appeared on the big stage, the crowd went mad. Me, Ella and Faya joined in with the screaming and pushed our way through the crowd trying to get as close as we could.

I felt Nessa's absence for a minute and knew that wherever she was she'd be gutted. Where on earth was she? Faya grabbed mine and Ella's hands and we started dancing, swaying and singing as Ian Brown belted out his songs. We couldn't hear him very well. To be honest he didn't sing very well either. It was more a low drone which drifted across the late evening sky. The crowd looked at each other in disapproval we didn't mind too much. It was The Stone Roses. It really was Ian Brown up there. So we all danced and we all sang and we enjoyed the atmosphere and the excitement at Spike Island.

Chapter 34

Ella

I loved it, I didn't care that they were shit or that Ian Brown couldn't sing for toffee and they didn't come back on for an encore; apparently they never did. We were still all holding hands and singing at the top of our croaky voices as we made our way out of the venue. I was on such a high. It was partly the drugs but partly the natural high from seeing one of my favourite bands perform live. It was amazing.

We got to Bess's car, which the touts had charged us a tenner to park. All the back windows were smashed. For fuck sake, why?

We managed to clear out all the glass and reported it to some coppers who were on patrol. They were supposed to be making sure that trouble was kept to a minimum but they weren't arsed. They just shrugged their shoulders and said that we should be happy that nobody was hurt. I remembered the card in my pocket.

'Here you go mate. This is my Uncle Richard,' I said.

The copper jumped to attention immediately. I felt Bess's eyes glaring in the back of my head. He was her uncle not mine, but if it meant we got some help who gave a shit.

The coppers suddenly changed their tune and before we knew it, glass fitters had arrived to repair the damage.

'Just charge the sarge,' someone shouted.

I did feel a bit guilty. He would go mad but I didn't know that would happen. Bess didn't look too pleased but she soon put her face straight when her car windows were all fixed and the car was safe to drive.

We put the cassette on full blast and virtually flew back home down the M62 totally euphoric; a top time was had by all.

I sat back in the car and reflected. It was only a matter of weeks and I would be working all over the world. It was hard to imagine it was happening. I looked up front and could see Bess's profile as she concentrated on her driving. The orange street-lights in the darkness flickered on her face, so it would become dark, then light, dark, then light.

My stomach lurched and the bile almost shot to the back of my throat. I'd not thought about the incident for a long time in any depth. I just wish that it had not happened. It was the biggest regret of my life. It wasn't right, I wasn't a lesbian, I liked men. I'll never know what had come over me. I also knew how it had affected Bess and the guilt she had was becoming too much to bear. She'd not looked at anyone else since and I wasn't daft, I knew why. She was definitely into girls and I wasn't sure if that was my fault or whether she'd always been that way. I didn't know how it worked, did you turn lesbian or were you born like it?

I looked at Faya and thought about Ness. I felt the tears forming in my eyes. I knew where she was heading and I just wish she would see sense. I didn't feel comfortable leaving her. In some ways she was more vulnerable than Bess, but they had each other. Ness had Faya and Bess had her beloved dad. They'd be ok. I felt a gulp in my throat and became suddenly very emotional.

I wondered what had happened to Nessa this weekend. I was sure she was safe. I just wasn't sure how far she'd gone for that prick. She was the nicest out of the three of us, and the kindest, warmest, friendliest person you could wish to meet. She was so mild mannered and her temperament was lovely. Me, I was too upfront and sometimes inappropriate with my honesty and Bess was the same to some extent. I would bear a grudge and fuck you off out of my life in an instant. Ness would always forgive and always saw the best in anyone. Bess didn't trust anyone, but no wonder with what had gone on in her life.

As we pulled up to the flat I could see Tony's car was there. I felt the relief coming from Bess and Faya. I was relieved but curious to know what the hell had gone on. We all must have felt the same as we couldn't get out of the car fast enough. We ran up the stairs and dived into her room, shouting for her. She was sitting on her bed, her eyes red. She looked exhausted, weak and defeated.

I asked her if she was ok. I could have cried myself. I hated what I was seeing. We'd known each other since we were tiny. This wasn't good. Bess sat on the bed and put her arms around her. I think Nessa had cried enough as she didn't flinch. She just looked helplessly at Faya with her big brown eyes.

Nessa, the girl with the wind in her hair and the sun in her smile was sitting with her beautiful auburn locks down her back all knotted and tangled.

'I just don't know what to do,' she said. 'I'm not sure what I'm doing here. It's like I'm lost in a world I don't even want to be in. I'm not even sure how I feel about him. It's like I want to make him right and I want us to live happily ever after, but I can't stand what he puts me through. I know he loves me so much and I feel like I'd be dropping him in it if I left him.'

At least she'd made some sort of admission. The next step was for us to try and get her to do something about it.

Chapter 35

Nessa

I thought about the night Tony took me camping. More accurately, the night Tony abandoned me at the camp site. I hadn't known whether to laugh or cry. I felt really spooked. The campsite was lit by only a couple of old fashioned street lamps which didn't give off much light at all. There were all sorts of noises, probably just the sheep but I couldn't be sure. It was like a scene from a horror film. I thought about the Yorkshire Ripper. What if he escaped and came after me?

The sheep seemed to be bleating my name in the darkness and I was really freaking out, struggling to keep a level head. I was sitting on my own outside a tent. I was too scared to get back in it. At least from outside I would see my would-be murderer or rapist coming. Then at least I'd have a chance of fighting them off. It was so quiet.

I wondered where the hell Tony was; the bastard. I would have gone to find him but I had no idea where his parents lived. I was paranoid that he'd taken me there and dumped me on purpose and was never coming back. That wouldn't surprise me.

I tried to make excuses for him. Perhaps he was having trouble getting little Sammy to sleep and was still trying to settle him. Deep down I knew it was more likely that he'd got in bed and passed out with or without little Sammy. I was fuming.

At two o'clock I was still outside the tent. A tight knot sat firmly over my bowels, I needed to poo. I felt sick with tiredness, nerves and the tension I was feeling.

At three o'clock I considered getting into the tent and trying to get some sleep but I was too scared. I'd really freaked myself out. I felt so lonely. I thought of the girls; they would have been going bonkers if they knew what had happened. They were probably tucked up in bed fast asleep.

Four o'clock came and went and there was still no sign of Tony. At Five o'clock the sun started slowly rising. The sound of the birds comforted me. I thought of my bed in the flat. I would have given my right arm to be there, in my own bed, fast asleep.

It got to six o'clock. I had been sitting there all night and was absolutely knackered beyond belief. My eyes were like lead weights in their sockets. They felt like someone had thrown a load of grit in them. I don't know how I managed to stay awake all night with nothing to do. My stomach was rumbling but I felt too sick to eat.

Eight o'clock, then nine o'clock came and I'd never felt so much anger. I wanted to scream. I wanted to pull the fucking tent down. In fact, I wanted to kick every fucking tent down. I was going to blow up with rage.

At ten o'clock my body couldn't take any more. I couldn't believe Tony wasn't back. Sammy wouldn't have slept for this long, no kid ever did. I was shaking and felt sick with exhaustion. I crawled into the tent shivering. I was freezing even though it was warm outside. It was my body reacting. I found a drink in one of the bags. It was baby juice but I didn't care, my mouth was like the bottom of a bird cage. I took a great big swig. I lay down on one of the sleeping bags and pulled the other one over me but I couldn't get warm. In the distance I could hear the odd car driving down the country lanes. Every time I heard a car my ears pricked up in the hope it was Tony coming back for me. I didn't want him;

I just wanted him to come and take me home. I fucking hated him. What an absolute toss pot. I dozed off.

The sound of a car woke me. I was disorientated for a minute and it took me a few seconds to work out where I was. I felt groggy and sick. When I remembered where I was the fury hit me again and I jumped up. I heard the car door slam and the sound of Sammy all happy and squealing with delight and shouting.

'Darling, sweetheart, Nessa,' called Tony. I tried to get my head together. I wasn't sure what my reaction would be. I looked at the watch on my wrist and couldn't believe what I was seeing. It was 8 o'clock at night. I almost lost my mind.

'Where the hell have you been, you fucking bastard?' I screamed as I scrambled out of the tent in rage.

He looked at me in sheer disgust, I felt like a low life scumbag for using such language in front of the baby but I was so angry with Tony.

'I beg your pardon,' he said calmly.

'Where the hell have you been?' I repeated. 'I was supposed to go to The Stone Roses. The girls will be there now. They'll wonder where I am. They'll be worried sick. You just left me here on my own all night and all fucking day.'

'I've had a really bad night with Sammy,' he explained. 'I don't need the grief, alright. We ended up calling a doctor. He had a fever and a small convulsion. My parents were out of their minds and we've been up all night with him. My parents are older and don't need the fuss to be honest. I've had enough grief from them. I'm not sure why I bothered taking Sammy to see them. They're not really interested anyway.' He continued. 'The doctor gave him some penicillin and it seems to have made some difference. We were exhausted so slept most of the day then my parents wanted to make sure we had enough to eat.'

The excuses went on and on. I couldn't believe his total lack of concern for me. I'd been left in a tent for nearly twenty four hours, no food, no idea where he was, all alone. To top it off I'd missed the gig of the year with my friends and he'd known how much I was looking forward to that.

I couldn't take anymore and burst into tears. He stood watching me like a helpless child while I sobbed and sobbed and sobbed. I'd had enough.

'Just get me home,' I said trying to take a breath between sobs.

'Would you drive?' he said. 'I'm absolutely shattered.'

I could have punched his stupid face but I didn't have any energy left. I grabbed my stuff from the tent and got us out of there as fast as I could.

I felt like a prize mug just doing what he asked and it just got worse. He insisted we drop Sammy off first which was completely out of the way. When we arrived I could see a very angry woman waiting for her son to be returned. She was also very attractive and I felt a pang of jealousy. My eyes were red from crying and my hair looked like it'd never seen a good brush. I couldn't believe it when she walked towards the car. No, no, no, I thought, don't do this. She tapped on the window which I reluctantly rolled down

'Thanks for having Sammy,' she said but didn't seem to mean it. 'You look like you've had a fabulous time.' I could tell she knew exactly what sort of a time I'd had. Her grin confirmed that. She knew she was better off out of it.

I drove back through Manchester feeling very confused. Tony sat silently next to me then he suddenly put his hand on my knee. I jolted with shock and looked at him. He stared at me as though he was penetrating my soul and my stomach flipped. The hairs stood up high on the back of my neck.

'Come back to mine,' he said. He was adamant. 'Please, I want you.'

I felt a twinge. I put my foot down and got to his place as quick as I could.

The sex was over quickly but at least there was some pleasure in it for me for once. I felt a bit better until he started to snore his head off next to me. I got up and got dressed; I wanted my girls. I had been an idiot, a total idiot.

Not long after I got home they walked in. I didn't want them to know how bad I really felt. It was embarrassing, but they could see it.

'What you going to do?' Ella asked her face full of concern.

'Not sure,' I replied. 'I feel trapped.

'Why are you trapped?' said Ella trying to keep calm. 'Fuck him off.'

'I can't,' I said, 'I'm pregnant.'

Chapter 36

Bess

What was happening to the three little girls who were once so innocent? Well innocent until Ella accidentally found out that her dad wasn't actually her dad. Innocent until Nessa found out her dad was a pervert. Innocent until my mum left me stranded with a drunken father.

Innocence certainly shouldn't involve asking neighbours for money for the electricity meter or avoiding the loan man because your mum couldn't pay. Innocence shouldn't involve putting an Alpine bottle under the Gas meter to stop the wheel spinning. Innocence wasn't being around guns and drugs all your life. Innocence didn't include going shop lifting instead of going to school. It didn't include knowing your Christmas presents were robbed from the local cash and carry because your parents were too skint to pay for them.

You couldn't be innocent robbing your dad's weekly wages so you could get food and warmth, nor could you be innocent shagging the landlord's son under a pile of coats while the other revellers inhaled on smoke strong enough to keep them going well into the night.

None of us were innocent. We were born wearing hard shells like jackets to protect us from the happenings around us. It was what made us who we were but Nessa's situation had just become so much worse.

She just couldn't keep that baby. She was a fool to think anything would get better if she was even thinking properly at all. She was deluded and we had to get her back on track. We'd come this far because, for all of our lack of innocence, we were good people. We had actually done ok whilst most of the people around us failed miserably.

When we were kids we were just poor and had to survive whichever way we could, but we'd grown up and gone to school. Some of our mates were never seen at school. They were undernourished and wore clothes that belonged to someone else. We'd turned out ok all things considered.

I went to bed late that night. The Stone Roses felt like a distant memory, but it was there somewhere in my mind and I smiled. The frown soon set heavy across my forehead as I thought of Nessa.

I don't know why but something made me get out of bed. I ran down stairs and dialled Nessa's number. Faya answered almost immediately.

'What's up?' I asked.

'How did you know?' she said, gobsmacked.

'I'm not sure,' I answered. 'I just had a sudden urge to call.'

'We're waiting for an ambulance,' Faya said. 'She's lost the baby.'

'Thank fuck,' came my thoughtless reply.

'I know,' she replied, relief flowing through her voice.

'I'll get my coat and meet you down there,' I said.

I put the phone down. Something felt strange. I wasn't sure if dad was in or not. My car keys were in the living room. I slowly opened the living room door and stretched my hand around trying to find the light switch. As I did someone grabbed my arm.

My heart felt like it shot out of my chest and I felt piss run down my legs as fear took over my body. The grip was strong and I couldn't move at all. My arm was wrenched hard and I was pulled into the front room and thrown about.

I was pushed hard onto the settee. I could see a figure in the darkness, but I couldn't make it out. The oven inside my stomach was on full heat and was spreading like a volcano throughout the rest of my body.

'Be calm,' I tried to tell myself. Then I felt a thud in my eye, another in my face. My attacker, burglar, or whatever he was, was punching me. I felt my teeth shake in my head. I fell backwards and my head hit the sideboard. I had to get up. I had to get away. Then I heard a car door slam hard outside.

'Dad,' I screamed, dad, dad.'

I was praying it was dad, praying he wouldn't be so drunk that this monster would be able to overpower both of us.

I was getting used to the light and tried to make out my attackers face, but he too had heard the car door and ran out of house. He bolted like lightning across the green. The only thing left in the room was the stench of stale alcohol which hung in the air.

Dad stumbled in and flicked the light switch. I groaned in pain, my face hurt. He saw me and stopped. He sobered up pretty quickly. I was in a lot of pain and could barely speak so I just cried.

Chapter 37

Ella

I woke up early and just lay there for a while. I had a shift at the pub but I really needed to get things ready for the cruise ship. My stomach churned every single time I thought about it, but I wasn't backing out. I only had a few more weeks to get organised.

I lay in my bed feeling the warm sheets on my naked legs. I stretched and gripped the sheets more for comfort, wrapping the soft flannelette around me. It was cool and soft and was stopping me from getting up. The sun was streaming through the windows and I could hear the sounds of the motorway not too far in the distance.

I enjoyed the silence of the usually chaotic house. Chaotic in a nice way, in a way I would never have again. I knew that once I'd left, even though the cruise ships were temporary, I'd probably never come back to my home and to my family. That thought was filling me with dread. It was a massive step for me, but one I had to take. Despite everything, they would always be my family, my brothers and Josie, mum and dad.

I thought about my dad. He might not be my biological father but he was my dad. I couldn't have chosen a better one. If they lined up all the men in the world I would choose Chris Parker every day of the week. He'd been my rock. He'd worked hard for us all. I smiled as I reflected upon my life; it'd not been that easy. We had had it difficult as children. Mum could barely put food on the table at times. Then there were times they'd pile us all in the car and we'd share a bag of chips and a bottle of coke. Those were the best times. I remember mum once having a Walnut Whip all to herself while she chopped up a Mars bar for us kids. I was fuming at the time, but looking back, so what? If she wanted a Walnut Whip to herself then so be it. As for dad, he would watch as we shared our bag of chips. He wouldn't take one single chip, nor would he have a piece of our Mars Bar. He wouldn't take a single thing off his kids. He was the best dad in the world and I loved him dearly.

As I lay there thinking about my family, mum suddenly burst in to my room.

'Bess was attacked at her house last night and Nessa has lost the baby,' she said so quickly that I almost didn't catch what she had said. 'I didn't even know she was bloody pregnant. No one told me. When did you find out? Is it that Tony's?' She paused and looked at me, her eyes narrowed. 'I thought you all hated him? What was she going to do? Was she going to keep it?'

I couldn't absorb what she was saying.

'And Bess is in a right state. Apparently she just came down the stairs and someone dragged her into the living room and kicked the shit out of her. I bet it was that Peter Lawrence again. He needs locking up he does, piece of scumbag shit. If John hadn't got home when he did she could have been raped or murdered.'

I was just dumbstruck for a moment and then my legs responded.

'Can you hear me Ella? You bloody deaf?' said mum.

I sat up sharp, the sun streaming through the windows suddenly disappeared and the day became very grey and dark, the story of my life. Just as things were turning for the better, someone would always drop a bombshell. One step forward ten steps back.

Chapter 38

Nessa

The pain was intense. It was severe around my abdomen. It felt like I needed the toilet and the top of my legs felt like they were burning. Then I saw blood everywhere. I don't know if it was psychological but the pain became worse at the very sight of it. My whole body became hot and I sweated profusely.

I needed to wake my sister. I was conscious she had work in the morning but I didn't have a choice. I would bleed to death if I just lay there. It wasn't stopping. I saw a towel that I'd thrown on the floor earlier. I leant over as far as I could and tried to reach it. I planned to put it between my legs to soak up some of the bleeding. I lost my balance and thudded hard onto the bedroom floor. It was the frustration that made me cry more than the pain.

'Faya,' I shouted. 'Please be awake, please wake up.'

She came running in and stopped dead at the sight of me.

'Jesus babe, are you ok? Let's get you up.'

I looked at her face, her beautiful face, the only member of my large family who gave a shit. She'd been like a mother to me even though she wasn't that much older. It was just me and her; we had a bond that was unbreakable.

I felt dizzy. 'Can you call Tony?' I asked Faya. She said she would after she'd called an ambulance. I hadn't even told Tony. What would he think? Probably nothing if I was being honest with myself. I felt dizzy again and tried to move, but it was getting harder and harder.

I heard a siren which I thought was a bit dramatic. I almost felt embarrassed. The paramedics made me stable and I felt at ease. They gave me some gas and air and off we went. Of course Faya came with me.

'Tony?' I asked.

She just shook her head. My stomach lurched even more. Tony had no idea of anything. He was an out and out bastard to me and I didn't know why. The tears streamed down my face. I was losing a baby and I was alone in the process because of this poor excuse of a man who somehow had managed to make me pregnant. I didn't even know how it had happened. He could barely perform most of the time never mind anything else.

I felt embarrassed as they rolled me into the hospital. People were staring and you could see them trying to guess what was wrong with me. The patch of blood might have given it away, but they stared none the less. I thought I saw Bess in a wheelchair with a swollen face. I had to look twice. I grabbed Faya's arm and pointed towards her.

'Jesus Christ,' she yelled. 'Bess, is that you?' You couldn't really tell it was her; it was only because I recognised her dad next to her looking worried sick.

I tried to sit up, but the pain across my stomach was too much and I went all hot and dizzy again. I lay back down and tried to listen to what was going on but I was quickly shunted away. I heard Faya telling her she'd be back in a minute.

Later Faya told me that Bess had been attacked in her house. She said someone had grabbed her as she went to turn on the light and battered her. She had been on her way to see me. I felt sick and it all exploded I couldn't hold it any longer. I needed to get off this fucking trolley now and go and see my beautiful friend who wouldn't hurt a fly. I pulled my gas and air mask off and tugged at the stupid tube thing stuck in the back of my hand.

'For God's sake,' I screamed. 'What's going on?' Then I passed out.

I fell into a deep sleep and in my dream there was no Tony, he didn't exist. There was just me and my friends and family. Then there he was. The sight of him made me cry. He was the most beautiful person that ever lived. He was walking backwards, his jet black hair thick and wavy, tanned skin glowing in his whirly windy way. He wasn't keeping still nor was he going with the flow, but he was moving further and further away from me, getting smaller and smaller which I couldn't understand. Why was he in my dream yet still running away from me?

I reached out. 'Please come back Si, please don't walk away,' I said.

Even in my dream he had is head down. His big brown eyes were looking at the floor, his mouth held to one side in his cock-sure way. There was a look of concentration. He looked up briefly and caught my eye but it was just for a second, and for a second I gasped as his gaze instantly hit my soul with that momentary glance.

The heat enveloped me. It was like his strength had burned a hole through my body. He reached out for me, but as I reached out for him he put his hand down. Not even in my dream could I get into his arms.

Where are you Si Bailey?

He walked away slowly, but he looked angry, angry with me, why? I ran over to him, he turned and pushed me out of the way. His elbow touched mine and again I gasped. It was like I'd had an electric shock, like if we touched explosives would go off. I turned around and he was walking faster and faster away from me. Why even in my dream did he do this?

He had no idea, or did he? This couldn't be all one sided, surely? It was too deep. I loved him. I decided to run after him, but he turned around and he looked angry, annoyed at what I was doing.

'I love you,' I screamed. 'I love you.'

I woke up sobbing my heart out, absolutely drained with emotion. I just wanted this thing out of me now and I wanted my life back. And I wanted Si.

Chapter 39

Bess

As luck goes, there wasn't much knocking about and I certainly wasn't having any; poor Ness wasn't either. All we needed was Ella to get knocked down or something and there'd be a trio of disasters. I felt sorrier for my dad than I did me; he looked devastated.

'What happened, Bess? Who was it?' he said. 'I'll fucking kill the bastard when I get my hands on him, I really will. Do you think it was Peter fucking Lawrence?'

I wasn't sure. I just remembered how frightened I felt at the time and the shock of it all. It was horrendous. I didn't think I'd ever be able to be in the house alone again.

I felt like everything around us was falling apart at the moment and the sights at the local hospital weren't helping either. There was a geezer who had broken his leg or at least he thought he had. He was being escorted by two coppers. There was an old guy in the corner who just kept making groaning voices, but he wasn't there to get treated. He was with his elderly wife who'd obviously had a fall as her face was a funny shade of purple.

There was a mum at the reception area, kicking off as her son had something in his eye. She was kicking off with the receptionist and she was kicking off with the kid for getting something in his eye. It was painful to watch.

'My son's eye is a right mess and if you don't get it sorted in a minute he's going to go blind you know, and whose fault will that fucking be? Yeah yours,' she said to the poor receptionist. Then she looked down at her son. 'What are you looking at, you little bastard? If you and our Jamie weren't fucking about, none of this would have happened,' she shouted and then slapped the lad hard on the head.

I couldn't even be bothered thinking about it. Normally I'd be pissed off with the mum, but whatever, it'd never change anything. Where we lived was rough. My attack just confirmed that you weren't even safe in your own home. I tried to go over what had happened but my face was killing me.

I put my head on my dad's shoulder and I tried to rest my eyes. I was knackered, tired beyond belief, but the pain was easing. I could smell the warmth of my dad's coat. As sleep rushed over me, she came, she was there, she was smiling and elegant and from a different world. She was beautiful and she stroked my head. She told me it was going to be ok and that she loved me.

'Mum, Mum,' I felt myself mouthing the words as I slipped deeper and deeper into sleep.

She walked over to me. I was lying down on a bed in a white clinical room. The sunlight was beaming in from a window. It made her appear ghost-like, but it was my mum and she was smiling gently as she always did. She stretched out her hand to me and held mine whilst her other hand stroked my forehead. I winced as I thought it was going to hurt, but it felt nice and I was instantly soothed. She didn't say anything she just smiled warmly at me. It made me cry and the tears streamed down my face. They were still there when dad gently woke me up to see the doctor.

After x-rays on my head and a clean-up of my face, it turned out that my skull was fractured just above my eyebrow.

'He must have hit you with some force,' the doctor said. It

was probably where my head had hit our living room wall at some stage. As we sat there, Uncle Richard barged into the room. He looked dishevelled and somewhat flustered.

'Bess, John, I've just seen a report, back at the station. What the hell's gone on?' he said.

He looked at dad for some sort of answer, he was angry. His face had a familiarity about it. Did he look like mum? The more his face was annoyed, the more I could see it or at least I thought I could. He stayed and took some details from us both. I had to go through the whole story again. I shuddered as I got to the part about turning on the light.

The following afternoon they said I could go home but I wanted to go and see Nessa and make sure she was ok. Tony was with her when I got there. He looked even more of a mess than usual. His hair was long, his breath smelt of beer, a smell I was very much familiar with and he looked like a good bath wouldn't go a miss. He had a scratch across his face.

I suddenly had a flash-back to the attack. I remember striking my attacker and catching his face with my nails. I shook my head to get the images from my mind.

Was this it? Was it Tony? No, it couldn't be, I'd just suffered a head injury and my mind was not functioning properly. After all, he was a posh kid and posh kids didn't do that.

I looked over at Nessa who just looked a mess, there was no other word for it and it wasn't about losing the baby, it was the whole thing. Then, the whole room lit up, as if someone had just opened the curtains and the sun came from behind the dark clouds. Ella walked in bearing cups of tea and packets of biscuits.

She looked at us both, in disbelief.

'Look at you two,' she said. 'How am I going to leave you both? I only went to bloody bed, woke up and look at the state of you.'

We were all subdued but we somehow managed to smile, she always had that affect.

Chapter 40

Ella

What a mess, I was going in a matter of weeks. I wasn't feeling good about leaving the girls and the situations they were in, both of them struggling. I had to keep telling myself that they'd be ok.

I went to visit them both at the hospital. The building was old red brick with a black tiled roof and huge windows. Inside was dreary. The walls were painted grey and some of the window sills had vases with dead flowers in. I walked along the grey shiny floors and was able to see my reflection as I inhaled the strong smell of cheap disinfectant.

I could see patients in wards that were just set back off the corridors all in white crisp sheets with a blue or orange knitted over-cover. The patients seemed old, with grey faces. It was as if they were waiting for their final curtain call and they were dressed ready to go back to their maker. I shuddered.

I walked along looking at the long glass windows and down at the beautiful ponds in the grounds. It had an eerie feel.

I searched for the ward where they were being treated. There was another corridor I had to take. It was narrower, colder, greyer with no polished floors, no long window. I'd taken it plenty of times with mum when I was a little girl. My brothers and Josie used to absolutely freak out and I used to make spooky ghost noises to scare them. I was smiling at the memories when I came to the door that said 'Mortuary'. I looked through the window in the hope of seeing a dead body or maybe a ghost or even a zombie with blood all down its face. Just as my imagination was getting the better of me, I felt a tap on my shoulder.

I froze on the spot; feet firmly stuck like they were in treacle. Fear travelled through my body faster than a bat out of hell. I turned around and it was Bess's Uncle Richard. He was grinning; he knew what he'd done.

'Jesus,' I said wafting my face to cool myself down. 'You frightened me to death,'

'Sorry,' he said trying to stifle a laugh. 'Were you looking for walking corpses?'

I smiled.

'Yeah, zombies with their faces hanging off,' I said and laughed.

'There's a little cafe just by the entrance. Do you fancy a cup of tea?' he said. 'I'm on my way to see Bess but could do with understanding what really went on last night. Have you got five minutes?'

I was in a rush to see the girls but I felt comfortable with Uncle Richard. I liked his eyes. He was warm and kind, but he was authoritative and firm as well and I couldn't help feeling safe with him.

He touched my shoulder, but caught my breast as he did so. We were both very embarrassed. He apologised profusely and we went for a brew. He ordered us a cake each and I devoured mine. I shouldn't have, I was piling the weight on, but I couldn't resist.

Uncle Richard got straight to the point, 'Who, do you think did that to Bess?'

For a moment I was taken aback at his abruptness and hoped he didn't think it was me. I looked at him blankly and he picked up that I was uneasy.

'Sorry love,' he said. 'It's just we need to catch this bastard before he strikes again,' he continued. 'It might be a pattern, he might be after you three girls or it might have just been a random attack.'

'Well, it's bound to be Peter Lawrence, isn't it?' I said. 'He's had it in for us three for years, hates us, always has done and he's a freak. He was outside my window the other week doing… well you know…'

I didn't want to be too descriptive in front of Bess's uncle. I couldn't bring myself to say he was wanking outside our window.

Richard acknowledged and commented. 'I've already thought about that and it's not trivial.

I thought about Peter. He had followed Nessa home off the bus once and we'd often caught him staring. He caused trouble years ago at the jubilee before Si Bailey kicked his head in. It had to be him I thought to myself.

I looked up and saw mum and dad walking quickly towards us. I beamed as I saw them both. They'd obviously come to see the girls too. My smile soon turned into a frown when I saw the look on mum's face I had no idea what was wrong with her and looked behind me to see if she had seen someone she wasn't happy with. As I turned back around she was up in Richard's face.

'What the fuck are you doing?' she said.

He looked as cool as a cucumber and held both hands up.

'Merely asking about my niece's attack,' he said.

'Yeah, well, fuck off,' she said.

She was fuming; dad grabbed both her shoulders. He looked at me with a look on his face that I couldn't quite work out and asked her to come away.

Richard stood up and dusted himself off then went to walk

away. Before he did he turned to me.

'Don't worry, I'll get whoever did this to our girl,' he said and walked off.

I was appalled with mum's behaviour so I stormed by her and dad. I didn't want to know what her problem was. She probably didn't have one. That's what people were like around here, rude with no manners. It more than cemented the fact that I needed to move on, needed to mix with different people and escape this bollocks.

Chapter 41

Nessa

The pain had been unbearable and drifting in and out of consciousness hadn't been much better. I wasn't sure where I was half the time or what day it was. I just knew that every time I went to sleep he was there, Si was there. It must have been a sign. I believed that he was thinking about me. I could feel him and I couldn't get him out of my mind.

I was finally back at home. The sun was streaming through the windows and I could see the blue skies from my bed. It didn't matter that if I sat up I would see hundreds of council houses, every single one of them the same. The sun made everything look and feel beautiful. The birds were on their best chirping mission and sounded beautiful and made me smile. I heard the children being taken to school, chatting and laughing, running and playing, dribbling footballs along the gravel path that was just underneath my window. In a way my heart yearned for those times when I was back at school, when I was young and innocent.

I looked around my bedroom. I felt safe and secure and I knew what I needed to do. Tony was nowhere to be seen. There was nothing more left in this shocking relationship and I'd do it once I'd mustered up the energy to pick up the phone. There would be no going back; he was a dead-leg. Despite his posh background and good education he was still a waste of space. He was scum and I had finally realised it. The whole relationship had been a disaster and I was glad I'd lost the baby. Who'd want a life tied to that twat?

As I lay there ruminating, there was a knock on the door.

I got up slowly to answer it. I spotted Beryl who lived on the landing opposite.

'Hiya love,' she said and craned her neck trying to look into my flat. 'You alright, love?' she asked.

'Yes thanks, Beryl,' I replied.

I didn't feel like talking much and wanted to shut the door as quick as I could.

Then I saw Tony standing there gawping across at Beryl, as though he was put out that someone was asking after me.

'I think you need to mind your own business,' he said to her, leaping to my defence.

The protection was unwanted. My stomach churned in annoyance, I was fuming.

I had no desire to see him and didn't want to make conversation. I just wanted him out of my life.

He was sullen and sulky.

'What's up?' I said. I couldn't believe it. I'd just nearly haemorrhaged and died and he stood there with a face as long as the day. Chin on his chest, eyes like a puppy, fucking pathetic. I could barely look at him. Looking at his face depressed me and made me feel ill beyond belief.

'I've lost a baby too,' he said, and burst into tears.

For a second I almost felt sorry for him but only for a second. Si's face popped into my head and gave me strength. Even if I never saw him again in real life, he was in my head, strong enough to guide me through my life. It was like he was talking from a million miles away, guiding me. He was there and he was saying get rid of this knob head.

I didn't know what to say to Tony. I just stared at him in disbelief. Actually I nearly laughed in his face, but I didn't have the energy.

'Do you even understand how I feel, Ness?' he whimpered.

'I never see Sammy and this would have been a chance for me to be a proper father with a wonderful mother like you and now you've blown that. How did it happen? Why weren't you more careful?'

On the side there was a huge vase of flowers from my big sisters and brothers. My first instinct was to grab it and smash it in his vile face, but I didn't. I just stared at him waiting for the rest of the bullshit that was about to come out of his mouth.

'Did they say when you could try again?' he said. 'I think we should try again as soon as possible. I just want a baby to love and to hold, a brother or sister for Sammy when he's here. I just want a stable life with none of the bullshit she gives me.'

I nearly laughed again. We must have had sex properly three or four times because for the rest of the time the man couldn't get it up or fell asleep half way through because he was so pissed. When he was sober he just wasn't interested in me.

'Go away Tony, I never want to see you again.' I'd said it and I meant it. I never wanted to see his disgusting face again.

He looked genuinely shocked. Surely he didn't seriously believe that I would take this shit from him forever. I half expected him to say 'ok that's fine' and piss off but he didn't. Instead he stared at me intensely.

'You've just lost my baby and you're asking me to go, just like that, like I'm the one who lost it,' he said. 'Look you won't feel right at the moment, you'll have a lot of pregnancy hormones floating around your body. You're not really in the right frame of mind to make a decision like that.'

His voice was getting on my nerves. I looked at him

again. I had no feelings for him whatsoever. Maybe a few tiny ones, mostly pity.

'Just go, Tony. It's over. It's got nothing to do with the baby, it's everything else,' I said as calmly as I could.

I tried to explain myself, but he just threw it right back at me, twisting everything I said. He turned everything around. I wondered why he was fighting so hard for me since it was clear he despised me and thought I was worthless.

He stood up. He looked like the mad professor gone wrong. I felt on edge, worried about what he might do to me. He came right in my face and put his nose on mine. His breath was hot on my face and I felt sick. I moved my head back, but he wasn't moving.

'You and your daft little friends are dead, do you hear me? You council scum; you're dead.'

Chapter 42

Bess

Once they'd patched me up at the hospital I felt right as rain. Dad and I had a nice stroll home. The sun was shining which made a change. The children were playing near the brook that ran gently through a small wood next to the hospital, trying to jump across without falling in. I smiled as I remembered our own childish games.

Dad looked down at me, and smiled a sad smile. I couldn't say much and just smiled back.

'I'm sorry, love,' he said.

I just shook my head. He didn't need to be sorry and my lack of acknowledgement said as much. Why was he sorry? He was the most beautiful man in the world, my rock; the only person who truly loved me.

We continued our evening summer stroll. I needed to walk, needed the fresh air and to take in the beautiful greenery that surrounded our deprived council estate. It looked almost like elegant countryside with stunning pink blossom trees lining the streets and the green grass verges with flower beds growing in the middle of them. It definitely was a case of the beauty masking the shit.

We passed the chippy and dad asked me if I fancied some. I couldn't think of anything better. We got a bag of chips each and drowned them in salt and vinegar. We sat together on the pub wall whilst we ate. I felt better already although I was dreading going into our house. Dad had tried to convince me it had all been made safe. He'd put a mortise lock on the front door and a bolt on the back gate which he said would deter any intruders gaining access to our garden.

'Are you ready love?' dad said once we'd finished eating.

We passed the red phone box on the corner of our road. I recalled Ella and me playing in there as little girls. We used to pretend that we were answering the phone and we'd chat on it for hours really believing there was someone on the other end. If we had a spare two pence we'd put it in the silver slot on the big grey box and phone random numbers and talk for as long as the two pence would last.

We'd once phoned a boy in my class called Tom and asked for his mum. We told her the teacher had snapped his Papermate pen on purpose. If we'd have known the trouble we would get into at the time we wouldn't have done it. I ended up in the headmistress's office every day for a week, repeating the story. Miss Young had grabbed the pen out of his hand and definitely snapped it, but of course the lying cow was denying it and only me and Ella would stand up for him. So it was kids versus teachers. Tom never did get a new pen or an apology. The recollection made me smile as I passed the phone box. It made me want to be a little girl again, a time when I all I had to worry about was Tom's light blue Papermate pen.

As we turned the corner, there was a racket going on outside our house.

'What the bloody hellfire is happening now,' dad groaned.

There was a marked cop car in the road. Uncle Richard and two uniformed police men were scuffling with someone on the floor. It was Peter Lawrence. He looked distressed and panicked stricken.

'Bess, Bess, tell them to get off. Tell them it wasn't me, please Bess,' he pleaded.

I didn't know what to do or say.

'Bess, Bess? John. For fuck sake, man, I'd never hurt Bess would I?' he shouted.

I couldn't be sure. I looked at my dad and he shook his head. 'He's a fucking weirdo, our Bess. Something's not right. Let them take him in and question him. If he's not done anything, they'll know love.'

I don't think there was any choice in the matter anyway. They handcuffed him and threw him into the back of the car. As the sky turned a hazy deep red, Peter Lawrence was carted away. His face was pressed against the window. He mouthed, 'you fucking bitch' as he was driven away. Why did I feel guilty? What the hell had he done outside Ella's? The man was a nightmare either way.

Chapter 43

Peter Lawrence

The feeling in my face as it was being smacked all over the place was excruciating. It felt like my head was bouncing of the walls. My teeth rattled and I bit my tongue. The next smack was even harder and stars appeared in my vision. I felt the warm trickle of blood from my lip which made me bite down even harder.

'You wanted me to do it, didn't you? It's what you wanted me to do so why you fucking hitting me for it?' I said.

It didn't make a difference. He wasn't stopping. I got another punch, this time in my eye. I felt it swell up immediately and grabbed my face to protect it. This wasn't going to stop.

'Fuck off out, now,' he said. 'Get the fuck off out. You did a good job.'

As the blood poured between my fingers I was confused. I smirked as I salivated. I'd done a good job. That's what he said.

Chapter 44

Ella

Bess and Nessa were both back home and safe. Peter Lawrence had been arrested. I still didn't know why Mum had kicked off about me speaking to Richard. Dad had gone quiet and my brothers were getting in to all sorts of strife. I was in the living room, listening to Josie pestering mum about going into Manchester with her mate.

It was getting warmer and the back door was open. I loved listening to the noises around me. They were familiar and always gave me a sense of security. I could hear the planes flying over. They seemed to be getting more frequent lately as more and more people were choosing to go abroad for their holidays.

'Jesus Christ,' I heard my dad's cursing. 'That was bloody low.'

I heard lawn mowers in the distance. As soon as there was a bit of sun people would cut their grass and their bushes, I found it bizarre. I looked out of our window I could see that our bushes were getting too high. I stared at them and drowned out the chaos while I remembered how we used to kick them to see if any caterpillars would fall out. Every now and again we would find the furriest biggest caterpillars and we'd all watch them, poking them gently with sticks to make them curl up. It was never long before Peter Lawrence would come and stamp on the poor things. Then we'd get stones and lob them at the back of his daft head.

I looked through our gate and could see a neighbour washing his car with a bucket of cold water and a big yellow sponge, fag in his mouth. Kids rode up and down the road on their bikes. I smiled. It was beautiful, proper art, and I was going to miss it.

Josie was growing up into a proper young lady and was slowly becoming my little mate. She was outgrowing the little sister role and could be a bossy madam, but she had a gentle soul and wouldn't harm a fly. We shared a bedroom and I didn't think there was any glue stronger to bond you together as sisters. We knew each other's idiosyncrasies. Her half of the room was tidy whereas mine was chaos, but we got it. We got each other and I respected her tidiness and she my chaos. Not that she had a choice. She would have it all to herself when I left and she'd love that.

The boys were growing up too and becoming a nightmare. Our Henry was ok but George was a little bastard and held no prisoners. Not sure why he was as he was but he had a chip on his shoulder that had come from nowhere. Mum and dad would have to sort him out before he went completely off the rails.

I had to go to the pub to speak to Lizzy and George about my leaving do. Originally Lizzy was going to have a celebration for the fact that Conny's murderers had been sent down. When I got the job on the cruise ships she decided to hold a party for me instead. I was over the moon. I wanted a DJ and a nice buffet. Lizzy had booked 'North West Soul' for me. I was feeling more excited about the leaving do than actually leaving.

I forced myself up off the sofa and set off for the Lion with all my plans playing around my head. I didn't know how I would pay for it all but Lizzy said she'd help and I knew she would. She loved me as her own and I was honoured, as she didn't like many people.

I smiled as I walked by a large family on our road. The kids had a paddling pool and the parents were downing copious amounts of booze. It made me smile. Their windows were wide open and there was the sound of some heavy metal band blaring out. It was quite painful on the ears but they were clearly having the time of their lives. I passed the green where I used to see a young Bess and Peter Lawrence play and jump about. I thought about calling in on Bess as I passed but decided I'd call in on the way back instead.

As I got into the pub, Lizzy's instantly recognisable voice greeted me.

'Ay, our Ella, they've only arrested that Peter Bastard Lawrence for the attack on Bess the other night,' she said.

'It won't be him, you know, even though he's a freak. He likes Bess,' I said.

'Well they've nicked the fucker,' she went on.

I knew her well enough to know that she thought he'd done it and I knew her well enough not to argue the case, so I nodded. I didn't know what else to say on the matter.

I went over to the jukebox, put fifty pence in and selected my favourite ten songs. I went behind the bar to bottle up and I noticed Tony sitting in the corner. He looked absolutely smashed. He was more than drunk, he looked wired. His hair was dishevelled and long. He had grown a scraggy beard which looked a mess. He stared at me through wide eyes but his stare wasn't welcoming and I wasn't sure what to do.

I walked over reluctantly. 'What brings you in here, Tony?' I asked.

'What do you mean, Ella?' he replied

'Just wondered what made you come in the Lion, you don't usually bother.'

'Is this a public house?' he responded. His body language

was aggressive and I hated to admit it but I felt a bit intimidated.

'Well, is it?' he said.

'Yes,' I answered. I wanted to tell him to fuck off but I couldn't. It was like I was stuck to the floor. I almost felt it would be rude.

'Then I can come in here as I wish, Ella,' he said.

'Course you can, Tony,' I replied and I spun on my heels, picked up an empty glass and got the hell away from him.

I didn't take my eyes off him. He unnerved me and it took a lot to do that. He was a psycho. I'd served enough of them to spot one when I saw one. Something wasn't right.

I went in the back to phone Nessa and she explained she'd ended it with him. The wave of relief that came over me was like a tsunami. I was so happy that she'd finally seen the light of day.

I went back to the bar and watched him stumble towards the door. He couldn't have timed it any better as Faya was just walking in. He stood directly in front of her menacingly and wouldn't let her pass. I could see the look of surprise on her face. He stared at her and put his face right up to hers.

'Your sister's a murderer, do you know that?' he shouted. 'That stupid slag killed my baby.'

Faya wasn't daft enough to take the bait. She continued to try and pass him without causing any fuss. He was drunk and clearly high on drugs.

Like hyenas, the locals had started to surround him. They didn't take kindly to outsiders messing with one of their own. He didn't care; he pushed on and on about Nessa being a murderer. Then Lizzy clocked what was going on.

'Get the fuck out of this pub now, you fucking freak. How dare you? Get out, you're fucking barred,' she screamed in her roughest, loudest, landlady voice with her husband stood firmly behind her.

He looked more shocked than afraid. It was probably her use of language and the brashness of her tone. We were used to it but that posh twat wasn't. He slinked away, but I knew he'd be back. He had a bee in his bonnet and I knew this wouldn't be the last of him. He was a piece of shit.

Chapter 45

Nessa

I was still in bed resting but I was getting bored. The pains and bleeding had reduced significantly. I stood up and looked at myself in the mirror. Stupid cow you are, I thought, staring at my reflection. I needed to get my life back on track, one way or another. I looked around my room. It was nice. My walls were covered in pink and purple split wallpaper with a big flowery border around the middle and I had flowery curtains and bedding that matched.

I was at college to pursue my dream of being a social worker. I'd messed up with Tony but I suppose it could have been worse. I was feeling a bit low and really needed to get back up.

I phoned Bess as I knew she'd just got home.

'I'm bored shitless,' she said.

'Me too,' I said. 'I'm just laying here thinking about rubbish stuff.'

It was true. My thoughts were not very productive. I was starting to get depressed. I'd done enough thinking and needed to move forward and get focused.

'Let's have a night in tonight,' I suggested, 'me, you and Ella. I can cook and we could have a beer or two, maybe a cheeky joint.' Even though we were growing out of it we still smoked the odd joint now and then. 'I'll phone Ella,' I added.

I could almost hear her grinning, 'Ok, sorted,' she said.

I cooked chilli. It was cosy in the kitchen and I was looking forward to the evening. Still in my pyjamas, I chopped onion and tomato, the phone rang. I put down the knife and went to answer it. There was nobody there.

'Hello, hello?' I said and rolled my eyes in frustration. I put the phone down; whoever it was would call back. I needed to get on with my cooking. A chilli was all I could muster. I wasn't a good cook. I'd been spoilt in a way by foster parents and then Faya who did most of the cooking.

The sun was shining through the windows. It made everything feel so much better. I felt alive and motivated. I could have done a hop, skip and a jump, but I didn't think it a good idea considering I'd just lost a baby and nearly bled to death in the process. So I put some music on and got stuck in to my cooking.

Ella was the first to arrive and was bursting to tell me what had happened that afternoon in the pub. She was still in full flow when Bess arrived a couple of minutes later. I winced when I saw her purple face and stitches where her nose had been cut.

'Jesus, that's enough to put me off the chilli,' I said and winked.

She laughed. 'I know, it looks like I've done ten rounds with Mike Tyson,' she said.

We discussed Tony and the fact he had called me a murderer, the idiot. I couldn't allow him to get to me. I couldn't believe he'd been aggressive towards my sister, the dickhead. He wanted to watch his step or he'd be getting it. It was too tribal where we lived, a great big family. If you hurt one of us, then one of us would hurt you.

We put the big cushions on the floor and I brought the food out.

'I'm starving,' Ella said and grinned. She always found comfort in food.

'Well there's plenty to go around,' I said and smiled.

'So go on,' I said, 'anything else happen with knob head?'

As I asked the question the phone rang again.

'For god's sake,' I cursed and jumped up to answer it.

'Hello, hello?' I said. Yet again there was no one there. I put the phone down. 'I keep getting silent phone calls,' I said to the girls.

'It'll be El Freako,' Ella said.

Bess looked worried. After what she'd been through she was on edge.

'It'll be alright, babe,' I said, 'it'll be something and nothing.' She didn't look convinced.

I started to dish up.

'I only want half a plate full,' Bess insisted.

'No way, I've made loads,' I said. 'You get it down you.'

'I'm on a diet,' she said. 'Look at me, I'm huge,' and pointed at her curvy figure. It suited her. She was a voluptuous young woman and she looked great.

She started telling us about the crazy things she'd been doing to lose weight and made us laugh with her antics. She told us that she'd gone with one of her customers to a posh salon in Gatley and got a wrap.

'Isn't a wrap something you eat?' Ella asked, stuffing her face with garlic bread.

'Not that kind of wrap,' Bess explained. 'First some woman takes your measurements and writes them all down and then you strip off to your knickers.'

I was intrigued.

'And then they put this cream stuff on you that heats up and wrap you in cling film all over your body,' she continued.

Ella and I nearly choked. 'Clingfilm?' we both screamed. I laughed my head off at the thought of Bess wrapped in

Clingfilm.

'Yes, bloody Clingfilm. They wrap you up in it dead tight, everywhere except your head.' She was laughing as she continued her description. 'Then the woman lay me face down on a table and started massaging me. She was stood, right next to my face and I was so tempted to stick my tongue out and lick her fanny. I was naked for God sake.'

I laughed so hard that I was worried I would do myself an injury.

'Beryl, who I was with, was going mental. She kept saying she was catching claustrophobia and she'd kick the woman's head in if she didn't un-wrap her.'

'You can't catch claustrophobia,' I said through tears of laughter.

Ella snorted like a pig which made me and Bess laugh even more than the thought of Beryl getting stressed out wrapped up in Clingfilm all slimy and slippery.

'Well we lost two inches all over our bodies,' said Bess smugly once she could finally speak again. 'And it felt amazing.'

She paused. 'It cost us twenty quid each though. When we came out we went straight into Greggs next door and got two pasties.'

The three of us roared and roared. I couldn't breathe and was actually concerned about my stomach but I couldn't help it, my mouth was aching. Ella pissed all over a cushion. Then one of Bess's stitches started to bleed. We all found it hilarious. And then the phone rang. 'Fuck off,' we all screamed in giddy unison,

Still laughing, wiping my eyes and making involuntary sighs, I jumped up, just in case it was important.

'Hello, Hello, ah come on, who is it? I know you're there,'

I said.

'Vanessa? Vanessa Brown?' said a voice I recognised instantly.

It felt like my heart stopped beating. My whole body went into shock and the hairs on the back of my neck stood up on end. My legs started to wobble and almost went from under me.

'It's me, Si.'

Chapter 46

Bess

Nessa fell to the floor in what seemed like slow motion. My stomach lurched into a frenzy of panic.

'What's up, what's up?' I said as I scrambled to my feet. Ella ran to pick up the phone. I went to Nessa.

'Hello, hello?' screamed Ella into the handset. She looked at the handset. 'No one there,' she said and looked at me. I slapped Nessa's face gently, she'd fainted. What had she heard? I felt scared.

It felt like something sinister was going on. I didn't think we'd heard the last of Tony and it was still on my mind that Peter Lawrence had been arrested. I'd not seen him or Uncle Richard since. Then there was the incident outside Ella's and the attack on me. Was I just feeling paranoid?

Nessa started to move in my arms. Her eyes opened and she blinked up at me. It reminded me of the day Skidder Barker had tried to batter her in the school playground. The day Nessa and I became one. Her face hadn't changed at all; she was beautiful.

'Do you fancy me or something?' she slurred.

I laughed. 'No I don't, but you are beautiful,' I said. 'Are you ok? What the hell happened? Who was on the phone?'

She blinked her eyes still vague and distant.

'I'll get you some water,' Ella said and went to the kitchen to fetch her some.

Ness took a gulp and we all cuddled up on the settee waiting for her to tell us what had caused her to faint.

'It was Si Bailey,' she said almost whispering. 'Si Bailey

was on the other end of the phone,' she looked at us both in desperation. We were gobsmacked. She must have banged her head as she fell.

'Are you sure it was him babe?' I asked gently. 'You've not been well, you've been very vulnerable and you've been having all those weird dreams, but...'

'No,' she said before I could finish. 'It was. It was Si. It was really him girls, I know it was.'

She looked from me to Ella and back. She had tears in her eyes.

'He asked for Vanessa. He always called me that. He said, "is that Vanessa Brown?" and then he said it was Si.'

There was silence as we all tried to absorb this. I was suspicious. We all knew Nessa had had feelings for Si Bailey since she was a little girl. Why would he phone her out of the blue? She'd been having strange dreams about him. It would be too much of a coincidence. But maybe she was right, maybe he had phoned her now. I felt mad for thinking it. Oh my god this was all so confusing. I was beginning to think that I still had concussion.

'When I got to the phone, there was just a dead tone, Ness,' Ella explained stroking Nessa's head.

'Jesus girls, I'm not delirious, nor am I mental. I know it was him. Why do you think I bloody fainted? I went into complete and utter shock.'

I believed her. I felt like I was going to faint. Oh my god.

'Well, how are we going to get back in touch with him?' I said going over to the phone

I picked it up, 'Hello?' I said to the dial tone. I don't know what I was expecting to happen.

'He's gone, you knob head,' Ella screeched and once again the laughter took over.

'Well you better get prepared, Vanessa Brown,' I said, 'because he's going to be back.'

We all screamed and jumped on each other.

If it was Si it would be a mad reunion. But what if Tony had pretended to be Si? The thought popped in my head before I could stop it but I didn't say anything. Maybe it was Si. Maybe the thread that held Nessa and Si together was really that strong. It would explain why she had dropped to the floor at the sound of his voice.

I'd had a great night with the girls but I needed to get home. Ella stayed with Nessa and once I was sure she was ok I left. As I pulled up outside the house I realised that, as usual, I would be home alone. As much as I loved my dad and understood he had a life too, I couldn't help resenting him a little. He was ok but I was frightened to death.

I walked slowly towards the house, the house I once loved. Or did I? Did I really have a normal happy childhood here, like Ella had? Normal people had families, mums and dads but not me. This house was just a shell, a shelter to keep me warm, but it didn't keep me warm, not anymore anyway.

I opened the front door anxiously. It was dark and all the lights in the house were off. I took a deep breath and looked around. The street lamp outside our house shone brightly. I stared at the big grey post with its big bright orange glow. We had bonded years ago, this lamp and me. It lit up my bedroom when it would otherwise be pitch black. It had comforted me when mum had gone. It had comforted me through all my terrors and nightmares and now it was comforting me again, guiding me into the house. I smiled at it as I stepped into my hallway.

Something didn't feel right. I didn't feel right. I couldn't go in. I ran out of the house and slammed the front door behind me. Someone was in the house. I knew it, I knew it. Where was I going to go?

I ran down the road and I as I turned the corner, I bumped straight into someone. He grabbed me hard and stopped me dead in my tracks. I was panting for breath. I felt like I was going to stop breathing.

'Where you off too love?' said a concerned voice.

It was Uncle Richard. The relief took over and I burst into tears and fell into his big strong arms.

'I thought there was someone was in the house,' I sobbed. 'I just can't turn this feeling off. All the time I think about what happened. It's taking over my life.'

'Come on,' he said. He was gentle. 'Let's go and see.'

We walked back to the house, his big arm around me. I felt safe and protected.

I opened the front door and stepped into our hall. He stood outside for a minute and looked around. I still felt uneasy but I knew he'd protect me.

We both checked the house together. I switched every light on as I wasn't sure what time dad would be in, if he came home at all that is. He didn't always. I was sure he had a fancy woman although he'd never tell me; probably because it was none of my business.

'You ok, now love?' Uncle Richard smiled.

'Yes, I need to get a grip,' I said. 'What's happened with Peter Lawrence?' I asked.

'They released him, love. No evidence, I'm afraid.'

Even though I knew deep down it wasn't Peter who attacked me, I felt uneasy that whoever it was, was still out there. Uncle Richard took out a cigarette and lit it taking a deep drag. He looked different. His eyes weren't as gentle, his mouth looked hard. In fact he looked like he'd been drinking.

'Sit down,' he said in a very demanding tone.

'I'm ok,' I said.

'Sit down,' he almost yelled.

I wondered what was going on. I sat down and he stood towering over me.

'I want to talk about the Parkers,' he said. His eyes were piercing, staring into the very depths of my mind.

My instinct was telling me to do a runner or was I just paranoid? Was Uncle Richard in some way responsible for what happened the other night?

My heart was racing. I looked outside and my street light flickered as if it too was panicking, as if it realised there was danger. My stomach was in knots and my mouth was dry. I felt queasy and my mind was racing. I told myself to stay calm.

'Do you want a brew?' I said. 'And then we can have a chat.' I tried to put on my most confident voice.

'No I don't want a brew,' he said mimicking my voice. He was still standing, towering over me.

My street-light outside was still flickering. Don't give up on me, stay with me, I willed. If the light went out, so would mine. I was being superstitious over a street-light, but it was my only solace. As he leant over me, I heard the familiar sound of dad's key in the front door.

Thank fuck for that, thank fuck he'd decided to come home. I prayed he wasn't pissed. Shit, my head was in overdrive. We could both be in big trouble here.

Chapter 47

Ella

I stayed at Nessa's; firstly because I couldn't get her to shut up about Si, and secondly because I was too lazy to move. I borrowed a pair of her pyjamas and it felt like we were children again having a sleepover. We got into bed and I chuckled.

'What?' Nessa asked.

'Just thinking about Bess and her wrap, and her saying she felt like licking the woman's fanny.'

We both started laughing again at the thought of her rolled up in cling film. For a second I got a strange feeling in the pit of my stomach but I pushed it away. It was done and dusted. I had to forget it.

I wondered what would happen with Si and Nessa. We'd heard the family had moved back down south but it wasn't like it was Australia. Just a few hours down the road. I wondered how she must have felt because even though she'd kept a lot of it to herself, we knew she was totally obsessed with him. She was in love with him and she didn't even know him, not really. But maybe one of us would find true love and after what she'd been through she deserved it. As I drifted off to sleep I heard the phone ringing. I leapt up.

'Ness, Ness,' I said but she didn't wake up. I ran to the phone wondering what I was going to say if it was Si.

It was still ringing when I got to it and I picked it up. 'Hello,' I said. There was silence. 'Hi, it's me, Ella,' I said, thinking the change of voice might put him off. It wasn't Si.

'Your friend is a murderer,' Tony slurred down the phone.

'She murdered my child. Your boyfriend was a murderer too and he got what he deserved, and your friend will get what she deserves. You're council scum, the lot of you. You're all deluded.'

I slammed the phone down, my heckles were up. I paced the hall for a while wondering what to do. So I did what all real northerners do, I went straight to the kettle and made a brew.

'What are you doing up?' Ness said. She startled me as she came into the kitchen.

'Robbing the flat,' I joked. 'I thought I'd root through all your stuff and see if there were any goodies I could sell in the Lion.'

I looked up at her. 'The phone rang again, babe,' I said. Her eyes immediately lit up and I shook my head quickly. 'It was El Freako being as charming as ever, the bastard.' I didn't think she needed to hear again how he thought she was a murderer. She had lost her baby. Although I was pleased that she didn't have to be tied to that scumbag for the rest of her life, she hadn't got rid of it out of choice.

'What did he say?' She actually started to laugh. 'I don't even know why I'm asking because I'm not interested,' she added.

'He called Conny a murderer and said he'd got what he deserved,' I said. 'He doesn't know what he's talking about the dick head. Are you ok?'

'Yeah, I'm fine.'

'You want a brew kid?' I said, trying to cheer the mood. 'We can drink them in bed then see if we can get back to sleep.'

So we sat up for a while drinking our drinks and again I giggled. 'Didn't we have a laugh tonight, babe,' I said. She smiled.

'I can't stop thinking about the phone call. I dreamt about him again, Ella. That's all I do. The dreams make me cry. I feel like we were once joined as one human, maybe in another life and then separated into two humans. I long for him, Ella. I feel like there's an unspoken understanding of each other, even though we've never really had a conversation, even though he's never done anything more than kiss my forehead,' she rubbed it subconsciously. 'And, you know what? I know I've not seen him for years, but deep down, I know he feels the same.'

I was too logical for all that bollocks but I loved Nessa and I knew she could be very spiritual in her thinking so I would never mock her. I just put my arms round her and nodded.

'Then if that's the case babe, it's meant to be and it'll all come good,' I said, and we smiled at each other.

Then out of the blue she asked me a question I wasn't expecting.

'What happened, Ella? With you and Bess, I mean. What on earth went on?'

I couldn't believe she'd asked me. I'd never openly spoke about it and I wanted to put it to bed forever. There was nothing to deal with, it was done and dusted.

'God Nessa, I don't think I'll ever know why I did it. It just happened. I know that's not much of an answer but I keep asking myself the same question all the time. The thought of it makes me ill. I hate the thought of it. I don't hate the thought of Bess. I love her but the thought of that...' I paused and looked at her. 'I think that's why I need to get away, but it will always be with me, it will always be there. The secret, the guilt, the fear; it could have ruined all three of us.'

Nessa put her arms around me. 'Well it didn't, did it? And you know what? You were just kids at the time, experimenting. Maybe you felt vulnerable, who knows. But it's only the same as you having a one night stand with some geezer. At least you knew her, knew she was free from any disease.'

'Jesus, I never thought of that. That's true. I don't even think Bess is a lesbian. I think it's all something to do with missing her mum and needing that female love and closeness, craving a woman's arms. I just think she went through something and I sort of hope so as she deserves to be happy. You know, marry and have a family.'

Nessa didn't seem sure. 'Her happiness will depend on what is right for her, Ella, man or woman,' she said.

I nodded in agreement. 'Yeah, I guess,' I said.

'Come on, let's get some sleep.'

I lay down next to my friend for our last ever sleepover. 'You want to spoon?' she giggled.

'Yeah I do,' I said, and we snuggled up. The tears rolled down my eyes, because a whole new world was ahead of me without Nessa, without Bess and without spooning but I needed to look forward.

Chapter 48

Nessa

My thoughts were pretty much about one thing. I knew the girls were convinced it was Tony playing with me but I knew that it had been Si who called.

He might have just called for a chat, but somehow I didn't think so. I knew there was a bond between us and that meant more than him just phoning to talk. We needed to be united, maybe now the time was right for him. For whatever reason, we'd been kept apart and that was meant to be but now, maybe, he knew that we needed to be together.

He was as rough as anything. He would never think like that. How could he? He wasn't educated; he wouldn't be capable of thinking on that level. I was being delusional.

Oh my god, that thought terrified me. I needed to find him so bad.

I knew no one believed me but we were soulmates. Throughout our lives and in previous lives we had gone through the same journey and it felt like there was an electric force between us. Looking back that force was so strong. It even stopped us from communicating. I couldn't even look Si Bailey in the eye.

If he felt the same, he would come and find me. Like Ella said, if it was meant to be, it was meant to be. I tried to think about something else. Thoughts of Si were driving me mad.

Chapter 49

Bess

'Alright, love?' Dad said as he came in.

Richard jumped and sat down on the other settee; his face changed. It became warmer. He looked like Uncle Richard again. I was relieved as it meant he probably wasn't going to kick off with dad. I could have cried there and then as the last thing we needed was more hassle.

'Want a brew kid?' my dad shouted from the kitchen.

'Yeah go on dad.' I heard the cold water tap blast on and the lid of the kettle click open. In his usual heavy handed way he slammed the kettle down onto the stainless steel sink, rattling the cutlery that had sat there patiently waiting to be put away.

I looked quickly at Richard, feeling a little bit braver.

'What are you doing? What do you want? Where did that come from?' I whispered. I didn't want to rock the boat with my dad.

Uncle Richard shook his head. 'There's a lot I want and a lot you want and we both have answers. I think we can help each other here,' he said cryptically.

Then he stood, dusted himself down and swiftly let himself out of the front door.

I sat there for a moment and tried to understand what had just gone on. What did he mean there was a lot I wanted? What was that about? Did he know something about mum?

It was getting ridiculous and too much had gone on. I wasn't sure I could cope with any further drama. I wasn't over the attack and my head was starting to hurt with it all.

I shuddered as I recollected the venom in his eyes. He had looked evil, wicked.

Dad came into the living room with a brew, almost spilling it. He was bladdered, but at least he was coherent.

'Do you want some toast love?' he asked.

'No ta dad, this'll do.'

I went to sit down. I was knackered and ready for bed. I'd just have this tea then I'll go up.

I nearly jumped out of my skin when there was a loud knock at the front door. Jesus, who would be knocking at this time of night? Dad looked at me, clearly wondering the same thing.

'I'll get it love,' he said as he stumbled out of the living room into the hallway

I bravely went and stood behind dad and couldn't believe what I saw. Peter Lawrence was in a right mess.

'What the fuck have you lot been up to?' he stammered. 'As if I'd do that to you Bess, I'd never hurt you, you know that.'

Someone had clearly hurt him though. His face was black and blue. I was gobsmacked, someone had taken something to that face; bare hands wouldn't be able to do that.

'Got nicked didn't I? And look what the bastards did,' he was salivating and had spit running from his mouth which he wiped with his sleeve, something he'd always done.

I looked at the night sky. It was clear and the stars were twinkling. As dark as it was, it was very early morning and I could just about hear the birds waking up gently in the distance. I could have stared at the stars all night. I could have actually jumped right up to them, sat on one and looked down at the mess we were making of the world and the mess that was going on right now in my life. A mess I didn't ask for and a mess I could feel escalating.

The volume of Peter's voice turned back up and I could hear it again as I focused on the moment.

'I mean it now, I'll get you bunch of slags. All fucking three of, you've had it. I'll fucking get you lot back one way or another, Bess,' he shouted. 'You bunch of fucking slags, fucking can't believe what has happened. See what's happened John? No way did I hurt your girl, you know that?'

Dad tried to calm him down but he was having none of it.

'Peter,' Dad said, 'chill the fuck out. Come in and sit down. Let's talk this through, eh?'

'Nah, no way, you're dead the lot of you.'

Dad shut the door in his face and we left him ranting. Then we heard a smash and glass shattered all over the hall carpet. He'd smashed the front door window with a brick then legged it.

'I've had enough, dad,' I said. I was shaking now. I picked up the phone and dialed 999.

Chapter 50

Ella

I woke early. I could hear the birds singing which always made me smile. Nessa's breathing was heavy next to me, almost a snore. She was fast asleep, probably dreaming about Si Bailey. I smiled as I thought about it. Then I thought about the days ahead. The party at the pub was just two days away. It was going to be ace. I wanted it to be the best send-off ever, something everyone would remember. George had all the food sorted. Lizzy had got the band organised and the DJ was booked. I didn't need to send invitations; people would just turn up, because that's what it was like. It was such a close knit community, all you needed was word of mouth and the party would rock.

There was so much I still had to do. I'd started packing but I needed to get some paperwork from Manchester. I was panicking I'd have nothing sorted. I needed to get a move on. I wanted to jump out of bed and do everything at once.

The knock on the door brought me back to my senses. I sat up; it was a bit early for visitors. I leapt out of bed and headed down the hallway, feeling like the bloody butler. There was another knock, a sharp rap. For god sake, Nessa would sleep through a bomb.

I opened the door. There was no one there. I'd definitely heard something. I stepped just outside and looked along the landing to the flat. It was nice in a way, tiled, with a rug and filled with plants. It was almost like the inside of the flat, cosy.

I went to see if I could see anybody running down the

stairs. I leant over the metal painted banister rail and looked down just in time to hear the huge entrance door to the block slam shut, then a car engine revved up as it sped off.

Weird, I thought. I turned around to go back into the flat and noticed a cardboard box next to the door. I was immediately suspicious. You didn't grow up around here believing things like this were presents from the tooth fairy. It had Nessa's name emblazoned in thick marker on the top of it.

'Nessa,' I called. 'Wake up babe.'

I was carrying the box into the flat. Then I wondered if I should leave it on the landing.

'Ness,' I shouted. 'Jesus Christ, Ness, Nessa.'

She came running out of the bedroom looking like she'd been dragged through a bush and then thrown back in again.

'What's up, you mad woman? Can't a girl get any sleep around here?' She half joked but I could tell she was pissed off for being woken up so early.

'Someone's just left this,' I said and pointed to the box on the floor.

'What the hell is it?' she said. She eyed it suspiciously. 'You open it.'

'No you,' I replied, but I thought about her recent experiences and didn't want her to go through any more drama.

I bent down and went for it, tearing the box like it was Christmas Day. It'd probably be something as shit as the presents I'd received all my life, I thought.

Nothing could have prepared me for what I saw in the bottom of the box. I screamed and threw it on the floor. A bloodied pigs head rolled out and landed right at Nessa's feet.

Chapter 51

Nessa

At first I couldn't work out what it was rolling towards me. It was only when it came to a stop that I realised it was a pig's head, full of fleshy bits where it's neck used to be. I couldn't believe what I was seeing.

I felt sick and heat rushed through my body making me sweat.

'Right,' Ella said. 'We need to phone the police.'

We heard the main door to the flat bang hard and footsteps running up the stairs. We looked at each other and panicked. We left the offending item where Ella had dropped it. Ella shut and locked the front door and we ran down the hallway into the bedroom, still screaming and grabbing each other.

'Who the hell would do that Ella?' I said. We both knew straightaway who we thought it was. It had to be Tony. He was convinced I'd lost the baby on purpose.

The phone rang and my heart stopped. If anything else was to happen, I swear I would have had a heart attack.

'It might be Si,' I said. Ella's face was a mixture of excitement, fear and 'get me the fuck out of here,' I almost laughed.

I ran over to the phone and answered it. There was nobody there. It was silent.

'You dickhead,' I screamed down the phone, for what good it would do me. There was no response, only heavy breathing.

'Say something you bastard,' I shouted. I was ready to confront this idiot. I can't believe I'd ever got involved with such a freak. Why hadn't I listened to the girls? I slammed the phone down so hard it almost snapped in two.

'I'll put the kettle on,' Ella said, her answer for everything.

'I don't want a brew, I feel sick, Ella, for God sake. What's this man doing to me? God, I knew he was a loon but this is taking it to the extreme.'

I shook my head.

A knock on the door startled us both and like frightened animals we ran into the bedroom, as quietly as possible, grabbing each other, shoving and pushing, our faces full of alarm and panic.

'Who the hell is it?' I whispered to Ella. I looked at her face. 'Why are you laughing?'

'I don't know,' she said. 'I guess I'm just so scared.' She made me laugh.

'For God sake the rest of the pig's body could be at the door and you're laughing,' I said. 'Are you off your head?'

'No, but the fucking pig is,' she said.

We both roared with laughter and fell onto the bed, unable to breathe, she was snorting like a pig, which made it even funnier. Then there was another knock at the door and something was slipped through the letter box.

We both sat in silence for a good fifteen minutes. 'Do you think they've gone?' I finally whispered.

'Don't know. I'm not sure.'

I could tell she was dying to laugh again. I was half annoyed with her now and half wanted to laugh with her. She was daft in the head. We'd just been delivered a severed pig's head, which meant I was in for it. Someone was out to get me and she was cracking jokes.

The phone rang again. I answered with a sharp 'Hello?'

It was Bess. It was so good to hear her voice. We both

started talking at once. She told me about what happened with Peter Lawrence. It did sound like he had it in for us but I wasn't sure that a pig's head was really his style. I didn't know if he even knew where I lived but I guess he could have easily found that out if he wanted.

She also told me about her uncle being a bit aggressive toward her and freaking her out. That went over my head a bit. She was probably just sensitive after the attack and reading too much into things.

I said goodbye to Bess. I could see a piece of paper hanging out of the letter box. Ella was behind me. She'd been listening to the conversation with Bess. She went and grabbed the note.

'This is becoming like a bloody armchair thriller,' she said and started humming the theme tune to Tales of the Unexpected, waving her arms and spinning around.

'You're a knob Ella Parker.' I said 'What does the note say?'

As she read it her face dropped and she became very serious. She handed it to me.

'You all love the baby sister.' I read out loud.

'What does that mean?' she said. 'I'm phoning Bess's uncle.'

I nodded. 'Yeah, maybe it's the best thing to do. It needs sorting.' He was already aware there was stuff going on so it made sense.

Where was Si? When was he going to phone back? It was imminent I was sure. I felt an electric force, like he was near. I couldn't explain it.

I looked at Ella again. 'Have you phoned him?' I said.

'Jesus, give me a chance. Do you think it's about Josie?'

I shook my head. 'I think that it's all bollocks. I mean, I'm a little sister. It could be about me.'

'But we can't forget what happened to Bess,' said Ella. 'That wasn't bollocks was it? And if it wasn't Peter, who was it? On the other hand, if it was Peter it needs to stop. Mind you, I can't see Peter doing anything to Bess and Bess said he's been attacked too. It doesn't add up.'

As we sat and pondered, Faya ran in full of excitement.

'Hey, girls, guess what?' she said and looked straight at me. 'The Baileys are coming to Ella's leaving do,'

Chapter 52

Bess

It was the night before Ella's party. I wasn't ready to say goodbye to my oldest, dearest friend. She meant the world to me. I smiled as I thought of all our years together, all the stuff we'd got up to and all the fun we'd had.

I remembered her as a little girl holding on to the big red pram, skipping happily with her mum. I was going to struggle when she left but I knew it was what she wanted and needed. There was nothing here for her. With everything that was going on, I felt like buggering off myself. It was getting ridiculous; physical attacks and pigs heads, what had we ever done to anyone? Obviously Peter was pissed off for being wrongly accused and that tit Tony was pissed off because Ness had lost a baby. The fact that she could have also died in the process didn't matter to him. I wasn't going to think about it.

I decided to go and see if Lizzy needed any help arranging any last minute party stuff. As I walked up the long road that ran through the estate, I couldn't help noticing the trees that lined the grass verges. They almost made a tunnel as their branches met in the middle of the road, as though they were crying out for each other, as though they needed to touch. You could just about catch the glimpses of sunlight bursting through them. It lifted me immediately.

I got to the pub before it opened. The place was full of the ghosts of memories past, of the shooting which would always stay with me. We'd had some good laughs in this pub too. You were always welcome and always felt like part of the family.

I let myself in. There was a small crowd around the bar. A few women were talking to Lizzy. She had some clobber on hangers and they were all oohing and ahhhing. I laughed. It was family allowance day so Lizzy was selling knocked-off clobber at a very reduced price. 'All good stuff too, none of your shite.' She would never change.

'Fucking hell love,' she said and she held her hand to her chest. 'You nearly gave me a fucking heart attack, then. I thought it was the Old Bill. Come in and shut the door, and make sure you lock it. Which dozy fucker left the door open?' she added looking around accusingly.

She continued her sales pitch. 'Here Janice, what about this Pierre Cardin jumper for your Bob?'

I laughed. It was like a bloody cattle market in here on a Tuesday morning. No wonder people walked around looking like the dog's bollocks. They looked more like they were from Alderley Edge, never mind one of the biggest council estates in Europe.

'Lizzy,' I interrupted. 'I'm going to nip to the Civic Centre, is there anything we need to get for Ella's do?'

She was on a roll and didn't really want interrupting. 'Just get some of those big pork pies, from the indoor market, love, nothing else. George has got it all sorted.'

She turned back to her punters and like a pundit at the Grand National went into her spiel about her goods.

'What do you mean fake?' she started to raise her voice. 'They've been nicked from Kendal's in Altrincham you cheeky fucker. If you don't like them fuck off. Do you think I'd sell shite? Any more of that and you can fuck off and don't come back, in fact you'll be fucking barred.'

There was no compromise. The luckless Janice had only

asked if it was a real Pierre Cardin.

'Bess, before you go, there are some nice dresses here for you and the girls. There's a nice one here from Benetton, it'll look great on you.'

'Ah, thanks Lizzy. Put them away and I'll pop round later with the girls.'

I hadn't even thought about what to wear. I used the payphone before I left to let the girls know that Lizzy had some good clobber. It was a beautiful day. I felt stronger and my face was healing. Nothing was going to get me down today. I had a bit of hair to do later, then a fashion parade at the Lion. I smiled, sometimes I loved my life.

Chapter 53

Ella

It was almost party time. Oh my god, I was nervous. I was worried nobody would turn up or the band would cancel or something would go wrong. It was making me feel ill.

Mum shouted up, asking if I wanted a brew. I wish I hated them all; it would make leaving so much easier. The boys ran around with pieces of toast hanging from their mouths. Our Josie was sitting in the kitchen pecking mum's head about this and that. She gave me a big smile. 'Mum said I can come for a couple of hours,' she said. She was chuffed as anything

'Ah did she now?' I said. 'Well you'd better come to the pub and see if Lizzy's got anything left for you to wear hadn't you? Come on, she'll sort you out with something.'

Her face was adorable as it lit up with excitement. 'Let me drink my brew and we'll see what she's got left' I told her. 'Go and get ready you can't come in your pyjamas.' She jumped up quicker than you could say Jack Flash and ran up the stairs.

Mum laughed. 'I've ever seen her move that quickly, Ella. Well done.'

She went quiet, picked up a pan and started drying it. 'I'm dead proud of you Ella. You've done real well for yourself. You've been abroad and now you're going to be working on a massive cruise ship. Wish my mum and dad were here to see it.' Her eyes welled up, which made me well up too.

'Well I'm not going yet, it's just my leaving do so save it till then or we'll be crying for the next couple of weeks.'

'You're a good girl, Ella. Go and sort your sister out. She's chuffed to mint balls.'

We all met at the pub. I loved being in there during closing time. George would call last orders about three o'clock and it would shut until around six. The smoky smell and stale beer lingered in the air. The blinds were shut so no-one could see in. That was Lizzy's rules. No fucker got to see what went on behind those blinds, she would say.

Bess was right. There was a right load of clobber, top clobber too. Ness was there, Bess, Faya, me and our Josie who was growing up fast. She was over the moon to be with the big girls. Well she was nearly fifteen. It wouldn't be long before she'd be hanging about with us properly.

We each picked out some clothes and tried them on in the pub. We had a good laugh together trying on various stolen outfits.

'Jesus, look at me arse in this,' I said, as I rolled a green dress over my body. 'I look like a crab apple.'

Oh my god, I was fat. Nessa put a red dress on and her tits fell out. 'With knockers like that love, you need something a bit higher,' Lizzy shouted and threw her a roll neck jumper.

We all laughed. Lizzy was also laughing. 'Pick your stuff and fuck off out. We've a lot to get sorted,' she said. 'Your clobber's on me girls. Fucking family we are and that's that and I don't want any arguing. It's sorted, George paid for it all anyway, fucking mug.'

We all knew better than to argue with Lizzy especially when she had done something so kind, so off we all went giggling with excitement at our new designer clobber for the party; my party.

Nessa and me got ready at Bess's. John was still working

and would more than likely be at the party later. He was at the pub every night anyway, so that night wouldn't be any different.

'I don't know how to wear my hair,' said Nessa, struggling with that beautiful auburn main of hers. She was holding it up. 'If it'd just stay like this it'd be fine, but it won't.'

So she got the hair drier and scrunched it all curly. Messy was in fashion. She'd cheated slightly as Bess had done her a demi-wave perm so it went messy really easily.

Mine was as straight as anything. I was contemplating a perm but for now it'd have to be the jet black bob that it had been forever.

'Leave you hair girls, I'll sort it,' said Bess as she came out of the bathroom. She looked stunning. She wore a mustard suit with black piping. The little box skirt showed off her legs and she had a little black camisole underneath.

'Wow, very sexy,' I said accentuating the words to make her feel good. She did look amazing.

I'd chosen a tight red dress, boxed off just over my knees and some huge knot-like earrings, Bet Lynch had nothing on me.

'Don't ask me to nod my head tonight, I might knock myself out,' I said. 'Have you seen these huge earrings, they're the size of boulders?'

'Where did you get them?' Nessa asked and I could see envy on her face. I laughed and nodded toward Bess.

'Fucking Joan Collins there,' I said. 'She's got everything, loads of perfume, about twenty watches, forty pairs of earrings.

'Borrow what you want Ness,' offered Bess laughing.

Nessa's face lit up and she rummaged through Bess's stuff and ended up with a fake pair of drop earrings that made the holes in her ears longer.

'Ella, there's a bottle of champers in the fridge,' said Bess 'I don't know how good it is, one of my ladies gave it to me. Probably knocked off, but go and open it, and there's a joint in that top drawer. Let's get the party started early.'

I didn't need to be told twice.

Ness put the stereo on and the latest hits blasted out as we finished getting ready.

Chapter 54

Ness

I stared at my reflection and couldn't believe how much better I looked. So I'd gained a couple of pounds, it made me curvy, voluptuous and my very full breasts added to it. After being with someone who didn't really want to come near me I could be forgiven for feeling a little bit shit but somewhere, if you looked hard enough, there was definitely a little tiny sparkle in those eyes. Yeah, I liked myself. I was gorgeous, and if Si was going to be at the party, he would think that too.

'Stop,' I screamed and the girls stopped dead. 'Sorry but what if Si Bailey *is* there tonight?' My legs were going to give way at this rate. 'What am I going to say? How can I look at him? It's no good, I can't go.' I had to sit down as the fear enveloped me.

'Get her a joint,' said Bess laughing. 'Jesus, Ness, you love the fella. What can go wrong?'

Ella started laughing. 'You've not seen the fucker for years. He might be a big fat bastard with no hair.'

'You're right helpful, Ella.' I said.

'What if he is dead ugly now?' she continued.

'He can't be,' I said dreamily.

'Ah, for fuck sake,' they both laughed. 'Get a grip, you big daft sod,' said Ella and we all laughed.

It was still light as we walked along the main road to the Lion. The trees that always longed to touch each were holding hands as though they were mirroring us.

Bess's beautiful blonde curls fell down her back, all natural and wavy. She was shorter than me and Ella but her beautiful blue eyes shone like the stars. She looked amazing. Her makeup concealed her fading bruises

Ella wore a red dress, her long jet black bob and straight fringe shining. She looked absolutely stunning as she walked down the street with us, her two best friends.

I thought I looked just as stunning as the other two. As we walked to the pub I daydreamed about Si Bailey. Would he be there? Would he show up in a horse drawn carriage and take me away from it all.

As we neared the pub you could hear the loud music and the DJ talking over the songs. It was already going full pelt. Through the windows you could see the disco lights, flashes of red, blue and orange, and reflections of the crystal ball as beams of light emanated in all directions.

We entered the pub and there was a huge crowd waiting for our girl. It went absolutely ballistic, banners, balloons, party poppers, the works.

The DJ played 'Simply the Best' by Tina Turner. She was made up. I could tell by her face and that was it, the night had started.

My mind had gone now and I couldn't concentrate. I could see Si's brother, Matthew, standing in a corner, fag in his mouth and pint in hand. He was still so cool. I wasn't sure whether to go over and ask where Si was but I didn't dare. What if I didn't like the answer? I needed to relax, enjoy the night and if he came he came and if he didn't, he didn't.

Chapter 55

Ella

I couldn't believe the reception or the number of people that had turned up. I spotted mum and dad in a corner. They waved; mum was beaming. The effort Lizzy and George had gone to was just amazing. I gulped as I looked around. There was a long table with food galore on it. There was every type you could think off. George had made huge pans of curry and huge pans of stew with bread and red cabbage. I sensed Conny's ghost smiling down on me and I felt a lump in my throat. How I wished he was here. How different my life might have been.

The DJ was blasting out 'Simply the Best' and everyone was looking at me and cheering. Some had gifts. I'd not thought of that. Lots of cards were floating about; I was so touched. The music stopped and the DJ said, 'Welcome Ella. Tonight's your night. Pick a song.'

I had to mingle and talk to everyone. It was amazing. I loved being the centre of attention. Ness was off looking for Si. I had to smile and prayed in my mind that he was going to show up. Bess was with my lot and her dad and they were all having a good laugh which was nice. I saw Matt Bailey.

He still caught my eye, he was handsome but I couldn't even think of anything like that now. It was the last thing I needed, but then again maybe I did need it before I left and why not with Matt?

'Where's your Si, then?' I said. 'Has he come with you guys?'

'Nah,' said Matt.

The slightly southern twist to his accent shocked me; it had been so long since I'd heard it.

'Bottle went,' he laughed.

My heart sank. For fuck sake, I didn't want any dampener on this night. I looked over at Ness. She was with Faya and some of their mates. One of her brothers had turned up so that would keep her occupied for a while.

The music just kept coming. The DJ was fantastic, people were getting drunk but everything was in hand. Lizzy made sure of that. I looked at her. She'd been a rock, my second mum. My life might have been different if Conny was still here but I might have still got itchy feet, who knows? No point dwelling on the past, the future was shouting for me.

I went and sat with my mum and dad for a bit.

'Can you believe you've pulled in such a crowd?' mum said almost in awe. 'Mind you, the free grub probably helped, people love something for nothing.'

I just nodded. I looked at her face and could see that she was so proud right now. Dad looked pleased too and I loved that man for what he'd done for me growing up. He was my dad, no matter what.

D Train came blurting through the speakers and everyone went mad, dancing to the beat and singing along, 'You just don't know what you did to me, yeah, yeah.'

Everyone was smiling and the atmosphere was crazy. I felt happy. I loved it here, this was home and although I was going away, I'd never leave these people for good.

I'd already spotted Peter Lawrence in the corner and had been informed that someone was keeping tabs on him. Lizzy had instructed a couple of the regulars to keep an eye on him. They got paid in pints so were happy to do it.

Chapter 56

Bess

I had goose bumps on my goose bumps at the whole event and the fact that everyone was here for our girl. It was a massive turn-out and the atmosphere was like that of a club.

Lizzy and George had definitely pulled out all the stops. They clearly thought the world of Ella. They thought the world of all of us; we'd all been through the mill and back. The DJ blasted out some top tunes and everyone was dancing wildly; it was electric. There were old eighties classics mixed with a bit of Motown for the older ones. Even I got up and danced at one point.

'Hiya,' said a voice from the bar which took me by total surprise. It was a girl who I worked with years ago at William's salon. I think her name was Andrea.

'Hiya,' I shouted back, it was difficult to hear anything with all the commotion going on.

'Do you want a drink?' she asked with a twinkle in her eyes.

'Yeah, go on then. Lager and black,' I said.

'Classy chick,' she joked with a twist to her mouth that made me go weak at the knees.

Oh my god, here I go again. I wish it would just go away and I could feel normal like everyone else did.

'How come you're here?' I asked.

'I was told it was your best mates do so I just had to come,' she said.

Was she coming on to me? How did she know? Did I give out signals? It's not like I wore Doc Martins or anything. I didn't know what to say. I was gobsmacked. Thank god the music was so loud and the lights were low or my face alone would have lit up the room like a beacon.

I laughed as I clocked her Doc's.

'What you smiling at?' she said.

'Just ignore me, you'd never get it. I'm very complicated.'

This time I gave her my best Bess smile. I could tell it nearly blew her away and I felt back in control.

'Want to come and sit down?' I asked. Very assertive Bess I thought.

She nodded and we tried to find a quiet corner where we wouldn't have to lip read. She was a hairdresser too and lived in Northenden. She had apparently bumped into Ella in Manchester one day. Ella had remembered her and invited her along. She had probably realised that Andrea was a lesbian and decided to set us up. As it happened Andrea was better than any other woman I'd ever met in my life. We clicked instantly and were laughing, joking and sharing stories about William who had been an utter bastard to work for.

'What happened to him?' I asked.

'Don't know, he probably died of AIDS.'

'Jesus, you can't say that,' I screamed pretending to be offended but we both laughed at the darkness of the joke.

I wanted Andrea to meet dad. She didn't hesitate and I dragged her over to meet the real love of my life.

'This is John Holland, my lovely daddy,' I said in a silly girl voice.

'Hiya love,' he shouted over the music. 'Are you our Bess's girlfriend?'

What? I couldn't believe what I was hearing. He knew, but how? I looked over to Nessa, who was with her rabble and then to Ella, who was mooching up to Matt Bailey. Nah, the girls would never betray me.

'It's alright love, I'm your dad.' He said sensing my confusion. 'I might be an old drunk, but I'm not daft, you're my girl. I love you for whoever you chose to love. Makes no odds to me.'

Tears of relief filled my eyes. Not that this girl was going to be in my life forever, it wasn't about that. It was about not having to hide anything from my dad and not having to fear my own sexuality. I had him on my side and that's all that mattered.

He gave me the biggest bear hug he'd ever given me. He had tears in his eyes, he shouted, 'I love you so much Elizabeth Holland.' He squeezed me tight. 'I don't care if you're a lesbian.'

As he said it the DJ stopped the record and the whole of the pub heard what he had just screamed.

I covered my eyes in shock and shame. Ness and Ella ran towards me to help me with my embarrassment. Dad was mortified. Andrea sat down in shock. Then I heard Lizzy's voice from behind the bar, 'and if you don't like it, you can fuck off,' she said.

Everyone seemed to decide there and then that if Lizzy said it was ok then it was ok. My goose bumps got bigger as everyone came over and hugged me, reassuring me it was ok.

Ness looked at me. 'What?' I said, still in shock.

'At least none of them knows you licked Ella's fanny,' she said.

I looked at Ella. 'Shut up,' she said. 'Before the fucking DJ stops this track.'

We all screamed with laughter and had a massive three-way hug. My girls, I loved them heart and soul.

I went and sat with Andrea. I felt free, liberated; my true self once and for all and it had been as simple as that.

Chapter 57

Nessa

I couldn't stop laughing at John Holland accidentally announcing to the whole estate that his daughter was a lesbian. I'm sure my heart had actually stopped beating for a minute. I thought Bess was going to drop dead on the spot until Lizzy saved the day. So that was it, it was out there. It felt strange, but I was relieved and I knew she would be. Ella had done the right thing by inviting this Andrea bird. She seemed to be hitting it off with Bess.

I looked around me. The pub was buzzing. I don't think I'd ever seen it so packed before. The music was awesome, a bit for everyone. The flashing lights were on full force with the disco ball spinning fast.

The DJ announced the buffet was open; music to my ears. We all queued up with our paper plates and plastic knives and forks while he played some quiet tunes.

'You alright Nessa?' Ella said. She was getting a little bit tipsy

'Yes, I'm good babe.'

'He's not fucking here though,' she said and made a stupid sad face, like a pout.

I smiled again although the thought of it didn't make me want to smile, it made me feel ill. What was going on? He'd called me or had he? What with the pig's head and cryptic notes not to mention Bess's attack, maybe he hadn't. Deep down, I was sure it was him.

The noise of everyone chatting away around me was like a comedy scene of its own.

''Ere Beryl, grab us two of them bread rolls, our Kirsty can have one for her lunch tomorrow.'

'Get plenty of that stew down you, Kev. There's nothing in for your tea, when you get back.'

'Wrap it in a napkin if your not going to eat it now. Waste not, want not.'

'Any doggy bags Lizzy?'

'Where've you knocked this lot off from George?'

And so the banter continued. I smiled to myself, there was nothing like it.

Peter Lawrence came and stood next to me. He was being watched very closely so I felt ok. He was getting difficult to look at as he got older, as rude as that sounded. He always had a wet mouth like a sick dog and it was enough to put me off my buffet.

'You lot have had it man,' he spat.

'Fuck off Peter,' I scowled. 'You're full of shit. Get it done and shut the fuck up threatening.'

John's mates came a bit closer but the last thing I wanted was it kicking-off tonight so I shook my head at them and they backed off.

'Your mates a fuckin lezzer, you're a fucking murderer and Ella's a...'

'A what Peter?' I interrupted. 'Come on think.' I was almost laughing now, it was that ridiculous.

He gave up. 'Ah, fuck off. You're a bunch of slags all of you.'

'Yeah we know, we know. Just go and have a good time mate or I'll have to speak to Lizzy about you.'

He was shocked at my response, but I wasn't going there. The man was clearly unwell and I wondered why he'd never got any help,

The live band was setting up in the corner. I shouted Bess and Ella over.

'You know, he actually looks like Bono,' I said and laughed.

'Let's hope he sings like bloody Bono,' said Ella.

When they came on, they started off with 'The Streets Have No Name'. We all agreed they were very good and joined in with everybody else singing along to U2 covers. Everyone was enjoying themselves. I was having an amazing time and Ella was in her element. About three songs in I was desperate for the toilet so I made a dash for it as quick as I could trying to get back to the dance floor as fast as possible.

It was on my way back that I saw Tony. He was coming through the front door with a look of hate and anger on his face. He was looking for me, I could tell. I stood still, the music was blasting and the noise of the people trying to talk over a live band was loud. I could feel my breathing becoming shallow as he saw me. I was rooted to the spot, I couldn't move. He was coming straight at me. I tried to look around for the girls, but all the faces were a blur. The thudding in my heart was becoming louder than the music. He was fast and he was furious, and before I knew it, he had me. He pulled my hair hard and threw me to the floor. I lay there on my back. He was kneeling over me, gritting his teeth hard.

'You fucking murderer, you killed my baby,' he screamed.

I tried to focus on what was going on around me. I could hear the band playing. I could see people's legs, their shoes. I could see Ella's high heels. I could make out Bess talking to Andrea.

He started to drag me across the floor, still on my back, my legs grabbing onto table legs through the dancers. I tried to resist and fight back but the more I did the more it hurt it me. Why wasn't anybody helping me? It was like no one around me could see what was going on. Where were the girls? Why weren't they running over?

Then, for the second time that evening the music stopped. The band stopped playing their instruments and the place went silent.

It was like a scene from a film. You couldn't have written it. Just when I needed him most, there he was. Everything I'd ever wanted, the man I had been waiting for, the man I dreamt about. There he was and he was going to save me.

Si Bailey screamed at Tony to get off me as he dived at him. Tears were in my eyes, as I lay on the floor, mortified, undignified, but electrified. Si dragged Tony off me. Luckily for Tony he managed to get away from Si and he shot out of the pub as fast as he could. I think Si would have killed him if he hadn't moved so fast.

I wanted to die but instead I covered my eyes with my fingers. I felt like that little girl, the little girl on the ground all those years ago when Skidder Barker had spat on my face at school. Si was there for me then and he was here for me now.

I could feel the heat, the electricity generated from his body. He wasn't fat and bald, he was just the same; he was beautiful. When I managed to move my hands from my face, I could see myself in his eyes.

He helped me up and pulled me towards him. He wrapped his big arms around me and held me tight. I felt whole, I felt complete and as the tears streamed down my face, I gave a huge sigh of relief. I never wanted him to let me go.

'I want you,' he said.

His voice moved me. It was the same soft and gravelly

voice.

'You've got me,' I said and felt like the grin was stuck to my face.

'Oh, I will have,' he said. 'I'm going to get you bad.'

I'd never felt anything like this in my life. Desire was taking over my body; from my toes, right up the insides of my legs, into my thighs, then so strong between my legs that it caught my breath.

'Let's go,' I said.

I winked at Ella, who winked back. I grinned at Bess who was wiping her tears. I grabbed his hand and we left the party to begin a journey of love and ecstasy, a journey that not everyone is privileged to have the opportunity to take, but I had my ticket and I was well up for the ride. In fact, no one would be able to get me off it. I finally had him. I was holding his hand. My Si Bailey

Chapter 58

Ella

At last she had him, her man. I felt jealous but in a healthy way. She was my girl and she deserved to be happy. I knew Si Bailey would make her happier than she'd ever been.

Bess had her woman. It wasn't as deep as the love Nessa had for Si but it might be one day. Her secret was out in the open at least. I could already see a change in her, it was as if she had suddenly been set free and I guess in a way she had.

I looked around. Tony had well and truly gone, absolute idiot. What would have happened if Si hadn't have shown up? For starters Tony would have been kicked to death by the mob. It made the hairs on the back of my neck stand up. Si truly was her knight in shining armour.

Peter Lawrence had also gone; Nessa had sorted that nuisance out.

I went over to my family feeling emotional. My brothers were having a whale of a time. My mum and dad were enjoying themselves too, I could tell. They were having a ball with John Holland and his cronies.

'Where's Josie?' I said, looking around.

Mum shrugged. 'Toilet, love?' she said half asking me.

I headed towards the toilet, but people were stopping me, asking me about Nessa, asking me who Tony was, asking me when Si Bailey had come back to town. I was getting a sense of panic now. I was probably wrong, but I'd not seen Josie for a while and my instinct was telling me something wasn't right.

Matt Bailey grabbed me. 'We going to dance baby cakes?'

he said.

I tried to be calm. 'Just give us a minute, Matt. I can't find Josie.'

He must have picked up on the seriousness of my voice and offered to help me look.

'I'm probably being stupid,' I said. 'But a lot's gone on lately. I can't even begin to tell you.'

'It's ok,' he said. 'Let's find her.'

She wasn't in the toilet, she wasn't in the vault and she wasn't back with my family. Matt and I went outside and she wasn't there either.

'Maybe she's walked home,' he said.

'Nah, she wouldn't do that,' I said. 'She's barely fifteen and too much has gone on, she wouldn't dare go without letting us know and getting someone to walk her back.'

I wanted the music to stop. I wanted everyone to go home. I just wanted Josie. I went to find Lizzy who grabbed the microphone off the DJ, 'Jo, Josie, Jo-Jo, you here love?' I waited for a response.

Mum stood up. 'What's up?' she said. 'Where's our Josie?'

Then everyone was looking, again that local loyalty, like one of our sheep was missing and we needed her back in the fold. Everyone left the pub and started shouting her name up and down the long quiet road. The trees were blowing gently in the wind. There was no other sound apart from the locals calling Josie's name.

Then someone shouted, 'quick, phone the police. Phone for an ambulance.'

My mum's screaming sent chills through my entire body and it felt as though the whole of the night stood still. Dread gripped me like asphyxiation.

With Bess at one side of me and Matt at the other, I

ran towards the scream and towards the crowd that was gathering. In the distance I could hear sirens. The tears were coming now. 'Please God, please God,' I begged, 'don't do this, please.'

Matt and Bess grabbed my hands as we approached the scene. The scene where my baby sister had been raped, strangled and left for dead.

Chapter 59

Nessa

We got back to mine. I was lost for words. I had no idea what to say to Si. I felt painfully shy and I think he did too. We both laughed nervously and then he became serious.

'Do you know I've always loved you? It was always you, nobody else,' he said

I did know because I'd always felt the same. There had always been something between us; the time with Skidder Barker, the time with Peter Lawrence and the time in Blackpool. There was a strong connection between us that couldn't be explained.

'I just had to come and find you. I couldn't have carried on without you baby,' he continued

He called me baby, my stomach muscles tightened and again that warm feeling flooded my body.

He asked about Tony, he wanted to know who he was and why he was trying to hurt me. Although I felt embarrassed, I had to tell him what had happened, leaving nothing uncovered. I explained that Tony was a big mistake and how when I was in hospital I dreamt of him, Si.

'I've missed you so much. I've missed you all my life. You might not believe me, but you've been on my mind constantly since I was a little girl, since the first day I saw you. There's something about your very presence that just draws me to you, like an electric force,' I said.

He grabbed my face and pulled me towards him.

I started to shake, as soon as he touched me. I could feel electric waves all over my body again; I knew he was going to kiss me. I'd waited for this moment for ever and my body trembled. I felt his mouth touch mine and his tongue quickly dart into my mouth. It was soft and gentle at first, then passionate and fierce. He was pushing down hard on my mouth. I wanted to climb inside him. If I could have got under his skin I would. I wanted him so bad, my body was weakening and I couldn't take it anymore.

We kissed standing up, grabbing, feeling, pulling at each other's clothes, an energy flowing between us all the while. I grabbed his hand and dragged him into my bedroom. I noticed the blue lights flashing outside. They almost lit up the room as they drove past. I heard the sirens but blocked it out. Nothing unusual for around here and I couldn't think about that right now. All I could think about was him. My desire for him was making me ache, I was moaning through our kisses and our instincts took over.

We ripped off each other's clothes; all the while our eyes remained locked, looking deep into each other's souls. I closed my eyes for a moment and remembered him as that cocky boy with an attitude of someone beyond his years and as a teenager so confident. Underneath all that I knew there had always been vulnerability within, a little boy who needed something, but even he probably didn't know what that was. I knew that behind the bravado and fighting that this boy was beautiful, this boy had a warm gentle side to him, and I loved him with all my heart.

He lay on top of me, flesh on flesh, electric sparks, buzzing on my skin, my legs were trembling.

'You want some of this baby?' he said and guided my hand to his cock. It was huge, I gulped.

I knew this was going to be animalistic. I always knew it would be, like Neanderthals. There was going to be no surprises here. It's like we'd done this before, in another life maybe, but it was the bonding of two people who had always meant to be one person.

I grinned. 'Of course I want it. I've always wanted it.'

It made him more eager. He was trembling now as he entered me slowly, teasingly, his eyes never left mine. I shook my head. I couldn't believe this was him

'Is it you?' I whispered. 'Is it really you?'

'It's me, baby,' he whispered. 'You ready,' he said with his lips touching mine.

'I've always been ready,' I gasped.

I pushed my body hard onto his. I couldn't wait any longer. The desire, the need, the lust was too much. Then we were there, we were unified and the sparks were about to cause an inferno within. He touched my breasts. He had them in his mouth. He disappeared down the bed and put his head between my legs. I'd never felt pleasure like it. I lay back, as he expertly used his tongue, soft gentle strokes, again sending my body into spasms. I arched my back, pushing myself onto his face. I had never wanted a feeling, a person so much. I screamed as I felt an explosion starting from my toes. I wasn't sure I was going to be able to handle it, it was so intense.

The throbbing and pulsating pleasure I was feeling between my legs, my first orgasm made me throw my head back, grip the head board for dear life and scream. As I did the tears rolled down my cheeks. I'd waited years for that.

I pushed him on to his back.

'Oh, you know what you want lady, don't you?' he said.

'I do, Si Bailey, I certainly do. I want you.' I straddled his cock and slowly sat myself down on it, bit by bit, taking in every single inch of it. It felt hot, it felt smooth, it felt deep, it felt right, as I moved slowly up and down on it, with his hands guiding my hips. I could feel him deep inside me, feel the heat. I bent down and kissed his mouth and as I did, I exploded again.

The feeling flooded my body making me weak. I exploded all over him. I wasn't sure what had happened. I'd ejaculated all down his big firm cock. This sent him wild. He picked me up and bent me over so my arse was firmly in the air. Not once did I think of how I looked, I didn't care, it was beyond that, it was beyond anything I had ever known. This was sheer ecstasy, sheer Nirvana, and as he pulled my cheeks apart, he thrust himself into me, pulling my body onto him while he was behind me, climbing me, as I pushed back onto to him, wanting to feel his masculinity inside me.

The fiery passion enveloped us once again and this time we both screamed. We were both reaching peaks of desire and couldn't take any more and the volcanic eruption between us had us panting, moaning and making noises I didn't know I was capable of.

We both fell into a heap of nakedness. I lay there in his strong arms. He reeked of masculinity. I kissed his face hard and he returned my kisses. I knew that we could never be separated again. As I lay there, I felt whole, I felt one, I was unified with my soulmate once again, because we'd been here before and we would be here again for eternity.

'I love you, Vanessa Brown, always have and always will.'

'I love you too Si Bailey.'

Chapter 60

Bess

We were surrounded by chaos. It's like we were in a horror movie. It was Josie, little Josie, she was in a heap on the floor.

Christine Parker and Chris Parker were being helped by police women. Josie, on a stretcher, was carefully being put in an ambulance. The paramedics were being gentle with her. I couldn't hold back, I broke down and started to sob like a baby. I remembered this little girl in her pram. I remembered her bouncing about on her mum's lap. I remembered she used to tease me and pull my hair as a toddler. She was always a lovely baby, a lovely toddler, a lovely teenager. Why would anyone do this?

Ella couldn't go in the ambulance, only her parents. She came over, she was in shock; she looked disorientated and lost. I hugged her and we both shared a moment of grief that left us lost for words and sobbing our hearts out for Josie.

The ambulance drove away with its sirens on. The police were asking everyone questions. The night chill was beginning to set in and I felt cold. In the distance you could hear the noise from the pub. The atmosphere was that of bad news. I could feel it from where I was stood. I looked at Ella.

'Do you want to go to the hospital?' I said. 'Or you can come back to mine. We'll get a cuppa.'

She shook her head. 'I'd better get home with our lads. Will you come with me?'

I saw Andrea walking towards us.

'Someone just told me about your sister. Fucking hell

love, are you ok?' she said.

It was a stupid question. Of course she wasn't ok but I didn't say anything. It wasn't Andrea's fault.

'Listen, I'm going to go back to Ella's. You and Matt want to come and keep us company?' I said. 'Is that ok with you Ella?'

Ella didn't care. She was shivering now so Matt put his coat around her and we all walked back to hers with Henry and George, who for once were very quiet. They were in shock; we all were. I grabbed Henry's hand to give him a bit of morale support and he gripped mine hard

'I'll fucking kill whoever did this,' he growled, 'with my bare fucking hands.'

Christine Parker had left a light on and the telly. It was something we did back then to make people think there was someone in and deter would-be burglars. The boys got their coats on and went back out. God knows what they thought they were going to do. Ella went straight to the kettle.

'Go and put something more comfy on,' I insisted. 'And I'll brew up.'

The sombre mood in the house was unbearable, I don't think I'd ever felt anything like it. There was nothing we could do but wait.

The front door burst open. It was Nessa and Si. They'd only just heard what had happened.

Nessa ran straight to Ella and held her tight. Ella broke down again.

'I'm in shock,' Nessa said.

'We all are. You should have seen her,' I whispered so that Ella didn't hear me.

I started to cry again. I wanted to be strong for my friend, but I couldn't help it. Josie was my family too, or as good as.

The three of us hugged tightly.

Si was demanding to know what had gone on. Henry came back; he clearly didn't know what to do. George was still out.

We told the Baileys about Tony and the pig's head. We filled them in on Peter Lawrence threatening us and wanking outside Ella's window. We talked about me being attacked in my own home and about Uncle Richard and how aggressive he had been the last time I'd encountered him. He'd said we could both help each other and I recalled how intimidated I felt by him.

'And don't forget the note, Ella,' Nessa said. She was rummaging through her bag now. 'I've got it here.' She read it out loud, *'You all love the baby sister'.*

'What the fuck's been going on here?' said Si. He was pacing in the living room. 'Haven't you got the police involved? Bess gets attacked; you get a pig's head through your door and now this?' He looked furious.

'Matt, Henry, get your coats on. Whoever just raped Josie will not be in a good state right now. They won't be able to hold a conversation. So we're going to fucking start with Lawrence, then that piece of shit Tony and then your Uncle Richard and we're going to find out who the fuck did this.' He said. 'You girls stay here. We'll be back.'

He pulled Nessa's face towards him and kissed her hard on the lips. You could see it was special between them. Whatever it was they had, you'd want it. It was beyond love, it was deep and even I knew that.

Andrea went home. The situation was so out of the ordinary and it was tough on her. I gave her a kiss on the cheek and thanked her for coming. She asked me to call her and I would, but for now I let her go and went back to my girls.

Ella was distraught and for once we didn't have much to say. We just took in the moment, and waited for the boys to get back. Christ knows what they were going to do, but when Si Bailey said something would happen, it would happen.

Chapter 61

Peter Lawrence

I was rocking on my bed, the stench was pungent. The house hadn't been cleaned since dad fucked off. There was rotting food on the floor in the kitchen and mice and rats had a free run of the gaff.

I was shaking. I didn't mean for that to happen. It'd all gone too far this had. He hadn't told me that he was going to do that to poor little Josie. I felt the bile rise in my throat but I couldn't be arsed to move. I just threw up where I was, all over myself and the floor. It didn't matter, the house was rancid anyway.

There was a knock on the door. It was that Bailey freak and his cronies. What the fuck did they want? I wasn't sure whether to let them in or not.

I opened the door and stood there with sick all down my shirt, wiping my mouth on my sleeve. They were actually being quite friendly for some reason. They didn't have a clue what was going on. Mind you, I didn't have a clue either.

Chapter 62

Ella

My stomach was churning, waiting for the boys to get back, waiting for the phone to ring. I was glad I had the girls with me.

I looked around our living room at our floral cottage settee and bamboo chair in the corner, our green carpet, and stone fireplace. The pink lampshade made it look cosy, while the floral curtains matched the sofa and made it look sickly. We had a big unit in what you could call the dining room with pictures of all of us on it. I couldn't look. I didn't want to see my sister's gorgeous chubby baby face, the picture with the orange dress and her hair done up like pebbles. I could see it in my head and I couldn't remove the image from my mind.

I screamed. 'Why? Why her?'

Bess ran over to me.

'Come on now, she's not dead. She's going to be ok. Remember, she's a little scrapper. She's had you lot to deal with all her life and she's a tough cookie. She'll get through this,' she said.

'Let's wait for the lads,' Bess continued. 'And let's wait for your mum and dad to phone home. They will when there's some news, you'll see. Come on, let's get strong for Josie. She's going to need us all. I'll brew up and I'm going to put some sugar in your tea, it'll make you feel better.'

The phone hadn't rung all night and at one point I got up to check it was on the cradle properly. It was three a.m. and I was knackered. The effects of the alcohol had well and truly left me. They had well and truly left us all. Where the fuck were the boys?

As I thought about them they came in. They were hyper, all talking at once and I couldn't understand what any of them were saying.

Si had been right. They'd spoken to all three of them and one of them was out of sorts, unable to talk straight. They knew who had hurt my baby sister. I walked over to the phone.

'What are you doing?' Si asked.

'I'm going to phone the police,' I said.

'No don't,' he said. 'He'll only get away with it. I've got a plan, but we'll have to stick together and do this without cracking if you really want to end all this. You girls can finish this fucker off if you want. Are you up for it?'

I looked at the girls. There was no doubt in my mind and no hesitation on their faces. We'd been through thick and thin and put up with so much, but this had pushed us over the edge. Through life we had been bound together and now we would act together for Josie. This prick had a lot to answer for and he was going to get what he deserved.

Chapter 63

Ella

We waited for the monster; the creature that had raped my little sister and left her for dead in the street.

We were doing this for Josie. I couldn't cope with the image of her face in my mind. She had been in intensive care for weeks; coma-induced due to the extent of her injuries.

The plan was in place. We'd gone through it meticulously. Only Bess, Nessa, Si, Matt and me knew what we were about to do. Henry had some involvement. He didn't need to know the full extent of it but he wasn't daft, he was mine and Josie's brother and he would be prepared die for us.

The beast had no idea that we knew what he'd done. The beast actually thought that we were here to meet, greet and entertain him.

Bile rose in my throat. This was not playtime in school, this was real. It was going to happen and the consequences would be serious.

I had the complete support of the girls; they were doing this for Josie. After all, they'd known her for nearly as long as I had. They were my friends, my soul sisters, and I'd never felt such love and loyalty as I did right then. They hadn't been forced in to it; in truth they appeared to be more up for it than me.

We were sitting in a seedy hotel bar in Manchester. We didn't look like council estate scum. We looked more like high-class call girls. We looked sexy and dirty just as we intended. He was going to want us all, badly.

I nearly heaved at the very idea of what we were about to

do. My stomach felt like something had died there and was rotting away. Nessa broke the very long silence.

'You both ok?'

I shook my head. Bess shook hers too. We couldn't speak.

'This is wrong,' I hissed, starting to panic

'How can this be wrong?' Bess hissed back. 'Get her a brandy, Nessa.'

'Your baby sister will be damaged for the rest of her life. She might have caught something off that bastard. She might never be able to have sex again, she might not be able to have kids, and she might not even be able to fucking walk, Ella. You heard the doctor.'

Never in all these years had I seen Bess so viciously angry, but she was right. Nessa came back with a Brandy. I downed it.

Then the beast arrived.

'Be calm,' Nessa said in a whisper. 'We can do this. We're doing this for Josie.'

He came over, bold as brass, hard as nails and without a care in the world. Josie's face flashed through my mind. My demeanour must have changed because he became awkward. You could tell he was wondering what was going to happen.

'Ladies,' he grinned.

We got him to order and pay for drinks then we went upstairs to the hotel room that he'd pre-booked.

It didn't take long to get him going, he was like a dog on heat. We were playing the part well as he lay on the bed. I felt like throwing up. Nessa stripped off seemingly without a care. She wore suspenders, stockings and killer heels, she looked cool and confident.

I stroked his face. I felt sick to the pit of my stomach.

Bess stripped off. She wore a red Basque which really

enhanced her breasts. She pulled his trousers off. He was groaning.

'You dirty slags, you dirty fucking slags, give it to me, all of yer, I want the lot of yer,' he said.

Nessa bent forward and started to go down towards his hard disgusting cock. She looked the part, she looked thirsty for it. She was licking her lips and flicking her hair so it brushed against his balls.

'Come on you slag, give it to me.' He was stiff; rock hard. I was repulsed and my legs trembled like jelly.

Don't do it, I thought. I almost said the words out loud. Don't go that far, please Nessa don't do this.

She picked his manhood.

I gagged.

Then I could see the syringe in her hand. There was nothing in it but air. It would kill him for sure, causing air bubbles to block his arteries resulting in instantaneous death.

I leant across, stared into his eyes and said, 'You fucking monster.' I nearly spat in his face. Peter Lawrence; the fucking beast.

Then, as if the dawn had burst upon his world, the realisation of what this was, who we were, rushed across his face. Bess was about to plunge the syringe through his skin but the door of the seedy hotel room burst open and there stood a dishevelled, mess of a man, Richard. The room fell silent.

'It wasn't me', Peter shouted. We all froze. 'It was your uncle Richard. It was him. He raped your sister.'

All at once a shocking clarity of truth hit home; Richard, the rapist.

I'll never understand why Richard was there at the hotel that day. Perhaps he just wanted to make sure Peter kept his mouth shut. Maybe he wanted to kill him; maybe he wanted to kill all of us. No matter the reason, he was there and his sudden appearance set off a chain of chaotic events.

Our plan was shot to pieces. Richard looked wild, staring at us frighteningly. I couldn't take my eyes off the man who had raped Josie; I couldn't understand why he had done it.

There wasn't time to think. I spotted Si and Matt in the corridor outside the hotel door. They were silently creeping up behind Richard. I thought the noise of my heart thudding, trying to escape from my chest, would break the silence and disturb Richard's contemplation. My heart felt like it was at the back of my throat and was about to jump out of my mouth.

I wondered if Peter Lawrence could see the Baileys and whether or not he would say anything. It felt like a lifetime passed before Si flew into the room and threw Richard onto the bed. Peter tried to get out of the way as though he had seen this as his opportunity escape but Matt pushed him back. Richard wasn't taking it and he lashed out at Si. The scene became an obscure mess. A room full of semi-naked girls, a naked dead beat with limp dick, a rapist and two brothers who meant business.

It came from nowhere. Peter had spotted the syringe which lay redundant on the floor and Bess spotted Peter eyeing it up. You could see the cogs going in both their heads. Peter was going to use it and Bess was silently willing him not too.

He was quick and, amongst the muffled chaos, he didn't hesitate. Peter Lawrence took the empty syringe that was meant for him. Coolly and calmly, he got up and went to the tumble of bodies; his eyes clearly focused on his prey. As quick as a shot, before anyone could move, he buried the needle hard into his enemy's neck.

Chapter 64

Bess

It was morning and the rain pelted against my bedroom window. The sound of the water hitting the glass would normally have been comforting but not this time. As I tried to piece together the events of the last few hours, the rain became an incessant beat in my head, forbidding my mind to think naturally. I was tired and in shock.

Then I heard dad run up the stairs and into my room.

'Bloody hell love, you won't believe it?' He was talking at a hundred miles per hour in his haste. 'Richard has been found dead in a hotel room in the middle of Manchester. Seems he'd been with some prostitutes and they've robbed him. Dirty bastard; he's always been a creep that one. He's got his comeuppance now. He has only got what he deserves love because…well I need to tell you something…'

He took my hand softly and sat on the bed as if he was going to be the bearer of bad news. 'The police got an anonymous tip off. They believe it was him who raped young Josie'. He looked at my face for any reaction, and then started apologising. 'Jesus, Bess, I let that man into all our lives again and he's gone and done that,' he said.

I sat up in fake shock and tried to look as though it was news to me. The sound of the phone ringing down stairs broke my performance and dad went to answer it.

I heard him screaming with what sounded like joy. I was totally and utterly confused.

I jumped off my bed, still numb from shock, still weary from the stress of the last few weeks. I went downstairs; dad was still holding the receiver.

'They've found your mum, Bess, they've found your mum,' he said.

I wasn't sure what to do. I couldn't speak, I didn't believe him, I couldn't believe it, it was simply too hard to take in.

I held my head in my hands and I sobbed. I sobbed for Ella, I sobbed for Josie and I sobbed for Ness and Si, I even sobbed for Peter Lawrence. I sobbed for my dad and I cried for my mum.

Dad hung up the phone, 'Come on love, we're going to get your mum.'

We waited for the authorities to pick us up. I didn't think my head had room for anything else and now this bombshell. They'd found my mum, but found her where? As dad and I sat in shocked silence my mind shifted back to the hotel room.

It was Richard. Of course it was Richard. Only after the event did it all became clear. After Peter Lawrence had stabbed him with the empty syringe, causing him to have a massive heart attack as we all watched in shock and horror. Only then did we learn the truth. At first there had been a deadly silence and a murderous stench that filled the room where a dead man lay.

Si spoke first, 'We need a plan.'

Nobody responded. I couldn't think of a plan; a plan to do what? Buy a strong pair of scissors from the local hardware shop and start cutting him up. Place his body parts in a plastic bag. Stick him in a freezer. What plan? I shuddered at my own sick thoughts. In the end we stuck to our original story of the robbery by prostitutes.

'You'd better start fucking talking', Si said to Peter.

Peter sat shaking on the end of the bed. Saliva was building up around his mouth but right now it didn't bother me.

'Are you going to phone the police?' He looked at us all in sheer desperation.

You never grassed on your own, although it would have been the easier way out. 'Just tell us, what the fuck has been going on,' Si snapped.

Peter told the story in a garbled mess the best he could. Our understanding was that Richard had employed Peter to help with the harassment of us three girls. Peter was adamant that he had no idea about Josie's rape or who had attacked me.

It became apparent that Peter was just doing as he was told. Richard was intimidating and it was clear to see Peter was still frightened to death. He shook as he spoke, 'The bastard never even paid me a penny, thought I was going to be loaded, you know rich. He did give me a few digs though,' and he had the cuts and bruises to prove it. 'I killed him for Josie', he said almost with pride, 'made me fucking sick he did, doing that to her'.

I'm not sure if I was just delirious but I suddenly realised a strange sense of loyalty from Peter. When he picked up that syringe, we had all thought he was going for Si and he very well could have. The room had gone into a total frenzy as if it was some crazy gangster movie, but it wasn't a film, it was real life and none of us were innocent.

Matt had jumped up immediately with panic in his eyes as he thought his brother was about to get it in the neck, off the local lunatic. Nessa threw herself on the floor putting her hands over her head in preparation for her own self-protection of what was to happen to her boy, her beloved boy. Ella and I had clung to each other for dear life, staring into each other's faces almost begging each other with our eyes for it not to happen. In actual fact Peter Lawrence hadn't gone for Si as we all first suspected. Instead he killed Richard, Uncle Richard who had raped our little Josie and left her for dead.

Peter waffled on about Richard's relationship with Chris Parker. Eventually it became apparent that Chris had also been a victim of Richard's vile predatory ways. He had raped her and the result was Ella. Ella covered her mouth and started to gag as the reality sunk in. Her real father was Richard.

The final scene was a blur of me Nessa and Ella sitting in a tight huddle shocked, exhausted and sickened by it all. The result was that the right man was dead although his death was not by our hand. He'd brought it on himself, his past would out and his demise would be justified to all those that mattered.

And then I was waiting. Waiting to go and pick up my mum.

As we drove to the hospital in Macclesfield, my dad and I held each other's hand tightly. It was surreal. Before we knew it, we were entering a consulting room. I looked around thinking how my whole world, our world, had gone from a flat plain to this bumpy roller-coaster ride. I felt as though my emotions were on the front seat as I took each climb waiting for the sudden fall on the other side.

The waiting room was bright and calm, cosy in fact considering it was in a hospital. There were big planners on the wall and a large computer monitor on an uncluttered desk. Outside the grey skies and rain reflected our mood. A smartly groomed woman, possibly in her forties, explained what had happened.

Once again Uncle Richard was at the centre of chaos. He

had been holding my mum captive for all those years like some sort of prisoner. The detail was grim. It was difficult to absorb what I was hearing.

We found out later that mum had been aware of what had happened to Christine Parker and Richard had wanted to protect himself while returning to haunt poor Christine's family. Josie flashed through my mind and my tears welled up. The bastard had offered to help my mum during her spat with dad and subsequently never let her go. The police had only found her as a result of investigating his death.

I felt a warm glow in my belly, which filled my whole being. She was near; I could feel her presence. I closed my eyes and willed her to be there. I was certain that the human heart couldn't possibly beat as fast as mine was doing right at that moment. As my pulse raced I opened my eyes, looked around and took a sharp intake of breath as the moment arrived, the moment I had dreamt of since I was a tiny girl. There she was, my mum, my beautiful mum, who I'd thought never came back for me that day. She'd finally come back for me.

She was accompanied by a woman police officer who looked kind. I let go of my dad's hand and ran to the frail, exhausted woman who I loved with all my heart and soul. Her face lit up immediately as she whispered, 'Bess, you're my little Bess?'

Through her frailty she held me tightly to her chest as we both sobbed uncontrollably. Dad soon joined us and we all held onto each other for dear life. I looked into my dad's face as the tears rolled down his cheeks and I smiled at him through my own tears. They blurred my vision and made his face look dreamy as though he had a soft glow. 'Bet you could do with a drink right now, hey dad?' I said.

We both grinned as he held the back of my head. 'I love you Bess, I love you so much'.

And I loved him.

Of course mum had a long way to go. She was admitted to Withington Hospital where they specialised in psychological trauma. But she would soon get better; I had no doubt about that.

It is said that out of chaos comes order, well, we have had more than our fair share of chaos.

Chapter 65

Nessa

I sat and watched him sleep. The dream like reality hit me fast, he had come out of nowhere and this time he was staying. My heart was in a constant flutter and my mind was all over the place. This was more than love, this was deep. We were like one being, split into two, and this was the joining of two souls. We had spoken about lots of things over recent days; in fact we had hardly slept a wink. I wanted to know so much. Why had they left? Where had they gone? Where were his parents? He said that one day he would tell me everything, and I knew that was that.

He stirred and turned over in his sleep so I could see the back of his dark neck, and I instinctively leant over and kissed it. He had told me that he had loved me since the day he saved me from Skidder Barker when she battered me in the playground and that even as a little boy the feelings were so strong that they confused him. He said he was never able to bring himself to speak to me or say or do anything about it. He had the very same block I did when I used to see him. He told me that he had thought about me every single day and while he had girls here and there no-one had touched his soul, not one gave him the electric shock of sensation he felt when he saw me.

I had told him about Tony, the miscarriage, the fact that we now believed Tony attacked Bess in her own home, the mental abuse he had put me through. He had reassured me that, after what he'd seen in the Lion that night, Tony would never bother me again. I didn't ask. I'd heard enough.

He looked peaceful as he slept. I thought about the night in the hotel, which would remain fresh in my mind for as long as I lived. I had a flashback to Peter Lawrence and that syringe and how we all thought he was going to plunge it into Si's neck. I shuddered and the tears tumbled down my face.

Si turned over as though he sensed my moment. His beautiful dark eyes were drinking in mine. He didn't say anything, he didn't have to. He pulled me close to his chest. He stroked my hair and kissed my tears. I looked up at him and still couldn't believe it. I had him, my boy, I was never going to let him go, and I knew I was his girl, our souls were one, they always had been and they always would.

Chapter 66

Ella

Things had settled somewhat, on our large council estate, the buzz appeared to be back but nothing would be the same again. We did however, have to move on. Mum had been understandably devastated about the whole Richard thing. Dad, our rock, assured us all was going to be ok and that little Josie had enough love around her to pull through. Peter Lawrence would never be part of the gang but he got the occasional nod if he was spotted. Even if you were enemies round our way you could still be thick as thieves.

Bess had her mum back and she was receiving medical help so things were looking better.

Ness had her boy and I really hadn't experienced anything like it. They were so in love, it was beautiful and I wondered when I'd stop getting goose bumps and a lump in my throat whenever I thought about them. He wasn't just her hero, he was everybody's hero for what he did that night and for the fact he could have died doing it.

As for me, I was going on the cruise ships. I was getting a coach to London, then flying to Miami to join my team. I had asked for a delay in my start date due to family circumstances and it had been accepted. I had thought about whether I should leave but dad was right, Josie had all the love in the world. Plus she had mum, who had herself survived a similar ordeal, so I was confident she would love and guide Josie in the best way possible. Everybody else was sorted. It was the right thing to do.

I walked up to the Lion as I thought about everyone I was

leaving behind. I needed to say goodbye to Lizzy and George and have one last half a lager with them. As I walked into the pub, the memories of the last few years hit me in the face. So much had gone on; Conny, shootings, more shootings, rape, love, laughter, friendship and family. The Lion was our central hub. I needed to let it go but also never forget.

After an emotional goodbye with Lizzy and George, I headed to Manchester and the whole clan was waiting for me at Chorlton Bus Street Station. I nearly died but was so pleased that they had all come to say goodbye. It was hard keeping my emotions in check as I looked at all their faces.

Mum, dad, my brothers and that baby sister of mine whose eyes I didn't want to look into but did. She looked straight into mine and it was like looking in a mirror; the image so familiar that I had to shake my head to clear my mind. She gave me the sweetest smile which set me off as I let go my first sob.

Nessa stood with Si and Faya, her face glowing. She stared at me and I smiled as memories flashed through my mind. We would laugh if our backsides had been on fire. I giggled, and mouthed 'love you kid.' At that, her eyes welled up.

Bess had her arm linked through her dads, who winked at me. I loved John Holland with all my heart and I winked back. Andrea was with them. For a second I had a flash-back to the night that should never have been. I looked at Bess and knew she was thinking the same. I gave her a knowing nod that told her I loved her with all my heart.

Matt was standing with none other than Peter Lawrence and I rolled my eyes in an affectionate way. I didn't mind him anymore. He'd killed the man who raped my mum and my sister, the man who was my father through a crime so sick that I could never forgive him. I shuddered at the moments we had shared, the moments he tried to steal behind my mum and dads back, but he was dead; time to put him to rest.

As I gave the driver my suitcase I saw them out of the corner of my eye running towards me. One with auburn hair with the longest eyelashes you'd ever seen, and the other with curly blonde hair and eyes bluer than the ocean. I saw them as six year olds laughing and giggling, scared and frightened. I saw them as thirteen year olds; Ness, dangly and scruffy, and Bess, prim and proper. My whole body started to shake as they ran at me with tears in their eyes. They held me so tight I thought I would die. We had something so strong between us. It was genuine love and a bond beyond belief. We held onto each other for what seemed like hours, and our eyes said it all. We had done the right thing for all of us because, if someone hurt one of us, we were all hurt. We did it for each other. As we looked up we saw Josie chatting to Faya, and we all burst out sobbing.

'Thank you, my girls, my sisters, my family,' I said to them both. 'I'll be back soon and we'll do it all again,' I laughed nervously.

Emotions ran over and there were lots of hugs and kisses.

'Time to go,' the coach driver shouted.

As I boarded the coach, I looked at my world, the world I was leaving behind to begin another. I knew that I would never meet anyone like any of them ever again.

And as the coach pulled away, my past flashed before my eyes, I could see little Bess on the playing green, Ness getting attacked by Skidder Barker and Si rescuing her. I remembered the shabeen and I remembered Conny. How could I ever forget any of them?

'Bye!' I shouted through the window. I watched until they all became tiny dots gabbing about the life that I was no longer part of. They would soon disband and go their separate ways.

I sat back and thought of the months gone by. I'd probably have nightmares forever, and then I thought about Peter. My god, he was just a lonely pathetic creature loved by no-one. The boys were sorting him out. He'd be ok. I gulped back a tear and looked ahead of me. That was the only way to look, forward, to my new life.

I'd be ok but I was not so innocent after all.

THE END